D1539868

Advance Quotes for *FIRE OF THE DARK TRIAD*

"… [A] mind-blowing narrative … *Fire of the Dark Triad* is a
perfectly timed, incredibly smart page turner — a real must-read!"
BORIS LOKSHIN, INTERNATIONAL FILM AND CULTURAL CRITIC

"The novel *Fire of the Dark Triad* predicted
the current pandemic long before its appearance."
SOLOMON VOLKOV, CULTUROLOGIST, MUSICOLOGIST

"*Fire of the Dark Triad* [is] a mesmerizing otherworldly story."
EDWARD RUBIN, WRITER, ART CRITIC, CURATOR *ARTES MAGAZINE*

"Thought-provoking … *Fire of the Dark Triad* is science fiction
for a reader who wants to be intellectually stimulated and
values imagination and skill. Do yourself a favor:
Sit down for a moment, start to read … see if you can put it down."
PATRICK LOBRUTTO, EDITOR AND AUTHOR

"Full of twists and turns, *Fire of the Dark Triad* is an
unusual science fiction story spiked with philosophy and
some mathematical thinking."
PROFESSOR KARL BARDOSH, NYU TISCH SCHOOL OF ARTS

"Asya Semenovich is a great talent … I literally swallowed
Fire of the Dark Triad, hoping that it would never end."
NINA ZARETSKAYA, DIRECTOR OF "MARRIED TO MATH"

FIRE OF THE
DARK
TRIAD

ASYA
SEMENOVICH

CONTENTS

DEDICATION

To Bruce and my Dad

What would your good be doing if there were no evil, and what would the earth look like if shadows disappeared from it? After all, shadows are cast by objects and people. There is the shadow of my sword. But there are also shadows of trees and living creatures. Would you like to denude the earth of all the trees and all the living beings in order to satisfy your fantasy of rejoicing in the naked light?

Mikhail Bulgakov, *The Master and Margarita*

PART I:

HALL
OF
MIRRORS

EARTH

A small mouse-like animal was stuck on an outcrop of boulders in the middle of a fast torrent. Let's call it Fitzy. It was one of the first mammals on Earth, and it lived on a lush grassy field at the foot of a large dormant volcano. The ground had been shaking under Fitzy's feet for its entire lifetime, so Fitzy more or less ignored earthquakes.

But this morning a particularly strong shock had triggered a landslide, which changed the route of a nearby stream and flooded the meadow that Fitzy called home. Fitzy's family had just enough time to climb onto a rocky bluff before it became a small island. They were now huddled there, sharing body heat and waiting for the water to recede. This was nothing out of the ordinary – they would retreat to higher ground every time water rushed downhill after heavy rains in the mountains.

Fitzy was positioned in the center of the pile, its body nicely warm and dry, but it was getting desperately bored. It wasn't naturally aggressive, but it felt that if it stayed still any longer, it would bite its neighbor. It wasn't Fitzy's fault. The little creature happened to carry a peculiar personality trait – its brain needed a constant stream of stimulation just to stay content.

Fitzy burrowed its way out, ignoring the angry squeaks from all directions, and started exploring the patch of grass above the water once again. Nothing had changed since its last inspection, but suddenly it heard a loud noise – another earthfall completely blocked the current. Fitzy froze and listened, but soon everything became quiet again; too quiet, in fact. The stream around the island slowed down and stopped. Fitzy realized that a way out had become available.

The remaining puddles were still too deep, but Fitzy kept jumping from one slippery stone to another, not giving itself time to get scared, until it reached the base of the mountain. As it scampered uphill, the dam overflowed, and the water burst out, completely covering the meadow below.

Fitzy stopped and picked up the familiar scent of its species. Soon it would find a mate and have offspring, some of which would inherit this vexing trait that just saved Fitzy's life.

Millennia passed.

The moon was full, the barren tree branches didn't block any of its light, and Gunt could easily evade the remaining patches of porous snow on the ground as he made his way to the usual meeting place. He left his camp right after a village kid brought him a red pebble, the signal that she needed to see him urgently. He had been waiting for her message since this afternoon, when his tribesman arrived from home with news that a wooly mammoth had been killed. Food was already being prepared for the feast in honor of her marriage with the chief. Her wedding party was to leave tomorrow morning.

Of course, they both knew that it couldn't have ended any other way. Their love was doomed from the very beginning, but during their brief meetings they never talked about it. In fact, they barely talked at all, trying to quench their thirst for each other. Whenever they parted, he couldn't think about anything except for their next time alone.

This night they had to face reality. There would always be the memories, he tried to console himself.

He thought about the first time he saw her. She and her father had come from their village three mountain ranges away to ask for peace and protection. She was beautiful even though her face and posture were understandably tense.

Her tribe was in trouble. Many men had been killed during a botched hunt, and now the village was unable to defend their hunting territory from the riverside people. The chief liked her. His wife recently died during childbirth, and he offered marriage as a guarantee for truce and cooperation. It was a very good deal for her tribe.

She was supposed to return home and wait for word about the big kill. Gunt, together with two other hunters, was assigned to protect her on her way there and back.

She nodded when he introduced himself and politely smiled. She seemed relaxed now, probably because the peace agreement had been reached. He was sure that she didn't notice it, but he touched her hair during their first short exchange.

He remembered the morning when they left for their trip, which was supposed to take six days. She was in a great mood, and they chatted a lot, all five of them, including her father. Gunt was observing. He noted how direct and earnest she was, how loyal to her people, how dignified.

For all practical purposes she was unattainable.

But he noticed the look she gave him when she thought he wasn't watching.

He knew right then that he could win her, and it became his obsession. The obvious insanity of it in the current setup made him want her even crazier. He let his instinct play the game – his subconscious was fantastic in recognizing emotions and reflecting them back to their owners. This always worked, and she wasn't an exception. He was on her territory without having to break any boundaries. He turned her into his mental accomplice before she even realized it.

And he definitely knew that he won when he held her hand a bit too long helping her to cross a rough stream, and she didn't take it away.

They became lovers once they reached her village. They met in the shelter of nearby forest caves every night. His head was spinning.

But now they had to end their affair, tragically. Tomorrow, Gunt and her wedding party would leave for his village.

He entered the familiar clearing in the woods, and she immediately appeared from the shadow of the eroded mountain wall. She was very pale.

She looked at his face and said, "I had a dream. We'll have a child. Let's run away. I brought food for several days."

He thought he didn't hear her right. "What are you saying? Your whole tribe will be slaughtered!"

"I don't care. I love you too much."

She stepped towards him, but he stopped her, putting his hands on her shoulders.

"We can't do it. You won't forgive yourself if we do. We have to say goodbye."

Her eyes were wide open. The next phase would be tears, he thought. It was better to end this conversation now.

"Goodbye," he said and walked back toward the forest.

He started downhill, towards his camp, not bothering to avoid snow patches anymore. He had just lost her forever. The forever part hurt especially badly, but there was something noble about it. He had sacrificed his own happiness for the sake of people he didn't even know.

You might believe this bullshit to feel even better said a sober voice in his head – but you don't care about these people and you know it. You don't care about people in general, except for yourself … but in any case, you're right, you needed to stop.

Gunt shook his head and with relief switched into his base self, the owner of the sober voice. He needed a break from the volatile personality that he employed for his emotional thrills.

Indeed, it was dangerous. He didn't want to become hunted by his tribe, the best men in the mountains. And even if the two of them escaped to the steppes, they wouldn't survive by themselves, and who knew if any local clan would accept them.

It wasn't worth it. The best – the hunt, the game – was over. She threw the lives of her people to his feet. Passion didn't get any better than that. He knew that all excitement would go downhill if they got together. She might be pregnant too, and any tribe they ended up with would expect him to stick around her for good.

He imagined her getting old and shuddered. How could others stand sleeping with the same person forever? They probably cheated, he thought, or if they couldn't get away with it, in which case they must be depressed and resentful. Anyway, he was sure that it was better for her to stay with the Chief. He would be a better father for their child.

He finally saw a campfire light in the distance and thought that the other guys were probably resting, preparing for the journey tomorrow. They were happy to go back. They said that they missed their families. He didn't understand it, but it wasn't his fault. He didn't know that he was different from most other people. The moment he got what he wanted, he became desperately bored and restless again.

It ruined him and the rest of his personality type for long-term relationships and caused a reproductive disadvantage, but evolution, for some reason, decided to compensate for this.

It gave Gunt charm and deceptiveness to lure in the next victim, self-confidence and boldness to initiate the affair, lack of empathy and guilt to discard and move on.

He was outfitted for the *Fast Life Strategy*, as scientists would call it much later.

Gunt wrapped himself in several layers of fur skins and lay on the ground. Looking at the fire, he relived the emotions of the last conversation. A warm feeling flooded his chest. But that was enough, he told himself. This story was over. He noticed a girl when he came down to their village yesterday. She had an even nicer body and looked happy, for a change. She was glancing at him.

The tribes would be mixing now, and he would win her soon, he thought before falling asleep. He had what it took.

Thousands of years elapsed.

The queen of the high plains stopped her horse on the side of the mountain and looked at the city under siege in the valley below. It was far, but she could see that her vanguard troops were standing in front of the drawbridge rather than advancing towards the gates.

"Why aren't they crossing?" she turned to their commander who had just arrived to give her an update. He was galloping all the way here, his hair drenched with sweat, his gray stallion foaming at the mouth.

"An enemy squad is defending the entrance, your highness."

"I see. But you previously reported that you had killed all the fighters."

He wanted to say something, but she impatiently waved at him to shut up.

"Never mind … so what are you waiting for? Just finish them off and go ahead with your looting."

"They're …" he hesitated.

"What?" She raised her eyebrows. "I heard your people aren't afraid of anyone."

"You better see, your highness. You should decide."

He was a good commander, she trusted him. She knew that if he couldn't make the call himself then it was serious enough, and she had to take a look.

"Fine, tell my son to catch up. We'll ride down together. I'll wait for him here."

Her ten-year-old son and his people were staying closer to her main forces, but not too far behind, so she waited in the saddle, looking at the city below.

They made a big mistake refusing to surrender, she thought, and they had an idiotic reason too – they swore to defend their faith from barbarians. She didn't give a damn about their religion. They could have carried on with whatever nonsense they worshiped as long as they accepted her as a ruler. But they decided to fight. It was pathetic, and she dealt with their small army in a quick battle.

That was one thing that she definitely cared about. She strongly disliked morons who had the stupidity to annoy her. In her ideal world, she would be doing whatever she wanted, and pissing her off wouldn't even occur to people as a possibility. Maybe it was the definition of power, she asked herself? Anyway, whatever it was she always knew that she deserved it. And, incidentally, she remembered herself at a very early age. She knew that she was exceptional, and she knew that she had to keep it a secret. But she had already stared attracting attention when it became apparent that she had never lost a single fight. She was offered a prominent position. People liked her charming personality, and she was always logical and fair. She became an adored leader.

She heard the approaching sound of pounding hooves, and then her son with his guards appeared from the other side of the ridge.

She waved in the direction of the city, and trotted towards the road leading to the valley. The two groups merged and assumed a proper formation.

She and her son rode in front, next to each other. They didn't talk, but she periodically glanced in his direction with immense pleasure. She loved him. He took after her. He was exceptional too; he had the same focus and intensity in his eyes. Thankfully, he got nothing from his father, her late husband, the king.

Her marriage was the second step to the place she deserved. She didn't know that she owed her charm to Gunt's genetic heritage, but she used it to provoke and secure the king's obsession with her. He was a mediocre lover and had no value in general, so she got rid of him quickly. She did it for the boy's sake too, even though she never told him who was behind the assassination of his father. She needed all of the power to herself to be able to give her son the empire he deserved. Unlike her meek husband, she was extremely good at conquering new lands – Gunt's genes were critical for that too. Successful wars required the same traits as illicit affairs: controlled aggression, fluid intelligence and cunningness, just taken to the next level. It worked well, and her military victories confirmed her conviction that she was exceptional.

She stopped her horse to evaluate the standoff at the bridge. She was close enough now to see a group of people defending the entrance, and there was something unnatural about them. The figures were the height of her son and had similar child proportions. Their fishnet armor and helmets looked ridiculously oversized, and the way that they held the heavy adult swords in their hands was laughable. It, probably, was the city's attempt to appeal to her female instincts, she thought, and it was very stupid of them.

"I repeat, what are you waiting for?" she asked the commander. "Kill them and tell our people they can have the city till tomorrow morning. Then we march."

The commander nodded; his face didn't flinch. He turned his horse and took off towards his troops, shouting commands on his way.

She couldn't see the arrows, but most of the small bodies fell, and her warriors galloped across the bridge, occasionally striking the ones who remained standing.

She imagined what would soon be happening inside the walls.

"We'll stay in tents outside," she said to the boy, "it will be nasty in the city tonight."

He shrugged his shoulders in response. "They shouldn't have pissed you off."

She smiled to herself. He was very smart for a ten-year-old.

It was too early for him, she thought, but when he got older, she would make sure that he had his first pick of the women in defeated cities, and she would bring along the ones he fancied to keep. They would be treated well as long as they would bear his children. She needed heirs.

A thousand years passed.

It was the dawn of the 21st century. Garrett, a former New York financier, was watching the news on a private boat that peacefully glided over azure Mediterranean waters.

Pictures of one of his clients, taken in a family circle, in political meetings, in front of election rallies, replaced each other on the flat-screen TV. If anyone asked this happily smiling man on the screen how he defined his relationship with Garrett, he doubtlessly would call it a close friendship. But nobody could ask him anything anymore – this morning he hanged himself. He went all in investing into Garrett's fund, and lost everything including the money he borrowed from his relatives and business partners.

He shouldn't have been so dumb and greedy, thought Garrett, listening to the details of the investigation.

"Wasn't it obvious that the return was too good to be true? What was he thinking?" the anchor was questioning the guest analyst.

Probably nothing, thought Garrett. Thinking wasn't the guy's forte, and he preferred to simply trust his charming friend. Garrett was good at making friends, which was very useful because he needed a number of rich and powerful people for his Ponzi scheme to work.

Gullible dummies with predictably pitiful behavior, he thought. It was their own fault that they believed in his bullshit. He won because he was smarter. It was an exciting game, for sure, but he was careful, and he always walked away in time. He moved his money to an anonymous offshore account, took a jet to Europe, and disappeared before the shit hit the fan. He heard his name and tuned back into the news.

"… It's very similar to Garrett Hall's case. To remind the viewers, last month Hall's sailboat was found drifting in the Pacific. After unsuccessful attempts to get in touch, a Coast Guard unit went aboard," now it was the analyst speaking. "There was nobody there, but they found a suicide note. Hall apparently jumped off the boat wearing his scuba lead weights. He apologized to the victims of his exploded financial operation and said that he killed himself out of shame and guilt. His body was never recovered."

They had no clue that this scenario was absolutely impossible for the simple reason that Garrett carried the same personality trait as Gunt, the queen and a number of other people across the generations. A twist of evolution wired their brains differently. They didn't know what conscience was in the same way that blind people couldn't experience colors. Unaware of their deficiency, they assumed that they were simply smarter and more flexible, and it was only fair that they created their own rules, leaving conventional morality to the rest of the world. They always existed, peppered throughout the population, and they mostly stayed under the radar.

But evolution didn't deal in precision. Sometimes they broke laws too boldly; sometimes things that they desired were too dark. Those who derived pleasure from killing became serial killers, those who enjoyed power and mass murder became bloodthirsty dictators. Self-confidence misfired into grandiosity; boldness into recklessness; opportunism into cold manipulation.

At the end of the 19th century, the nascent field of psychology identified these malevolent aberrations and gave each of them a name: *Narcissism, Psychopathy, Machiavellianism.*

Later it was understood that these sinister traits always intertwined, and the scientists coined the new term *Dark Triad.*

The Dark Triad personality was the most dangerous type, the worst of humanity. Aggressive, selfish, uninhibited by morals, they got whatever they wanted, ignoring the cost, because they never paid. Nature had armed them with the perfect tools – they used charisma, lies and manipulation to pass the cost of their actions to others. Unscathed, they traveled through life leaving destruction on various scales in their wake.

Recognize them, stay away from relationships, screamed the headlines of the tabloids. Beware of Dark Triad leaders, learn to identify them by the discernible traits, be sure never to elect them, cautioned venerable publications.

However, as ominous as they sounded, the Dark Triad warnings were mostly lost on the background of other alarms constantly going off on Earth. Regional conflicts, financial crises, shrinking natural resources, pollution, global warming – the number and severity of issues grew like a deadly snowball. The conscientious part of the world desperately tried to prevent the approaching catastrophe, but there was too much darkness in human nature. The planet's future looked seriously dim.

And then against all odds humanity got a chance. By a complete accident, scientists stumbled onto a game-changing discovery. According to their new theory, at the very end of its creation the Universe unfolded into an infinite number of identical copies glued along their multidimensional edges. They were called *Mirror Worlds* in the first news announcement, and the name stuck.

In the beginning it was a purely academic concept, but after several decades, physicists learned that the matter connecting Mirror Worlds created observable singularities in space. Moreover, some of them were located right in Earth's backyard, inside the Solar System.

Theoretically, the science said, they could serve as gates to other copies of the Universe. Over the next several decades, astronomical amounts of money were poured into researching the space singularity. But the gate matter turned out to be impenetrable for transmissions. There was no way to see the other side. The doors to the other worlds remained locked, and the excitement about them gradually died down.

Hope was regained overnight when a breakthrough discovery of the specific magnetic properties that allowed physical objects to pass through the singularity field. Another century later, scientists came up with technology to build spaceships capable of crossing over to the adjacent worlds.

The first unmanned shuttle was sent to the other side through the closest singularity in the vicinity of Saturn's orbit. It was programmed to simply pass through the border, quickly collect data and return home.

Earth held its breath, but the suspense didn't last long. The drone came back within several hours with a pot of informational gold.

According to its records, crossing the boundary registered as a momentary glitch in navigation systems, and then the shuttle exited the singularity in seemingly the same location of the Solar System as its entry point. The Mirror World indeed was an identical copy of the known Universe.

Expeditions sent through other singularity gates reported that there was no trace of intelligence or its previous existence on the other Mirror Earths. It seemed that evolution simply skipped that step there.

Physicists processed the new data and adjusted their theory. It was determined that all Mirror Worlds periodically developed minor perturbations in their gravity fields, breaking the exact symmetry. Among other things, it slightly affected water distribution and formed different weather conditions on Mirror planets. A climate pattern on Earth prompted evolution to create an advanced intelligence.

Humanity felt lonely once again, but it didn't grieve for too long. In practical terms, the new reality meant that an infinite number of uninhabited copies of Earth were available for colonization. There was enough space for everyone who cared to have a world shaped according to their preferences. Earth's governments, relieved to export domestic conflicts and to solve resource problems, enthusiastically encouraged the idea. In a joint effort they built mega ships for freight transportation and together signed a document promising full support to settlers until their civilizations reached technological self-sufficiency.

Mass migration took off like an explosion.

Logistically, some new worlds preferred to stay under Earth's governance, creating the United Commonwealth, but the majority requested independence, which Earth granted without dispute. Armed conflicts were at an all-time low, and everyone seemed to breathe an enormous sigh of relief, until the imperfection of human nature completely shattered this utopia.

The problem started when some seceded colonies demanded support well beyond the original agreement. This angered many Commonwealth citizens, and under the weight of internal political pressure, governments started ramping down on free aid.

When a developing world was refused a free upgrade of medical software, a group of terrorists snuck a biological weapon across the Earth Mirror border as an act of revenge. The virus wiped out a third of Earth's population before a cure was found.

It was later argued that the scale of the disaster wasn't intended, but the Commonwealth's response was brutal and final. Special squads descended on all independent planets, annihilated their spaceship fleets and released nano-organisms that chewed up and rendered unusable all advanced hardware and machinery. The Commonwealth's troops waited until everything that could lead to a restoration of modern technology was destroyed, sent the bots a command to self-destruct and departed for good, leaving behind camouflaged satellites to keep an eye on the cutoff civilizations.

Earth buried its dead, and the survivors began to put the shards of their lives together. They tried to process how this could have happened and recoiled in shock: the terrorists were monsters in human form. It was clear that there was something wrong with them on a deep psychological level. Indeed, scientific measurements of their brain functioning revealed a pattern that correlated with the Dark Triad personality type.

For the first time, Earth's population looked into this phenomenon seriously.

Low agreeableness, tendency to violate the most basic norms of behavior and a distortion of the emotional sphere were among the main symptoms at the high spectrum of the traits. Throughout history, Dark Triad people left a scorched-earth in the lives of individuals and created wildfires of hatred and cruelty on massive scales.

Every single person lost someone they loved in the epidemic, and people unanimously swore to prevent this from happening ever again. A high precision test was uniformly adopted to evaluate the intensity of this Dark Triad mental distortion, and countries across the globe introduced a cutoff score for some professional occupations and political positions. Couples were expected to share this information with each other to expose potential cheaters and emotional abusers. The presence of the trait was quickly nicknamed the "Curse of the Dark Triad."

It wasn't a future anyone wanted for their kids, but fortunately, curses were a thing for medieval times. By this point in human progress, genetic engineering had already eliminated inheritable diseases relating to human bodies. Laws prevented DNA adjustments to cure mental disorders, but the current epidemic tipped the scales in the other direction.

Political movements fueled by outrage called for removing the Dark Triad personality from humanity's genetic pool for good. A few cautious voices warned against playing with fire. But the fire was already out of control, argued the rest.

The majority easily won, and constellations of genes responsible for the Dark Triad were allowed to be replaced on embryonic levels with benign donor materials.

Over generations, the condition became more and more uncommon. Crime statistics went down, and there were changes in other areas too. Political systems rebuilt themselves as one functional entity, and strict moral principles became prevalent in all fields of human activity. It was only a matter of time before discrimination against people based on their DNA was considered a violation of human rights, and the practice of eliminating the Dark Triad trait from the population was labeled as genetic self-cleansing. Any tinkering with the genes linked to personality characteristics was once again banned.

The test remained available for self-exploration purposes, but it became illegal to ask for anyone's score, and socially unacceptable to bring up this subject. There was no way to find out how many Dark Triad people were left on Earth.

Meanwhile, surveillance reported violence and instability on all closed Mirror Worlds without exception. As these societies became more and more technological, they experienced a greater and greater likelihood of self-destruction. At some point, Earth's moral responsibilities vis-à-vis the former colonies became a hotly debated topic, but finally a strict non-interference policy was accepted as the only ethical solution. Even sharing secretly collected information with the broad Commonwealth audience was considered a violation of independent civilization privacy. Only a small intelligence community retained the right to review spy satellite records.

A few more centuries passed.

PART II:
HEADHUNTER

EARTH

I woke up drenched in a cold sweat. It took a moment before my heart began to slow down, and the familiar sight of the navigation room pushed the nightmare from my head. I rolled out of the pilot chair and fought an irrational desire to turn on all the internal lights.

"Kir," I asked, "did you wake me up?"

"Your level of adrenaline was nearing the threshold. Besides, we're entering Earth's orbit."

Our psychologists advised against cultivating a personal relationship with an implanted chip, but it was very reassuring to hear Kir's voice.

Earth guard systems requested identification, the usual procedure for everyone coming from the Mirror Spaces, and I initiated the arrival protocol.

"Nick," said Kir almost immediately, "we can't land. The Cyber Safety Department has turned on a Red Alert for all ships arriving from Earth3, citing cyber-implant contamination. We're told to dock in the quarantine area." He paused for a second and added, "Nick, I'm positive that my systems are clean."

Of course, they were, I thought. I didn't believe for a moment that this check was related to contamination. It would be too much of a coincidence, and I didn't believe in coincidences anymore. It was an information leak that certain people were trying to stop, that much was certain.

The border control cruiser escorted my ship to the quarantine hangar entrance – standard procedure in cases of suspected contamination, even if it felt somewhat menacing. Nothing personal ... but I didn't even try to pretend that it was true. The gates closed, and I surveyed the interior of a huge holding area, letting Kir deal with the landing.

All the other parking spaces were empty; and the only person inside was a woman in a Cyber Safety uniform. Kir opened the hatch. I stepped out and waved at her as I walked down the stairs.

She addressed me from several steps away, "Welcome to Earth. We apologize for the unfortunate delay and will send you on your way as soon as possible. Can you please grant us permission to run diagnostic software on your cyber-implant?"

Another standard procedure for cases of suspected contamination, I thought.

"No problem," I said giving her my most charismatic smile. "How long will this take?"

She stopped and looked at me with the cold resolute eyes of an interrogator. How unusual for friendly Cyber Safety personnel, I noted. Except that she most likely wasn't from Cyber Safety and didn't care about appearing nice. She was testing me: citizens with nothing to hide wouldn't pay attention, people trying to smuggle critical information might get nervous.

"We cannot provide an exact estimate at this moment, but we'll make sure that you're comfortable during your wait," she said, smiling tightly.

I told Kir to allow all cyber safety access. She nodded in acknowledgment, and gestured for me to follow. We passed through the metal gate to an internal corridor and entered a room that was decorated pleasantly enough, but nevertheless lacked a certain touch of care with which Earth usually treated her citizens. They didn't even bother to imitate natural light.

I sat down in the only chair, which felt pristinely unused. Cyber contamination protocol hadn't been invoked for a very long time.

I wasn't surprised when Kir turned on a widespread security breach warning. They went beyond running diagnostic software – so much for standard procedure. I wasn't the only one who didn't believe in coincidences, and my connection to the stolen information was obvious.

Let them look, I thought. They wouldn't find anything. It would be a big overstatement to say that the situation was under control, but things were going as planned, at least for the time being. As for the delay – I still had several hours before the timing would become truly critical. I praised myself for such rational and restrained thinking.

According to quarantine rules, I had to use their proxy to contact Earth. Not that it mattered, since Kir's communications were under surveillance anyway.

I took a deep breath, preparing for the conversation, which would determine if my plan had any chance to work.

"Kir, request a connection to Hilgor," I said finally. Listening to the gentle sound of the outgoing ring I silently begged for Hilgor not to reject my call. The truth was that I would most definitely get killed in the very near future if he wouldn't take my call now. And incidentally, my life wasn't even the highest stake in my game.

□   □   □

A young man, Hilgor, a recent transplant from a Mirror World, was standing at his window wall looking out onto a multileveled flow of traffic connecting skyscraping sectors of the great city of Berlin. He seemed to be deeply immersed in his thoughts when a sudden shift in the building brought the sunlight directly into his eyes. "Damn it," he said, shielding his face with his hand.

A large dog in the middle of the room stretched, sighed and turned onto his back, his shiny fur looking particularly black on the pristinely white surface of the floor.

"Damn these narcissistic buildings, Riph," repeated the man stepping away from the window. "I get they desire to look their best, but what about me?"

The dog ignored the question and went back to sleep. He didn't have a problem with tower behavior unlike his master who sounded mildly annoyed. Architects programmed skyscrapers to periodically change shape in order to achieve their best appearance under different light conditions. None of the modern windows had the ability to block the sun, however. Generations of Commonwealth's people had received retinal filters and self-protecting skin as a part of their standard birth package, so the brightness regulators had been redundant for some centuries now. But the man wasn't born here. In fact, he arrived to Earth only three months ago, and, in spite of the best efforts of his hosts, minor issues like this kept popping up in his day-to-day experiences. The external walls of his apartment needed to be replaced with some transparent photochromic material, but he kept forgetting to order it.

Of course, it was Hilgor's own decision to refuse implanting any hardware upon arrival to Earth. Instead, he wore the assistant chip on his wristband, and his residence and his flyer had to be rigged with custom devices, but he preferred to deal with the corresponding inconveniences.

He walked to the corner, which remained in the shade regardless of the building's orientation, and sat down in a shabby-looking armchair, blatantly contrasting with the sleekness of the overall room design, and refocused on the conjecture he had been trying to prove.

"Hilgor," said the chip through the surrounding audio speakers, "you have an emergency call from Orbit. Nick is online. Would you like to accept?"

The man abruptly got up, and his expression quickly went through the degrees of surprise and hesitation.

"Fine," he said finally, "two-way audio."

He didn't have implanted optical displays, and he didn't feel like searching the apartment for his goggles, which made up for this disability. But most importantly, it was easier to control his voice than his facial expressions. He wanted to hide his bitterness.

A soft chime signaled the beginning of the open connection, and then a familiar voice came from the room speakers.

"Good evening, Hilgor. How's life?" Nick sounded perfectly casual, as if they had parted just yesterday. "Listen, sorry for disappearing – I have been extremely busy recently. I had to leave Earth for a while."

"Busy?" asked Hilgor. "What do you mean – busy? How is …"

"I'll tell you everything," said Nick quickly. "But can we talk face to face? It's important."

Hilgor had to admit that he was rather keen to finally find out how Nick's extraordinary story ended. His pride briefly fought with his curiosity, and then he replied in a similarly casual tone.

"Sounds good, Nick. I will send you the meeting location. When do you want to meet?"

"The sooner the better," said Nick, and Hilgor picked up on a note of relief in his voice. "I just need to go through a couple of things on Orbit before I can land, but it shouldn't take long."

"How about if I go now, and you join me when you can?" asked Hilgor. He knew that his work session had ended anyway – it would have taken much less than Nick's sudden reappearance to forget about mathematics.

"See you soon, Hilgor. And thank you."

The chime announced the end of the connection, and Hilgor approached the sleeping dog.

"Wake up, Riph, and let's go. We're meeting Nick tonight," he said and headed to the door.

Hilgor decided to go to their meeting place on foot. It would take Nick some time to get to the city even if he landed right away, so there was no rush. In general, Hilgor preferred walking over taking a flyer unless he was in a hurry, and not just for Riph's sake. After three months, Berlin still seemed infinite, still had the attraction of an unsolved mystery. Hilgor almost regretted that the feeling of warm familiarity would soon replace the burning curiosity of the initial encounter.

A sudden wave passed through the pedestrian flow, and he quickly scanned the surroundings. Someone had upset the strange rhythm created by the precision with which people walked past each other in order to avoid close proximity, an old habit formed during the epidemic times. Hilgor, who was now used to such glitches, immediately identified the culprit. A woman had looked in his direction for too long and, distracted, stepped into someone's buffer zone. This happened around Hilgor all the time in spite of the fact that his tall, lean figure and chiseled face with very bright blue eyes didn't stand out at the slightest. It was Riph's fault. Nick had explained that there were almost no dogs on Earth because people had simply lost interest in keeping them as companions. The woman turned away, and the smoothness of the crowd's movement was restored.

Hilgor kept walking on one of the highest street levels. Nothing here resembled his planet, but the pathways that crossed at seemingly impossible angles above and below had already been developing a pattern in his brain. He wasn't focused on geometrical puzzles at the moment, however. He was thinking about Nick. There were very few people in his life that he could mentally refer to as friends, and this was a word he had started applying to Nick in his thoughts.

Of course, in the very beginning of their relationship Hilgor had been suspicious, if not paranoid, about Nick's motives. But that was understandable, given the circumstances of their acquaintance. One day Nick simply showed up in Hilgor's life and introduced himself as a secret agent from Earth. Nick patiently waited until Hilgor went through all of the proper stages of mental shock before filling him in on the details.

According to Nick, Hilgor had something that Earth lost and desperately needed back. Hilgor didn't quite get what *it* was from Nick's explanation, except that it possibly had something to do with his ability to do mathematics. He clearly understood, however, that at some point it was considered so undesirable on Earth that it had been almost bred out, and Earth did just fine without it for several generations. But recently, said Nick, they got some bad news. Military intelligence issued a warning that some cutoff Mirror Worlds would reach a technological level and would be able to cross Mirror borders within a century. Almost all of them were aggressive, and their sentiments towards Earth didn't leave much hope for peaceful encounters.

At that moment, it was still possible to preventively invade the developing civilizations and throw them back technologically as had been done once before. But generations of people grew up ashamed of their ancestors for doing precisely that. It was beyond impossible to repeat such an inhumane deed again. The only ethically acceptable solution was to build a solid defense system, and Earth invested its best resources into a space shield design. Groups of highly intelligent engineers and scientists came up with excellent ideas, but in spite of all of their efforts, the program development got stuck in the initial stages. After several decades, Earth realized that it had a serious problem. The Mirror Worlds were catching up. Time was running out. Concerned voices started asking what was wrong.

The answer was both unfortunate and obvious. Their failure to launch a suitable defense system was just one example of overall progress stagnation. People did notice that their civilization hadn't significantly progressed in any fields for a while now, but life had been so comfortable that they hadn't considered it too worrisome.

This time, they were finally forced to figure out the reason why this was happening. The computational power available for pattern recognition was almost unlimited now, so it didn't take long to find the cause: the rate of human advancement was reversely correlated with the elimination of the Dark Triad from the population.

Earth had to look into something it didn't like to remember, and the longer people investigated the history of the matter, the more they understood why the defense program was failing.

Dark Triad people were known for their selfish and asocial attitudes, but these same traits, viewed from a different perspective, turned out to be little more than an evolutionary mistake. In fact, it was rooted in a neutral quality of mental unrest, which, in turn, translated into a fierce lust for anarchy and a burning desire to change the status quo. They fought boredom by their inherited desire to explore new territories and the imagination to develop new things. They weren't afraid of anything when they were engaged in an obsessive hunt for fresh experiences and extreme emotions. They broke boundaries and took high risks for things that most other people didn't care about in the first place.

In other words, they had the madness to see something that didn't exist and the obsession to chase it at all costs. But was this really a mental illness, as it was initially defined, or was it something else? Could it be a kind of violent creativity? Creative drive? Nobody knew, but without it Earth was losing the survival race.

The solution came to everyone at the same time. The trait was still available on the closed Mirror Worlds, and Dark Triad personalities could be imported to the Commonwealth to rebuild an environment where mundane reality could be disrupted again. It was understood that they wouldn't care about the moral side of such disruptions, but Earth didn't have a choice and had to take the risk of inviting evil back.

Psychologists dusted off the old Dark Triad test. Now someone had to go to the cutoff civilizations, quietly and covertly search for people who had a high enough score and convince them to move to Earth. A new profession was born – *Headhunters*.

Nick was a headhunter. He brought Hilgor here because Hilgor passed the test.

Hilgor didn't know how he felt about it, not even after he had spent several months on Earth and finally understood all of the layers of the issue. Of course, there was nothing to complain about in practical terms. Everything was just as Nick promised. Hilgor received ridiculously high amounts of money from the government, and he could work on whatever he wanted.

At some point, he was asked if he would be interested in the space shield program, but there was absolutely no pressure. It was a decent challenge, and he still had plenty of time to do his own research, so he joined the project group with sincere enthusiasm.

Everything had been good on the surface, but Hilgor still didn't feel completely at ease. It was hard to blame him really. There was something unhealthy about the fascination with which Earth's population viewed Dark Triad outliers.

Dark Triad. Dark Fire. Friendly Fire. He watched the super-alert eyes of local people during their interactions with him and imagined a similar wordplay in their minds.

Hilgor turned into a small alley, and Riph confidently headed toward a familiar door in a white porcelain wall. The dog stopped to sniff at some protruding object in front of the building, and then, satisfied, lifted his leg. Hilgor looked in a different direction, pretending not to notice. This object was probably a work of art just like everything else on Earth. It was another thing that Nick had told Hilgor during the flight. You see, he said, they collected a lot of art over the centuries, and they disdained wasting precious space with generic patterns. Hilgor remembered noticing this sudden "they" during that conversation.

The plaque at the entrance announced that it was an architect's rendering of a place without a character. The installation represented a small fast-food place with an automatic food dispenser from some period several centuries ago. The artist was talented enough to achieve the desired effect. The place felt perfectly and refreshingly ordinary.

Hilgor dropped his jacket on the hard white bench and threw the leash on a plastic tabletop that flashed with ancient headline news and bright advertisement clips. Riph immediately stretched out on the floor, obliviously blocking the aisle. There was nobody to inconvenience. The place was empty.

Hilgor had to step over the dog to get to the vending machine in the back corner. Unfortunately, coffee wasn't on the list of options, so he toggled the stimulant level of some synthetic drink from the past to the highest setting and watched a tall glass fill with cold amber liquid. The running text on the display cheerfully wished him *good morning* in several modern and archaic languages.

He agreed with the vending machine that he wouldn't be going to bed soon. It wasn't even clear when exactly Nick would arrive.

"Riph, we will try to help Nick," he said to the dog. "We both like him a lot, don't we?" Riph responded with a slight movement of his tail recognizing the name even from the depth of his sleep.

APPROXIMATELY SIX MONTHS EARLIER

That morning, as so many mornings before that, started with the sensation of a gentle breeze on my cheek. I waited for a moment and opened my eyes to the familiar sight of a vast unobstructed seascape. It was early; the ocean was still dark in the low angle of the morning sun, and the wide strip of beach had a deep yellow color. I got up and put on a linen robe that hung on a chair next to the bed.

"Good morning, Nick," said Kir.

Folding the external walls of the room was the only form of wake-up call that I allowed Kir to use during my vacations. I had the luxury to drift from my dreams slowly, hovering over the images before they melted away. There were no urgent decisions to make, no place to rush to.

I stepped out of the room and sat on the porch, my bare feet touching the cool sand, and stared at the boundary between the dark sea and the pale cloudless sky, well defined at this hour.

In several minutes, I heard a familiar flutter of wings, and a seagull landed on the ground nearby. It had unblinking yellow eyes with a small black dot of a pupil, long orange beak and a distinct dark mark along its light gray back. It tilted its head and looked at me.

"Morning," I said, "how was your fishing?"

It came almost every day now in what seemed to be a gesture of genuine greeting. There was no obvious material gain since I never bribed it with food.

For a while we sat silently and looked at the line of the horizon. Then the bird flapped its wings and took off in the direction of the ocean.

I got up, walked to the edge of the water and stretched. The curved beach was completely empty except for the pile of large white cubes that formed my house.

In fact, there wasn't another living soul anywhere near my rented artificial island in the middle of the Pacific.

Sometimes I wondered if it was a sign of getting old that I preferred this solitude to the maddening energy and psychedelic beauty of big cities. I immediately felt embarrassed, though. Thirty-two was a far cry from advanced age no matter how you looked at it.

I dropped my robe on the dry sand and stepped into the calm water, so transparent that I could see schools of tiny fish scurrying close to the bottom. I carefully walked around the cluster of small corals and decisively plunged in. As usual, the water felt bitterly cold and dense at first, resisting my rapid movements and instantly driving away the remains of my morning dullness, but after several energetic strokes, it became much friendlier. I slowed down and switched to a steady pace in a straight line away from the beach. All Kir's feeds were still turned off, and pristine snapshots of the bright blue sky and the pale green water underneath replaced each other in measured beats.

For a while I didn't think about anything, enjoying the freedom of the ocean.

Finally, I asked Kir for the morning update. A bunch of irregular blobs popped up in the backdrop of my vision. I focused my eyes on a large red bubble in the forefront, making it expand, then slowing it down in mid-stroke. The combination of stock market fluctuation and my recent expenses sent my account to less than 20,000 credits. By itself, it wasn't a reason to worry – I could easily afford my current lifestyle for a couple more months. But I had made an agreement with myself that reaching this number served as a signal to start a new contract. After another couple of strokes forward, I abruptly changed my direction towards the beach.

The vacation was over.

When I stepped back on the shore the sun was significantly higher and the line of the horizon blurrier. I quickly showered and donned a light summer outfit.

Behind the folded wall, the ocean was gleaming in the sensual heat of late morning, but I hardly looked at it, feeling the familiar chill of excitement down my spine. The game was on.

I ignored the basket of fresh produce delivered in the middle of the night, picked a random precooked meal from the pantry and chewed as I ran up the steps to my study. I sat on the lonely armchair in the middle of the windowless room, leaned back and snapped my fingers to activate the hand controls. Kir projected the home screen onto my retina, and I navigated to the familiar interface of the contract assignment program.

As always, I sorted the list of Mirror Worlds by environmental danger coefficients. It was directly linked to headhunter compensation: the total bounty amount was calculated based on the Dark Triad score of a delivered target and the difficulty level assigned to their home planet.

I checked out the top place first and paused in surprise. I had never seen anything like this. Not a single headhunter had ever been registered in that sector, although its award coefficient was more than ten times higher than average. It was totally baffling that I never ran into it before. I whistled and asked for detailed information.

Facts about Sector M-237 began filling the space around me.

People of Beta Blue, as they called their planet, didn't know much beyond the fact that at some point in the past, they were a part of some technologically advanced civilization with the label "Earth" attached to it. However, the local regime worked this potential to the maximum. Media, controlled by the government, warned that the Commonwealth was planning to launch an attack to reclaim the planet. News was filled with ominous reports about secret Earth agents infiltrating research and defense facilities. The imaginary spies were elusive and impossible to catch due to their superior technology, but alleged traces of their malicious activities were exposed daily. Admittedly, being an actual earthman in this situation would have its difficulties.

By the early afternoon, I felt that I couldn't absorb a single additional fact, but it didn't matter. I found out everything that could affect my decision.

Surely, there was a risk. Headhunters were on their own – it was a part of our contract. Nobody would come to help me if my cover was blown. On the other hand, the chances of this happening were minimal considering the means at my disposal. This planet was in a period of wild technology expansion with no coherent laws yet in place and a very inquisitive government to boot. I figured that Kir would be able to hack into Beta Blue's vast digital net and manipulate local computer systems, making me both omnipresent and invisible – a virtual ghost with rather unlimited power. In addition, I was positive that it would be easy to convince a discovered target to defect. Dark Triad outliers didn't do well in totalitarian worlds thanks to their inherent hatred for any kind of rules, totalitarian regimes being the most annoying.

But most importantly, there was the challenge factor. I wanted to be the one to score in the place where nobody else had.

All in all, it was fair game, but I momentarily hesitated before applying. It was very strange that I had never heard of Beta Blue before. They probably just adjusted its rating, bringing it to the top, I told myself. I really wanted to go to this place.

"Kir," I said, "get clearance for M-237."

"Right away," said Kir.

I got up and walked downstairs. The clearance was nothing more than approval from an algorithm that matched headhunter experience with the estimated Mirror World difficulty, and I had never been denied a request. I knew that I would be wound up until I received permission. I had never learned to take rejection well, even when it was formal and impersonal.

"Your request for Sector M-237 has been approved," said Kir before I reached the main floor.

So, this was it. My future for the next several months was set.

I stepped out onto the porch and looked around. The sun was almost touching the surface of the ocean, and both the sky and the water glowed with a warm golden color; cicadas peacefully chirped in the trees behind the house. I was moved. This place had begun to feel like home, to the extent that the notion of home was applicable to my nomadic life.

Walking to my flyer I noticed a seagull silhouetted against the deepening blue of the evening sky. I wondered if my friend would be upset facing the closed wall of my bedroom in the morning. My heart unexpectedly ached for a second, but I consoled myself with the hope that the next guest would be kind to it too.

BETA BLUE

As usual, there was a blink in all ship systems when it crossed over the Mirror World boundary into Sector M-237. I immediately paused all the navigation programs and ran diagnostic tests. For unknown reasons, the singularity crossing always created some damage, and its severity was impossible to predict.

I wasn't too lucky this time. Kir estimated that it would take him almost two weeks to repair all of the corrupted software. But I wasn't complaining. The longer it took, the more time I had to complete pre-entry preparation at my own pace.

The blue planet started slowly filling the external camera screen, and I had a usual momentary conviction that I had accidentally made a loop in space and come back to Earth, but I reined in the desire to ask Kir for location confirmation. Instead, I told him to camouflage the ship and start blending with Beta Blue's computer network. By now the cabin fever kicked in, and I couldn't wait to start the field operation.

First, I ran a singularity-scoring program on digital profiles of the planet's inhabitants. The top hits tended to correlate with a higher intensity of the Dark Triad trait, although admittedly, this technique wasn't precise, gave a lot of false-positives and failed to pick up any-one completely avoiding the net. But I was fine with that. Our purists would spend months assimilating with the local population to look for subtler signs, but I didn't have that kind of patience.

The highest score belonged to a Remir Autran, and I asked Kir for his summary.

Remir's anomaly was obvious. Files that he periodically posted on random obscure websites spread like wildfire. They contained music, the old, archaic style that existed on Earth before artists learned to directly engage the subconscious levels of the brain. This style was still popular at home, albeit mostly among a modest group of connoisseurs.

He was approximately my age, less than a year younger. Kir didn't find anything particularly noteworthy about his early years. He came from an average middle-class family, dropped out of engi-neering school during his senior year and never touched the techni-cal field again. He didn't have a steady job. He had a history of erratic behavior and marked periods of heavy alcohol use. These were all good signs, very indicative of the Dark Triad type. Moreover, his per-sonal life seemed to be a mess, and the list of women he was involved with at one point or another guaranteed to take a long time to review. I impatiently interrupted Kir before he got into specific details.

"Kir, forget about women. Bring on a sample of his work – with video."

A screen opened in the center of my vision.

Remir, tall and very thin, stood in a circle of blue light. He was wearing a casual Beta Blue outfit – a loose robe on top of a gray shirt and light pants. There was a small pale scar in the corner of his mouth, which gave his face a slightly mocking expression, as if all his seriousness was just a sham.

He tossed back strands of ash-colored hair and looked straight into the camera. A large screen of the performance system interface lit up in the air.

At first, Remir touched the virtual surface gently as if getting himself comfortable, and it responded with the deep sound resembling a waking avalanche. He nodded to himself, moved his fingers across the glowing rectangle, and a jubilant melody burst out into the air like some mighty creature celebrating release from captivity.

I turned off the audio to better focus on Remir. Apparently, it was hard to keep the magic going. His face became contorted, his hair was dark from sweat, and he squinted as if to protect his eyes from the screen's brightness. I thought that he definitely had an aura of feverish intensity that I had learned to associate with Dark Triad personalities.

I turned off the feed.

"I think we have a decent chance here," I said. Of course, I didn't expect any response, but I liked to run things by Kir all the same. "The singularity score may not mean much, I give you that, but overall, he looks promising. Where is he now?"

"He lives in the main city, but for the last 25 days he has been staying in a hotel in the town of Oren," answered Kir.

"What's so special about Oren?"

"Nothing. Singularity score is low, population size low."

"Puzzling," I said. "What's wrong with living at home?"

"Nick, here is a relevant audio recording. It was made 26 days ago by the Ministry of Internal Affairs."

I heard the beeps of a communication device.

"Mr. Autran?" the woman on the phone sounded very calm.

"Speaking," Remir's voice was slightly hoarse as if he had a mild cold.

"Mr. Autran, we have a problem. In fact, you have a problem. We're sure you're aware of it."

There was a long silence.

"The president didn't appreciate your joke about his re-election campaign," continued the voice. "He was very upset, actually."

"I … it was a private conversation." Remir was clearly caught off guard. "In any case, there was nothing offensive."

He suddenly seemed to regain some confidence, "The president must have gotten the wrong interpretation."

"Do you want me to play you the recording?" The woman sounded sincerely helpful.

There was another period of silence.

"I didn't think so," her voice was openly smug.

"We want you out of the city until election day. There better be no noise from you during that time. Then you can come back on the condition that you'll publicly support the elected government immediately upon your return."

"I wouldn't enjoy doing that. I am not that much into politics, you might have heard that," said Remir in a friendly tone.

"Perhaps you don't quite understand. I don't think you would enjoy losing your city residence permit either. And you probably wouldn't enjoy having to distribute your work through the official channels. Understandably enough, the Ministry of Culture may not appreciate your style. Not to say that we have been, shall we say, negligent, allowing you to share your music informally despite the amount of network traffic it creates. You might have heard that some critical public functions were slowed down for a while after you posted your last release. I don't think you would enjoy it if we fixed this glitch."

There was a pause.

Then the woman continued, "The president got fed up, frankly. Leave the city before the end of the day."

The line went dead.

"So, he left," I said. "Not exactly heroic behavior, but civic courage is not a part of our requirements. Plus, what would you have done in his place?" Kir was silent. "Anyway, what's happening now?"

"The election is in two days. Remir is scheduled to come back the morning after that and will be heading straight to the news headquarters for a live interview."

"Excellent," I said, "let's pack."

Later that night, Kir landed my small passenger shuttle on a flat clearing in a mountain forest. I stepped onto the grass, slightly slippery from the evening mist, took a deep breath of cool fresh air and looked around.

On the north side, the trees climbed up a steep slope until they gave way to bare gray cliffs with wedges of snow in between. To the south, I saw a cluster of lights in the middle of a large valley below. It was Oren, the town where I was supposed to find Remir. I zoomed in; at close range its buildings resembled a herd of marine creatures exposing their backs above the dark waters of an imaginary sea.

The flyer slowly lifted off, stopped at treetop level and suddenly vanished as the vehicle's surface switched to a frequency invisible to the naked eye. It would be locked in this position until my return. Earth's security didn't allow headhunters to use any machinery on the closed planets out of concern for accidental exposures.

Before disappearing into the forest, I looked back and had to exercise some imagination to believe that the shuttle was still there.

"See you soon, don't get too lonely," I said and walked away.

The downward terrain was relatively tame, and I was able to descend in an almost straight line, only rarely having to go around patches of glacial moraines, where the ground was too unstable. A couple of times I skidded on steep slopes, but steadied myself by grabbing low tree branches.

Soon the ground flattened out, gradually leading me to the edge of wheat fields. It took me another hour before I finally reached the industrial yards that defined the boundaries of Oren. I started making my way through empty passages between the lots with parked agricultural equipment. Live security patrols had become obsolete long ago by the comprehensive net of electronic surveillance, and with Kir deleting my image in real time from all cameras I didn't have to worry about being inconspicuous. Even if I was stopped and questioned by a random police unit, there shouldn't be any problem. Kir had already run the identity creation program through the planet network, and there were no inconsistencies in the history of my digital construct. It was impossible to tell that I never existed, and in the worst case I could only be fined for the minor offense of not carrying an ID card.

I finally entered the residential district on the other side of the warehouses and immediately noticed that the place had a distinct air of shabbiness. Random pieces of trash were strewn on the sidewalks, and blotches of electronic graffiti flickered on peeling walls of the grotesquely shaped concrete structures. As I got farther away from the outskirts, the streets became cleaner, but the incongruent jumble of city blocks still looked way more prosaic than it had seemed from above.

After a few more minutes, I reached the hotel, where Remir had been staying since his arrival. Before going in, I quickly surveyed the interior through the multiple security camera feeds. Fortunately, the lobby was empty. The lights were dimmed, and a holographic message hanging in midair behind the counter indicated that service would resume in the morning.

I told Kir to unlock the doors, walked in and settled in the chair in one of the curved corners of a weirdly shaped room. Having studied the pattern of Remir's behavior, Kir predicted that waiting wouldn't take too long. To pass the time, I picked up a disposable news tablet from the low table, and a sentence immediately condensed on the empty gray screen: "Nick, would you like the latest update?"

I almost dropped it, but immediately recalled that Kir had already inserted my fingerprints into the central database.

"Sure," I said. Earth's surveillance satellites provided headhunters with an up-to-date overview of Mirror Worlds status, but I didn't have anything better to do anyway.

My curiosity was immediately rewarded. A big headline screamed at me in large red letters: ANOTHER ACT OF SABOTAGE BY EARTH AGENTS AT THE NORTHERN FACILITIES

I skipped the news summary and watched the live video coverage. A casually asymmetric, but still doubtlessly military structure was split in half by what seemed to be a major explosion. In a moment, the image of a burning building was replaced by menacing looking objects recovered on the scene of the bombing. They looked impressively real, and I mentally complimented the secret service artists both for imagination and graphical execution.

Kir's soft chime alert distracted me from this entertaining activity. I looked up and for a moment didn't recognize Remir in the hunched figure that stumbled out of the elevator doors. His hair and gray shirt were drenched in sweat in spite of the fact that the place had perfect thermal control, and his robe looked as if he had slept in it.

Without noticing me, Remir walked straight to the counter and punched some sequence on its surface. A small round bottle popped up from underneath. He unscrewed its top section, converting it into a glass and took several hurried gulps. Only after that did he glance at the room.

I put down the tablet, raised my hand in greeting, and he slowly approached. He looked completely different in person. The light in his eyes was gone, and so was the aura of desperate energy. His face had a haunted expression, and the glass in his hand was trembling.

"Why don't you join me?" I pretended to be oblivious about his condition.

He pulled a chair to my table and sat down. It seemed that he was glad to see another living soul.

I thought that things were unfolding quite nicely.

"How are you?" my question sounded almost mocking, but he didn't seem to care. He was sufficiently drunk.

"Yeah," he looked around as if determining the degree of hostility of various objects. "It hurts, the lights are too bright. If they would just turn the lights down, it would be much easier."

He took several more gulps, and the muscles in his face relaxed slightly. I watched, pondering my next step. Even though it was unethical to exploit his current state there was nothing technically wrong with it, and his shaky grasp on reality could be very useful for my first move.

"I am from Earth."

He didn't seem to hear.

"We're not aggressive," I continued, observing his reaction. "We don't plan to invade. Your news is made up."

He contemplated me in the most focused manner he could muster and nodded.

"No doubt. But … these…" he waved his hand in the air. "This place has *official* surveillance. You aren't cautious enough to be a spy, I'm afraid. Very funny of you, though."

I passed him the news tablet.

"Take a look."

He shrugged and took it in his hands.

"Kir, show him views from the security cameras," I said.

The screen flashed, and Remir's expression changed. He put the tablet on the table carefully, as if it was about to explode in his face. Then he pulled his chair away from me, and his images projected on the newsletter in different angles. And in each of them, my chair was empty.

A light panic appeared in his eyes.

"Who is Kir?" he asked and nervously looked around the room. "And … this …" he pointed to the screen, "this can't do that." He started to slowly get up not taking his eyes away from my face.

Now I needed to act quickly.

"I can do more than that," I said nodding towards the tablet.

Remir was backing away from me.

"Your depression, anxiety. The dark fog in your brain. Your insomnia." The timing was critical. "I can make it all go away."

I guessed correctly. Remir stopped.

"And the headache?" he whispered almost inaudibly.

"Right," I nodded, "and the headache."

"How … quickly?"

He was in my bio-transmission range.

"Kir, give him the basic psychoanalgesia," I ordered.

Remir's posture shifted as if a loose spring inside his body changed, now suddenly tight and stable.

It was very interesting to watch.

"I don't believe in talking to people in pain," I said, "I needed your mind back. It will wear off by tomorrow, though. I can't cure you, it's not my specialty."

His eyes were alert and clear, and incredulous.

"It just let go. All of it."

He passed his hand across his forehead, "How?"

I didn't answer, waiting for him to put it all together.

When he did, he stepped back again.

"Really, Earth?"

I smiled reassuringly, "Remir, we want nothing from Beta Blue at large. It doesn't have anything we care about. I'm here because of you. I might offer you something that you find interesting."

He processed that for a moment.

"Well, whatever you did," he said touching his forehead again, "I suppose you could have killed me if you wanted."

I continued to hold my reassuring smile. Kir was indeed capable of permanently shutting down a human brain. All headhunters' implants had this function as a last resort in self-defense situations. Fortunately, I had never had to use it.

"But you didn't," he continued, "what do you want?"

He was studying me with intense curiosity. He didn't seem afraid.

"Maybe nothing, I need to find out. And then I might make you an offer."

"To find out …"

"If you're very special."

Surprisingly, he didn't look intrigued.

"Why do you care?"

"I'll explain later. For now, I need you to wear this to run my test. It won't take long."

I pulled the silver mask with the psychometric device from my pocket and placed it on the table. It gleamed in the dim light of the room.

Remir gave it a thoughtful look, then shrugged, sat down and put it on. I watched as he sat very still, his body frozen in a program-induced trance, his face looking like a blind sculpture. Kir was monitoring all of the room's entrances, and all was well – everyone was still asleep.

After several minutes, the test result displayed in the center of my vision, and I mentally congratulated myself. Not only was Remir's score above the necessary cutoff, it was also the highest I had ever seen. I multiplied it by the Beta Blue difficulty coefficient, and thought that this time my luck was exceptional.

"Done," I said, and he took off the mask.

"What was that?" he asked, shaking his head.

The standard rule was to give him a break before going into detail. Not to mention that people would start waking up soon.

"You passed and I have a lot to offer you." I stood up preparing to leave, "But I have to go now."

"Wait."

They always protested at this moment.

"You'll have a wonderful sleep," I told him before disappearing behind the door. "See you soon."

The plan was fully formed in my mind by the time I stepped back out onto the sidewalk. Clearly, the best moment to suggest defection was right after Remir's mandatory interview. His emotional state would be rather unstable, and my job to convince him to go with me would be the easiest.

There was nothing else for me to do in this shithole where I could attract too much attention, so I headed to the central station and took the first train to the city.

The next several hours were unremarkable as the sleek underground express whooshed past most of the local stops. The few people who shared the flexible tube with me were dozing. I glanced at my reflection in the window and had a momentary dreamlike feeling of participating in some strange dress-up game at home. A loose robe and plain suit set, which Kir printed just before I left my ship, was an average outfit here for my age group, but it suddenly felt too weird. Thinking that I must be tired, I told Kir to let me know when we were close to the main city station and shut my eyes.

Kir woke me up when the train had already stopped at the platform. Passengers started filing out of the car and I followed the line. The moment I stepped outside, the intense sunlight of the early afternoon, humid heat and unsavory smells of the big city simultaneously assaulted my senses. But I found all of it perversely pleasant after the weeks of living in the sterile atmosphere of the ship.

The city definitely wasn't anything like Oren. Much wider streets weaved between asymmetrical high-rises; and the dense flow of pedestrians and heavy car traffic negotiated with each other at complex intersections. Curiously, there wasn't a single straight line in view: the extreme biomorphic style, usually a brief and harmless period in other worlds, had happened to gain the status of official state architecture on Beta Blue.

I switched from onlooker mode and focused on the immediate plan. Both theory and my own experience dictated that my next step should be temporary assimilation; it was critical that Remir became as comfortable with me as possible. Normally I would have to rub shoulders with people on the streets for some time in order to study local behavior at close range. In this case though, there was a perfect shortcut; the feeds from police drones and cameras of personal communication devices effectively covered every nook and cranny in the inhabited areas of Beta Blue. I could hole up in some low-key place, tell Kir to run a program that fused them together, and a virtual copy of the world would literally be at my fingertips.

I checked in to a nearby commuter hotel, took the elevator to the tenth floor and found my room in a curved row of identical doors; the handle acknowledged my fingerprints and granted me access. I examined the interior and admitted that, as compensation for its shabbiness, it was mercifully simplistic. I closed the blinds of the narrow horizontal slit that looked out onto the bowed side of a neighboring building and lay on the single bed, propping up my head with a pile of cheap, spongy pillows.

"Give me an aerial view," I ordered, closing my eyes, and found myself suspended in the air above the city.

The clusters of grotesquely elaborate buildings below made me think of a coral reef. I adjusted the viewpoint to eye level, and the scenery changed. Now I was standing on a very busy sidewalk. The world around me looked solid, with the exception of a few blind spots distinguishable by faded colors and blurry outlines – Kir filled in the missing details by extrapolation. The murmur of street noise captured by hundreds of personal device microphones added to the effect.

I focused on a random lovely girl hurriedly weaving through the crowd. Her face was flushed from running, visibly distressed. I told Kir to bring up her data. According to her home security video, she had accidentally let her cat out and spent almost half an hour luring it back in and now was on course to be late for her first job interview. Nothing in her personal files caught my attention except for a full collection of Remir's music, carefully sorted and frequently accessed.

Her bus appeared from behind the corner and came to a halt across the street. She stopped at the pedestrian crosswalk; her expression now desperate. "Kir, change the signal," I said, and the traffic light obediently switched. Cars stopped, and she darted across, just in time to jump inside the closing doors. I smiled and looked away.

For the next several hours, I wandered through the complex ecosystem of stores, restaurants and other ground level venues, observing nuances of local habits. People were going about their daily business in a manner typical for all big cities in all Mirror Sectors. For the most part, they looked reserved, even sullen and didn't smile or make frequent eye contact with each other, but they didn't look like a population on the verge of war with a super civilization. I wondered how many actually believed in that.

Deciding that I had enough information from the street level, I used drones to look into windows on the top floors. The crowd was left far below, and I hovered in space between the twisted pillars of high-rises. The data coming from one of the offices piqued my interest, and I told Kir to zoom in.

The stakes were high here. This group was trying to reverse-engineer Earth technology by studying a recently discovered artifact, an actual piece of an ancient energy generator, somehow missed by the nanobots.

"Kir, how far along are they in their research?" I asked.

The world around me suddenly froze.

"Kir?"

He didn't reply.

I opened my eyes and made a hand signal to turn off all external feeds. There was no response. My vision was blocked by the same still image of the room with motionless figures staring at their displays. For the first time in my life, I was blind. I sat up and tried to stop the cold wave of panic rising from my stomach. It simply wasn't possible. Kir never malfunctioned. I didn't have time to consider all of the possible ramifications when the picture started moving again.

"Nick, there was a problem. Their progress was stalled, but I couldn't determine the reason." Kir's voice was calm as usual. "The analysis overloaded my computing resources."

"But … Kir …" It didn't make sense.

"I ran the emergency diagnostics on all my systems. Everything is in order."

"Pause all programs," I said.

I never imagined how elated I'd be to see the dull interior of a shabby hotel room. Now I had to find out what happened. I couldn't afford glitches like that – Kir was my only advantage on this planet.

"Let me look at your logs," I said, and a system interface window opened.

I winced at the complicated tangle of pulsing surfaces, took a deep breath and began troubleshooting.

The results didn't make me feel any better. I could see that Kir had run into some logical inconsistency that sent him into recursive loops, but try as I might, I kept losing the thread. After some fruitless digging, I finally had to assume that it was one of those almost zero probability events that were mentioned in the implant liability contract. Nobody, including me, ever believed that they could actually happen.

There was a simple test to prove this theory by repeating my steps. I braced myself and said in an upbeat voice, "Kir, resume all programs. Check the research status again."

This time nothing strange happened. Kir positioned me next to a woman that was staring at her computing screen and twirling a strand of blond hair around her finger.

"Nick, they are stuck because of this person's error."

I wasn't sure if I should feel relieved or more worried.

"Why were you unable to identify this before?"

"Nick, I can't tell you. I don't know."

I decided to conclude that the statistics caught up with me on this one.

"Kir, let's go to a private location. But this time, intercept only hidden camera transmissions," I said.

Only one feed was available – it seemed that the government wasn't interested in the private lives of its population at large.

I looked inside the monitored apartment. An unhealthy-looking middle-aged man stood in the center of the room staring at his computer from a distance as if he was afraid to get any closer. I checked the recent network activity and saw that someone from the Homeland Safety Department had remotely accessed his system and purposely left the folders messed up, files randomly opened, their order rearranged. I checked the content and almost whistled with surprise; the man had been saving media images that claimed to capture sightings of Earth's military fleet. And there were pages and pages of his calculations and design drawings.

"What does he do for a living?" I asked Kir.

"He works as a commercial aircraft engineer," he answered.

"Why are they watching him?"

"The security services received a recording submitted by a nearby pub bartender."

"Let's listen to it," I said.

The lively music in my ears sounded completely out of place in comparison with the dead stillness of the man's apartment.

"Another round, please," a man said, sounding a bit shaky, "listen I have to tell you something about these Earth spaceships. I've done the calculations backwards and forwards. I can't get it out of my head." There was a rustle of paper, "See, there is an aerodynamic flaw. I don't care what technology is used to power them." He switched to whisper, "Keep it between us, but these things just can't fly."

I thought that the government was relatively humane. The man in the apartment had accidentally gotten too close to the truth, but he was still alive, just warned for now.

I took a sip of water from the plastic glass on my nightstand and told Kir to move to another random point in the city. After several more hours, the overall picture of a benign totalitarian state gained color and detail, and the city started to look familiar. I turned off the external video streaming and felt that the reconnaissance was more or less done.

I got up from the bed and stretched. There was one place that I had to visit in person: the Media Center where Remir's interview was scheduled. It would be center stage for the next step in my operation, and I had to check its surroundings properly.

I felt rather hungry by now, and it was dinner time here, but I never trusted local cuisines. I ate one of the nutrition bars that I brought from the ship and left the hotel in very good spirits.

◻   ◻   ◻

The sun was already setting, westward walls of the buildings were touched by the warm orange light, and the afterwork crowd slowed, having lost their midday energy. Women were openly checking me out as we passed one another, but I was used to this kind of attention on the closed Mirror Worlds. Centuries of human DNA improvements on Earth had done their job. Women aside, standing out was a major inconvenience for my stealth operations, but there was nothing I could do about that.

An especially attractive young girl gave me a smile, and I imagined her with tiny beads of sweat on her upper lip in my hotel room, her body next to mine on the wrinkled sheets of my bed.

Not now, I said to myself, business came first. I would have all the time between checking the Media Center neighborhood tonight and meeting with Remir the day after tomorrow. I quickened my step, thinking about the *Game*, as I referred to my main entertainment during working trips.

It so happened that my personal life was rather bleak until I'd started my headhunting career. Women from Earth were beautiful, intelligent and easy to get along with, and I had nobody but myself to blame for my failed relationships. I had tried everything, even conjoined cyber-mode, which made implants share their external feeds, but it didn't help. Instead of providing the desired effect of intimacy, I would feel choked. I was at a loss.

And then I met the women of the Mirror Worlds. The vast majority were of no interest to me, even ones whose looks were on a par with Earth's standard. There were some, however, that had a quality that I couldn't quite define, but it made all the difference, and it made the Game extremely exciting.

Everything usually began from a moment of explicit eye contact, after which I would instruct Kir to suspend any communications with me until further notice or in case of an emergency. I wanted a fair challenge and needed to level the playing field. Then the thrilling part would start. After the first cautious steps, the boundary breaking process would speed up, the wordplay would become treacherous, body language ambiguous, and, finally, the entire pretense was dropped and there would be an open acknowledgment of attraction. The sex that followed was incomparable to anything I'd ever experienced back home.

Unfortunately, the end was inevitable. My brief crashes had never had a sufficiently high Dark Triad score, and random people weren't allowed on Earth unless they were brought by the outliers. So, the Game had to end when I left the planet, well before any negative issues had time to surface, and the sadness at parting only added to the overall effect.

But it had to wait just a little longer, I repeated to myself. I was getting very close to my destination – by now I was already at the border of the Government District, the hilly area adorned with the spiral of the presidential palace at the top. I stopped at a convenience store, and, using the bank account set up by Kir, bought a set of props – a local communication device, sunglasses and headphones with a conspicuous microphone bead.

The streets here were significantly emptier since the state employees had already gone home, and awe-inspiring buildings appeared abandoned for the night. It was getting darker but the overhead lamps weren't on yet, which added to the feel of the evening desolation.

The Media Center, a relatively easy on the eyes imitation of a partially melted iceberg, was located on a plaza with a breathtaking panoramic of the city. I walked around the grounds until I knew the layout by heart, and again thought how exceptionally smoothly everything was going. And then I remembered the strange incident with Kir. It was a random glitch, I said to myself and pushed it out of my mind.

I was ready to go back, but before leaving I decided to stop at the observation deck for a quick view. I reached the edge, placed my hands on the rails that were still warm from the heat of the day, and looked at the cityscape below my feet. The flickering high-rise lights made downtown look unexpectedly alive, and it was the first time that the local architecture didn't annoy me. It was a good thing, given that there would be no escape from it until I left.

I gave the city one last glance and started walking downhill along a completely empty alleyway. The bright light of the night's illumination suddenly flooded the streets, and for a split second I didn't understand what had forced me to leap off the road. I pressed my back against the nearest wall and only then realized what triggered my reaction; there were two human shadows on the ground the instant that the lights went on. One started at my feet, and another, a longer one, stretched parallel to it.

In an almost inaudible whisper, I asked Kir for the full digital coverage of the area provided by the dense net of security cameras. Except for my lonely figure, the street was empty.

"Kir, replay the last two minutes of my eyesight," I said, trying to slow my pounding heart. I paused the recording at the moment of the flash and reviewed the snapshot. There was a clear image of two long shadows on the ground – the only good news was that I wasn't hallucinating.

"Show the location of second shadow's origin," I ordered in a low voice.

"Nick, it's a blind spot."

Keeping my back to the wall, I slowly inched to the area where the shadow's owner had hid. Of course, there was no one there now.

"Kir, increase the radius," I somehow knew that this would be futile.

It was. According to Kir, there were no people in the neighborhood.

Trying not to succumb to fully justifiable paranoia, I decided I'd run an analysis in the relative safety of my hotel room. Not relying on Kir anymore, I painstakingly cleared every sector around me visually as I started making my way towards downtown. However, all was still and quiet in the Government District, and there was nothing suspicious in the livelier Central City neighborhoods either.

I closed my room door, sat on the edge of the bed and tried to put things into perspective. Somebody had hidden in a blind zone when I passed and then disappeared without leaving a trace. I checked the detailed digital layout of the area once again, and in the end established that the video coverage had enough holes to allow for some non-nefarious explanation. There was some probability, however negligent, that a person happened to walk in my vicinity accidentally avoiding surveillance cameras. Fully unconvinced, I jacked up Kir's security settings to the maximum and went to sleep.

When I woke up in the morning, the sunshine outside was so uplifting that the events of the previous night seemed like a bad dream, except that Kir's recording of the mysterious shadow would be available to review at any time.

I moved the only chair out of my way and started pacing the room.

"So, Kir, let's look at all aspects of our situation. You must agree that the last two incidents were not only highly improbable, but also rather disturbing," I said aloud.

A shiver went down my spine as I remembered the feeling of suddenly going blind.

"What would you do in my place?" It wasn't a well-defined question, and Kir naturally kept quiet. "You wouldn't leave immediately, would you?"

I gave this thought proper consideration.

"In fact, Kir, you probably would. Because we don't know what happened."

I imagined turning around and going back to Earth empty-handed, with accounts of some incoherent incidents as an excuse. Then I thought about the outlandish amount of money I'd be leaving behind.

"But Kir," I continued, "we're almost done with the target. I should close the deal tomorrow. And then we can get the hell out of here."

I decided to interpret Kir's silence as a sign of approval even though it was clear that my judgment was clouded. Moreover, I knew for a fact that my strong inclination for getting involved in risky endeavors was my major character flaw. But then again, it was exactly what made me choose my job in the first place. I didn't want to leave.

"We'll proceed as planned, but with extra vigilance," I said firmly.

Now there was the practical question of what to do next. Remir would arrive tomorrow morning, and I was already prepared for our meeting. My initial plan was to start looking for a potential Game partner by hanging out at the bustling spots around the city, but given the way things were going, I needed to drop this idea and exercise restraint.

I felt robbed. The Game was a big reason I liked my job. But now, as nice as it would be, it wasn't worth the risk, not if I wanted to be on the safe side.

"Fine, Kir," I said bitterly, "I'll give up on women this time."

I spent the rest of the day playing some stupid games from Kir's collection and periodically checking on Remir.

He started drinking in the morning, and was pretty much out of it by the time he left the hotel for the station. There was precisely one remaining overnight train to the city, but he contemplated the departures screen in the waiting area with deep concentration as if calculating multiple options.

Finally, he reserved a seat and made a beeline to the small transit bar. When the PA system announced his train's boarding, he ordered another drink. I was a little alarmed, but Remir made it just in time, the doors closing right behind his back. He immediately proceeded to the restaurant car and settled at the counter next to an attractive brunette. Kir did a quick review of her digital history and confirmed that they didn't have any prior connections.

After a couple of stops, they were leaning very close to each other. She laughed and touched his shoulder when he whispered something in her ear.

Meanwhile, all the news stations were broadcasting a steady rising count of votes in favor of the only presidential candidate. I turned off the displays and, disappointed by the boring day, went to sleep.

In the morning, everything still looked completely safe. Remir's interview was scheduled to begin in little less than two hours, and his train was already approaching the city.

I checked out of the hotel and began walking towards the Media Center. According to Kir, a serious storm was approaching the local shores and the air outside had already cooled down. People on the streets were dressed warmer, but I was fine – my body easily adjusted to the temperature thanks to my genetically enhanced thermoregulation.

Remir's train pulled up to the platform, and I asked Kir to use camera feeds to follow him along his way through the city. And then, I abruptly slowed down in the middle of the sidewalk. Instead of the station arrival area, I was looking at the closed door of a guest room in the hotel where we had met two days ago.

I must admit, I didn't expect this development and automatically continued walking towards the Government District as Kir showed me the events with Remir from the previous night. According to video records, Remir and his female acquaintance got off the train after several stops and took a taxi back to Oren.

Let's not call it a failure, I tried to console myself, let's call it an incomplete success. Strictly speaking, nothing particularly bad had happened, at least not for me. It simply meant a slight change in my plans. Not that I was happy about extending my stay on Beta Blue, but it wasn't a big deal. The delay should not be too significant. Remir had just gotten himself into serious trouble with the authorities, and his psychological state wouldn't be any better after the problematic interview. Anyway, the beginning had been way too smooth.

By now, I was next to the Media Center plaza. There was obviously nothing for me to do here anymore, but before turning back I decided to make a brief stop at the familiar observation deck to figure out the logistics for my travel back to Oren. Unfortunately, someone was already there. A woman in an elegant, but very simple white dress with a short light cape was leaning on the railing and looking down at the city. Her clothes flapped in the strong wind, but she didn't seem to notice the chill, her pose was relaxed and casual. I turned to leave, and she suddenly looked in my direction. Dark sunglasses shaded her face, and her shoulder-length brown hair had been completely disheveled by the breeze. She was holding a plastic cup, and I noticed an expensive looking bottle of wine sticking out of the bag over her shoulder. I thought that it was a bit bizarre, but then again, I wasn't completely sure about local customs. Maybe it was completely normal for women to drink from disposable glasses outside government buildings in the morning.

She suddenly walked towards me, smiling. There was something slightly unnatural in her smile, but she was very attractive, which at the moment was the only thing I truly cared about. She stopped in front of me and pulled another plastic glass from her bag.

"This wine is excellent," she said cheerfully, "you have to give it a try!"

"Is there a special occasion?" I smiled back, accepting the container.

She didn't answer. Instead, she poured me the rest of the dark red liquid from the almost empty bottle.

"You aren't local," she stated.

"No," I agreed readily. It was pleasant not to lie. Unfortunately, it didn't last. "I'm a provincial reporter, came here to cover the elections. Live news from the streets, you know."

Apparently, it satisfied her curiosity since she didn't ask any more questions.

At the close range she looked even better. She was slender, not as tall and athletic as an average woman on Earth, but her proportions were nice, and a hint of fragility gave her some extra points in my eyes.

"It's very nice here," I said and took a sip of wine, pretending not to notice gusts of cold wind.

"True. Too bad that I don't come here often," she nodded.

"It's a beautiful city," I continued, "I wish I knew it better."

It was a blatant lie – the buildings below reminded me of a dead coral reef now, gray and petrified in the bright light of the morning. But I wanted to keep the conversation going.

She didn't say anything to this, however. I noticed that her lips were bluish and her teeth were chattering slightly.

"You're freezing," I suggested.

"Yes," she agreed. A vertical line appeared on her forehead, and she looked around as if surprised by her surroundings, but the strange expression quickly went away.

"Do you want me to show you the city?" she asked abruptly, and I almost choked on my wine. But I recovered immediately.

"I would love to," I replied with an enthusiastic smile, "but let me check the flight schedule." I took the local communication device from my pocket and changed my position so that she couldn't see the screen.

Kir, is she a security concern? I typed, holding my small tablet away from her.

"No, Nick," he said immediately.

I was about to ask him for details of her background, but then stopped myself. It would ruin the Game by giving me an unfair advantage. What Game, I thought, remembering my promise to be vigilant. But this was too appealing to pass up.

Remir could wait. Not much would change in the next few hours, and it was better not to analyze my decision-making process too deeply.

I put away the tablet and looked at her impenetrable dark shades. "There are flights every hour. I'm at your disposal."

"Perfect," she said quickly, "let's go. I agree that it's chilly here. It'll be much warmer at sea level. And the area down there is more fun than this government desert."

She looked at the empty plastic cup in her hand and turned, searching for a trash disposal. There were not any in view, so she crumbled the cup and stuffed it into her bag. Then she gestured for me to follow as she headed toward the stairs leading from the overlook.

"Lita, by the way," she said over her shoulder.

I noted that she didn't ask for my name.

We crossed the plaza, and she stopped by a stylish, but not particularly new car parked on the side of the relatively busy road. I hesitated for a second, remembering the empty wine bottle, but she laughed, apparently intercepting my concerned look.

"I'll put it in automatic mode," she said opening the door.

This meant that we would move at a snail's speed obeying all possible traffic rules, which was annoying, but safe. I got in.

She punched several buttons on the dashboard, the engine murmured, and the car gently pulled into the street. I quickly became grateful for the extremely conservative style of the autopilot; however, the descent she chose was so steep that I had to hold onto the armrests in order not to slide down. She was silent, and I didn't say anything either, waiting for further development.

Soon the road became flatter – we were approaching sea level.

"Listen, I've got an idea," she said. "Let's go swimming. And I'll take you around the city later, after the sun has gone down."

I thought about the storm warning, but decided not to argue. Lita fumbled with the console, and the car turned towards the coastline.

After a couple of sharp turns, a view of the rather stunning bay opened up in a distance. We exited towards a side road leading to the shore and drove under an overhead electronic sign, which flashed a warning about the park closure due to the severe storm.

I prepared a disappointed expression, but her face lit up.

"Great! There won't be any lifeguards today. We're safe," she said enthusiastically.

I wondered what exactly "safe" meant, but by that time the car stopped in the completely empty parking lot at the very edge of the pebble beach. We got out, and I noted that all service booths were indeed closed. The waves were huge, and strong whips of air violently jerked Lita's light dress. She took it off as if not noticing the cold, crumpled it into a ball and threw it on the front seat. Underneath she was wearing a tight silver leotard.

For a moment, I forgot about the storm. I already had a pretty good mental image of her body, but the reality notably exceeded my expectations. It was one of those rare occasions when the clothes didn't hide any faults.

"We are in luck," she turned to me, "we can go beyond the buoys!"

I glanced at the water. Large swells carrying white caps on their crests slammed against the shore like loud thunder and retreated back with an angry hiss. I looked at her with some concern.

She was hugging her shoulders, her legs and arms covered with goose bumps.

"The water is warm, we just need to get in," she said confidently.

I wasn't worried about myself, but I had no way of knowing her level of competence in the rough sea.

"True, but we could freeze when we get out," I didn't want to reveal my doubts about her swimming ability and appear overly cautious, either. "I would rather ..."

She took off her sunglasses. There were tears in her eyes, and it was so unexpected that I stopped mid-sentence.

"It's the wind," she said hurriedly.

Before I had a chance to respond, she ran toward the water.

"Wait!" I shouted, but she didn't stop and dove into an approaching wave.

Her head bobbed up some distance away from the shore, and she took off away from the beach without looking back.

I remembered the empty wine bottle and her strained smile on the observation deck, thinking that the whole thing was very strange. But something about her had made me guess that she would be an excellent Game player, and, in addition, at this point I was genuinely worried about her safety – the storm was fairly serious. It didn't seem like I had much of a choice. I shrugged and then undressed down to my brief and went in. Apparently, Kir evaluated the situation as an emergency because he was instantly present and opened a screen with maps of the local currents. It was a good call; however, I immediately noticed that Lita had entered the path of a strong drift, which was moving toward the open sea with the speed of a fast river current.

I caught up with her, dodging waves by diving underneath their crests, and touched her arm.

"Hold on!" I tried to outshout the wind. "You are caught in a rip!"

She stopped swimming forward, but it didn't slow her down. Then she understood. She turned around and tried to move against the current, but it kept pulling her back. I saw that she was getting really scared.

"Kir, find an optimal route to the beach," I muttered under my breath.

I quickly reviewed the displayed directions and thought that getting back was very doable unless she panicked. I gave her a reassuring smile.

"Don't fight it, save your energy! Swim after me!" I tried to keep my voice as calm as possible for a person who was being forced to yell.

She nodded and followed my lead towards the open sea.

It seemed to take an eternity to exit the current. When the surge finally let us go, the shore was a significant distance away, but at least it wasn't getting any farther.

Then we started our long swim back. I stayed nearby, ready to offer help, but she made it by herself even though her speed kept steadily decreasing, and she clearly struggled at the end. It took us so long that by the time we got out of the water the sun was starting to roll behind the dark cliffs. The wind had become even colder now, but we walked to the car very slowly – she didn't seem to have the energy for a faster pace.

Once we were inside, she turned on the heat, and sat quietly for a while, too exhausted to talk. I noticed that her knees and hands were shaking.

"Thank you," she said finally, "but how did you figure out the current?"

"Intuition," I replied, "and luck."

"I'm sorry. I would have sworn it was safe. I come here to swim all the time."

"It was a temporary anomaly, created by the storm."

"How do you know these things?" There was a sincere respect in her voice.

I reprimanded myself for the slip.

"I love open water," I said. At least it wasn't a lie.

"Today was a very strange day," she winced, as if remembering something unpleasant. But then she focused on me again, and I could see that she truly noticed me at last.

She brushed the wet strands of her hair from her face, and for a moment we silently watched each other. She looked away first and started fumbling around, searching for her dress. It turned out that she was sitting on it, so when she managed to pull it on, it was rather wet.

"I'll drive," she said, "I am as sober as I have ever been in my whole life."

She gave me a quick sideways glance and started the car. We exited the park at a reasonable speed, but once outside she accelerated so sharply that for a second, I missed the autopilot mode.

The sun was still up, albeit very low, but she didn't put on her glasses, squinting slightly when the light fell on her face. I looked at her profile and thought that her features were just right, the way I would like to draw a woman's face if I could draw.

"The city is ugly," she said suddenly. "Everything is the same; every damn building is a copy. They don't have any imagination."

"Who?" I asked. "Architects?"

She gave me a strange look and didn't answer.

I thought it would be nice to touch her damp hair and run my fingers through it.

"You're drenched. Do you want me to take you to your hotel?" she asked, not taking her eyes off the road.

"That would be good," I agreed, trying to sound casual. Things were definitely progressing in a promising direction. I gave her the address, and she nodded without slowing down.

We spent the rest of the ride in silence – she seemed to be completely absorbed with driving. I imagined moving my hands along her neck and down the curve of her back, but decided that I needed to think of something else for the time being.

She stopped the car at the entrance to the hotel parking garage, still not looking in my direction. It was my turn to make the next move. I was about to suggest that she come up for a drink when several displays flicked open in my visual field.

"Nick, there is an emergency. Your mission is in jeopardy," said Kir.

An ambulance was wailing its way through the streets of Oren. Inside, Remir was linked to monitors and sensors, his pupils the size of small pins, his face blank, his lips a dusty blue. The intercepted data showed that his vitals were dropping rapidly.

I swore to myself.

"It was an amazing day. Was great knowing you," I said in a buoyant voice and opened the door. I thought that I caught a brief expression of surprise and felt annoyed. The Game crumbled without ever starting, and I really liked her. I thought that she must feel disappointed too, but even if that was the case she didn't let on. Instead, she gently touched my hand and smiled.

"Goodbye," she said, "and thank you. You wouldn't know it, but you really helped me today."

I wanted to ask what she meant, but there was no time. If Remir was to die, my outlandish bounty would disappear into thin air. There was a moment of awkward hesitation, but fortunately her dashboard display showed an incoming call, and I quickly got out. The car immediately picked up speed and turned onto the main road at the end of the alley.

"Kir, what happened to Remir?" I whispered.

"Recreational drug overdose," Kir summarized the rows of medical notes scrolling down my vision.

On a hospital camera feed, the ambulance stopped at the entrance to the emergency wing, and I watched as Remir was rushed to intensive care.

"Kir, check train schedules to Oren for tonight," I said.

"The next train isn't leaving until morning," he replied.

Great, I thought. The only remaining option to make it in time was driving, which I'd have to do using a local contraption at a speed that was both unsafe and illegal. Of course, Kir would delete my car from police feeds, but still ... I sighed, accepting my fate.

"Find me the closest rental," I said, switching to professional mode.

"Nick, the hotel has a self-dispatch site inside its parking facility."

"Reserve me the best piece of crap they have," I said and walked toward the garage gates.

Within a matter of minutes, I was on the road to Oren. Kir took over the autopilot control, and I focused on Remir who had already transferred to the recovery unit after receiving emergency treatment. Through a video camera inside the room, I watched him lay motionlessly on a hospital bed, his body covered by a web of tubes and monitor cords. He was alone, and his condition was officially upgraded to "serious, but stable." However, Kir's data analysis predicted something that the hospital staff couldn't see yet – cascading organ failure starting in the very near future. I didn't have much time.

I told Kir to accelerate. The engine revved, and the car bolted forward, making me feel slightly unnerved; I didn't have to worry about violating speed limits, but this thing wasn't exactly designed for the tight turns and sharp lane changes that were now being asked of it. I was beginning to feel annoyed with Remir, but dismissed these unflattering thoughts, which were only unproductive.

Fortunately, the traffic was light, and I arrived safely, pulling up to the hospital with less than ten minutes to spare. I ran to the beehive-shaped emergency building, slowed down in the lobby, smoothed out my hair and assumed an air of busy confidence. The door for medical personnel opened, recognizing me as a support technician who had been called to fix an equipment glitch in Remir's recovery room.

I followed the directions to Remir's unit, ordered Kir to stream views from the hallway surveillance cameras and walked in.

Remir was conscious and slowly opened his eyes, apparently having heard the click of the shutting door. Dark circles under his eyes looked like bruises.

"Was it suicide?" I asked leaning over the footboard.

He recognized me.

"Hard to tell," his voice was barely audible, but his lips twisted slightly, indicating a grin.

"Well," I shrugged, "you'd better make up your mind. If I don't intervene, irreversible damage will start in less than five minutes."

A spasm went down his throat.

"Remir, your body is shutting down. There is only so much that your medication can do. I need to physically administer our drug if you want to live."

He nodded almost immediately.

I pulled a dissolvable patch from my pocket and plastered it to his hand. Then I sat in a chair in the corner and waited. It didn't take long. Monitoring devices showed the threatening signals starting to retreat, and Remir's face gained a faint color. He apparently felt the change too.

"Did it work?" his voice was hoarse, but noticeably more normal.

I got up and went to the side of the bed.

"You'll be fine. But you'll need to stay here for some time. You have to heal. I'll see you when you're better. The drug will make you sleep, to speed up the process."

I was about to leave, but a sudden movement in the hallway attracted my attention. A woman appeared from behind the corner, breaking the stillness of the empty corridor. She was walking quickly, looking at the unit numbers, and for a moment I forgot about Remir. As improbable as it was, I recognized Lita. She was even wearing the same dress, though wrinkled and without the cape. Astounded, I watched her approach our door.

She came in and went straight to the bed, her eyes anxiously fixed on Remir's face. Then she glanced in my direction and, as if momentarily losing her balance, she stepped backwards knocking off a plastic glass that was perched on the edge of a small nightstand.

"Lita, I'm fine now. And he is helping," said Remir quickly.

"I'm helping." At that moment, I understood exactly what had happened. I swore at myself for not having seen this sooner.

Not taking her eyes from me, she picked up the cup from the floor and put it back.

"Lita, we need to talk," with some effort, Remir turned his head in my direction. "How much time do I have?"

"Before you fall asleep? About five minutes." By now I had completely regained my cool. "By the way, don't worry, they don't have audio here, just video monitoring. See you later," I gave Lita a friendly nod on my way out.

I made my way down the corridor and out of the building watching the live feed from the hospital. There was no way to hear their conversation, but Kir has provided me with a transcript by reading Remir's lip movements. Lita, unfortunately, was sitting on the bed with her back to the camera, so I couldn't see her reaction to Remir's story about our midnight meeting in his hotel lobby, which he was recounting with his usual ironic half-smile. The pauses between his words were getting longer; he was slowly falling into the induced unconsciousness.

I found a cluster of mesh chairs on the lawn in front of the hospital entrance, picked up one and moved it slightly away from the others and farther from the illuminated sidewalks.

"Kir, show me Lita just before the time of Remir's interview," I asked, already having guessed what I would find out.

Through the lenses of the Media Center's security cameras, I saw her waiting on the plaza outside. She looked nervous and repeatedly hit a button on her communication device. According to Kir, she was calling Remir's mobile phone. There was no response, but she kept trying until she suddenly received an incoming call from a different number.

"Lita, he wasn't on the train," the person on the other end of the line sounded confused, but he obviously was trying to be comforting. Kir identified him as a Media Center employee and Lita's long-time acquaintance.

"We checked with the hotel; he is still there. Lita, don't call. He is not alone."

"I see. Thanks for the heads up!" her voice was unnaturally high.

"Lita, I am sorry. I know it's a mess. Hope it'll somehow work out ... good luck."

He waited for a moment, but she was silent, and he hung up.

Lita sat down on the wide steps of the building, then abruptly got up and went towards the observation deck.

"That's enough," I said. "Now, give me data on their relationship."

Kir did a great job presenting their three-year long love story in several sentences. The pattern was as clear as the logic behind it was incomprehensible.

They had met in the state-owned studio where she worked as a sound engineer, where he was making his first and only official recording. At that point, she had been in a stable relationship for five years. He became obsessed with her. The music he released back then was all written for her, and, incidentally, all pieces from that period were widely considered masterpieces. She left her partner and moved in with Remir. His first affair happened a year later. She left. He fell apart. He hysterically pleaded for her to return, and when she refused, he went into a steep downward spiral and ended up in jail on public disturbance charges. She bailed him out and went back to him. Over the next two years, this cycle kept repeating with minor variations; his other affairs, her periodic attempts to move on, his immediate crackups.

The mesh chair was remarkably uncomfortable, but I ignored it, trying to digest this information. I hadn't seen anything quite like it before. Whatever was in his head, Remir obviously couldn't last without her for long. And why did she continue going back? Was it love, or was it an attachment disorder? It was a philosophical question, and I didn't have the luxury to dwell on it. In any case, he was not going to leave without her, that much was clear.

I had to admit that things had gotten a little messy. But the Dark Triad outliers never gave me an easy time, and I was used to their idiosyncratic behavior and nervous breakdowns. Remir's overdose wasn't a big deal, really. And my accidental episode with Lita, in a way, simplified things. She was able to see that I wasn't some alien monster.

I decided that there was no reason to drop this case, even more so that there was a reason to hope that we were very close to completion. I just needed to tread carefully.

By now Remir was asleep, and a weary looking doctor was talking to Lita in the hallway. She nodded, quickly signed some forms he gave her and headed towards the exit.

In a moment, she appeared outside the hospital doors and slowed down, anxiously looking around. I stood up, waved to attract her attention and sat back down when she saw me. She hesitated for a moment and then warily moved in my direction as if she was walking on a tightrope. She stopped some distance away, her silhouette completely dark against the lights of buildings and pavement behind her back. I didn't get up. It was critical not to scare her now.

"Was he delusional?" she asked in an almost indifferent tone.

I switched to night vision to observe her expression.

She was watching me with disbelief and suspicion, her face contorted, eyes narrowed.

"No, he wasn't," I said calmly.

She was looking at me as if studying some frightening artifact, and I felt a somewhat irrational disappointment that there was so much repulsion in her face.

"Sorry that I left so abruptly. I didn't mean to." I purposely tried to override her fear with the memory of the day we had spent together. "I had to deal with this … emergency. I really enjoyed your company." It happened to be true, but that was beside the point now.

Her face assumed a strangely lost expression, and I figured that she was trying to reconcile two disconnected images in her mind. I leaned back and gave her my most disarming smile, hoping she wouldn't panic. Fortunately, her posture relaxed, as if she recognized a familiar person under a scary mask.

"Would you explain?" she asked, and there was no longer any edge to her voice.

"As you may have guessed, our meeting wasn't an accident," I kept my voice calm and casual. "We were both waiting for Remir to show up for the interview."

She pulled an empty chair closer to mine and sat down.

"Will he really be fine," she asked, "as far as you know?"

"I know that he will make a full recovery."

"He hasn't ever done that before," she was staring at the grass at her feet. Then she looked up at me again. "What do you want from him?"

I decided that I could tell her now. "He has very rare qualities and, hence, has an invitation to go to Earth. It's a much nicer place."

"Interesting," she grinned, as if I said something funny, "who would have thought?"

I wasn't sure what part of my sentence prompted this remark, but didn't interrupt.

She frowned, thinking. "How long will he be … recovering?" she asked.

"He will sleep for two days. Then he will be back to normal. Or at least to whatever he used to be, before this event. But this is not the best place to talk, Lita. I'm erasing our conversation from surveillance in real time, but some other visitors could come and sit nearby at any moment."

She nodded and got up. "Where would you suggest we go?"

"The hotel where Remir was staying. We'll be here for the next two days, we might as well settle in."

She tensed again, and I decided that it was time to bring the matter out into the open.

"Lita, you aren't afraid of me, are you?" I asked point blank.

I was provoking her, but it was worth the risk – whichever way she answered would allow me to maneuver our interaction in the right direction.

She hesitated for a split second, and then shook her head.

"I trusted you once," she smiled dryly, "and it turned out to be fine."

As we walked to the hospital parking garage, she still kept some distance from me, but now it seemed to be a calculated caution rather than genuine fear.

"Kir, book us two units in Remir's hotel, next-door to each other," I said.

"Who is Kir?" she asked right away.

"It's a computer chip; I use it as a personal assistant. I'll explain this too."

She nodded, and we temporarily parted ways, walking to our cars.

We drove through empty streets, barely touched by the light of the early morning, parked next to each other in the hotel's underground garage and walked to the elevator shaft together. I glanced at the reservation details.

"Lita, you are in suite 320, I am in 319 across the corridor. Your place or mine … to talk?" I asked her as the doors closed behind us.

She shrugged, "Might as well be mine; they are all identical, I'm sure."

She gained access to her room which recognized her finger-prints. I followed her closely, and we almost collided when she abruptly slowed, adjusting to the dimness inside. Our bodies brushed against each other for a brief moment, and she quickly stepped forward. I noted that the awkwardness was a little more pronounced than the situation warranted. And I reminded myself that this was nothing but work now.

"Light?" I asked.

"No, it's fine," she said and walked to the only chair in the far corner. Still ensuring that my movements were slow and non-threatening I sat on the bed on the opposite side.

Her face was hidden in the shadows now, and I had to enhance my vision again.

"So you are from Earth," she said, "I guess, I believe it. Are you typical?"

It was a tricky question. But I had to say something.

"Maybe a bit more adventurous. My profession is exotic."

She nodded in acknowledgment.

"Why do you need Remir? Is your population that much into music?"

"No," I smiled at the thought that our government would go to the trouble of sending headhunters to the Mirror Worlds in search of brilliant composers. "It's not so much *what* he creates. Although I'm sure the art crowd will be delighted. It's the fact that his mind works in a very special way," I paused, letting her take it all in, "and you are invited, as his partner."

She raised her eyebrows, but didn't say anything.

"Unless ... do you want to take my test? To see if you are special too?" I asked, slightly surprised by my question. Strictly speaking, I shouldn't have cared. Our contract dictated that only one outlier per trip was counted – the authorities didn't want to risk putting more than one egg in the same basket. My take-home pay wouldn't increase even if she passed, but I admitted that I was genuinely curious.

"No. Later," she said, "I'd rather see what your planet is like first."

Different people have different priorities, I thought.

My biometric mask doubled as a communication device, allowing non-wired people of the Mirror Worlds to access audio-video inputs. I pulled it from my pocket and extended it to her, not getting up. I wanted her to approach me, not the other way around.

"It has software that will give you the standard introduction. I swear it's safe to put this on. Do you believe me?" I asked.

"It's strange," she replied, coming over and taking it from my hand, "but I'm not afraid of you, for no good reason."

I waited until she settled down in her chair again.

"The informational program is interactive. It'll guide you, but you can ask questions at any time," I said.

She nodded and put the mask on. I knew that it would take some time, so I slid to the floor and leaned against the bedside. She was sitting upright, her spine not touching the back of the chair, her hands squeezing the wooden armrests.

"Yes," she was talking to the program now, "no preference."

She was still going through the initial set up when Kir suddenly turned on an emergency signal.

"Nick, I am malfunctioning again. There is an irreconcilable parameter conflict."

My heart lurched. Kir was my only significant advantage on this planet.

"What conflict?" I whispered.

"I intercepted improbable information from the news coverage of a failed missile test. Here is the culprit, Nick."

He connected me to the feed from a media helicopter that was circling over a swampy open area of a crash site and zoomed in on a small pebble in the middle of the scattered debris. The object's surface was mostly covered by the thick mud, but I could clearly see a segment of a serial number on its exposed part. It was written in Earth's modern numerical system.

"This belongs to a Commonwealth's surveillance drone, last year's model. It seems that it was accidentally hit by a missile part during the explosion," said Kir. "Nick, you told me there's no Earth presence here. I … Nick, you are getting a connection request."

For a moment, I sat frozen, listening to the chime of the incoming call in complete shock. It didn't make any sense – I was the only registered headhunter here.

"Accept," I said finally.

A dark-haired man with very intense gray eyes was looking at me from a communication screen.

"Nick," he said with a slight Earth Central accent, "we need to talk. Please go to your room right away."

The screen folded, but I didn't move. The only thought bouncing around inside my head was that Kir wasn't broken. I pulled myself together, shook off my stupor and looked at Lita, who sat still, intently peering into the space in front of her.

"Kir, pause her program and connect me to her audio," I said getting up. "Lita, I need to go now. Ask the device to contact me when you are ready, and I'll return as soon as I am able."

She nodded, and I left the room.

The man who called me a moment ago was sitting in a chair in the center of my unit. He raised his hand in a standard Earth greeting gesture.

"Sit down, Nick," he said, motioning towards the bed.

He was dressed in a casual local outfit, but the air of something decisively official about him was so convincing that I obeyed without question.

"JJ, Defense Ministry. I am speaking with you because we screwed up. I screwed up," he winced in obvious irritation. "I've been asked to ban any headhunters. It's bad enough here without them stumbling around like blind elephants. But no," his voice acquired a mocking tone, "I was told that a continuing ban on this sector was attracting attention and we couldn't afford a public investigation." He stopped himself.

"Sorry, Nick. Nothing personal. You were not supposed to see that drone. In fact, you were not supposed to be there in the first place. We couldn't keep this planet locked down anymore – the headhunter agency kept demanding an explanation. But we adjusted the parameters in your assignment system so that the difficulty threshold was prohibitively high. I have no idea how the program passed you. You must be outstandingly good, Nick."

I thought that I should probably be flattered. I couldn't enjoy the feeling, however, considering the somewhat eerie atmosphere of the situation. His next phrase didn't make it any better.

"In fact, we didn't have to tweak the parameters very much. That place is bad, Nick."

"Wait," I finally started putting the pieces together, "these explosions … was that really you?"

"Nick, come on. These guys stage the theater themselves. We sabotage their research in infospace. They don't even know about it."

I remembered Kir's glitch during my initial reconnaissance.

"Sabotage their research?" I understood the reason for the first error. JJ and company must have caused it while adjusting the data to cover their tracks. The blond woman didn't make a mistake; the slowdown was the result of our agents tinkering with her program.

"Nick, we're an emergency team. Last year our routine satellite surveillance sent an alert that this sector had successfully reverse-engineered some of our old technology. You know, from the pieces that were accidentally left over after the separation. We looked into it. Their classified research was on the verge of discovering the Mirror space structure and a way to cross the borders. And their military was getting to the point that it could penetrate our current defense system. By the way, don't be fooled by their archaic utilities. They don't bother about mass consumer goods."

"But … why didn't you …" I stopped myself before finishing the question. Of course, they were doing it secretly. Earth wasn't prepared to make fast decisions anymore. By the time the debate about the ethics of slowing down the progress of a developing civilization was over, Beta Blue's troops would be walking on Earth.

He read my expression and nodded in satisfaction.

"I guess you get it. You can expose us by reporting this incident to your authorities. Or you can delete your implant log and forget about it. Secret projects are wrong, Nick. Lying is immoral.

But people will die when the invasion starts. Hard philosophical dilemma, isn't it? Think about it. You can use this line to get back to me … to let me know what you decide."

"Am I … safe for now?" I didn't know how to ask him directly. But he understood.

"Nick, we're government employees, not assassins. If you choose to leak information and stop this project …" he shrugged, "the fallout is on you then. That's all." He stood up, "By the way, I might as well tell you – we have been following you here. No offense. Just a precaution."

I remembered the two shadows.

"Here's some free personal advice," he said, already touching the doorknob, "just go home. Forget about your target. The political situation is extremely unstable. It'll get nasty there very soon."

He left, and I continued sitting on the bed, struggling to reorient my view of the world. The transparency of Earth's government had been deeply ingrained in my mind, and the existence of a secret operation was as believable as a theory that the Grand Council was a gang of disguised non-humanoid aliens. But the man in my room was real.

I suddenly felt very unsettled. The world where rules were broken didn't feel safe anymore. I needed some time to calm down, put everything that just happened into one cohesive picture and determine my position with respect to all of its components. I hadn't made much progress in that direction, however, because Lita called.

She was waiting for me in the doorway, holding the mask in her hand, and after a quick glance at her face I realized that the balance of our interactions had changed. She was looking at me with an expression bordering on awe. This wasn't surprising. Seeing Earth for the first time in the program often had this effect on people. I had gained the new status of a being that belonged there casually, the same way she belonged to the everydayness of Beta Blue. And even though it wasn't a reflection of my personal qualities, I very much liked the result. For the sake of the job, I reminded myself.

She looked aside, apparently conscious of the way she was staring at me, and stepped back.

"Your program is very helpful. But …" she cleared her throat, "it feels so unreal. Can you tell me about Earth yourself?"

I thought that this was definite progress. She was relying on me for comfort now.

"Sure," I said. "Let's get inside and settle down. Make yourself comfortable."

This time we both sat on the floor across the room from each other, her back against the wall, mine against the foot bed.

"Lita, you'll need to put the mask on again. I want you to see things through my eyes," I said, and she nodded in agreement.

I began from the standard narrative, using my personal experiences as examples. I told her about the comfort and confidence from being surrounded by an old and friendly civilization. I gave her a glimpse of our vastly superior bio-technology. I showed her Orbit in its entire splendor and walked her through the streets of my favorite cities.

Before long, I realized that I was telling her as much about myself as about Earth. At least about some parts of me.

"It looks perfect," she said. "Is it perfect, Nick?"

It was the first time she had called me by my name.

"No," I said, "for me it isn't."

I knew that this was insane. I had never admitted this to anyone, let alone people from the Mirror Worlds. But I told her. Maybe it was my late and senseless revenge on Earth for my broken trust. Maybe her life was also so obviously messed up that I knew she would understand me.

I told her about the decadence of the Earth's population and about the boredom of ordinary jobs, where nothing interesting ever happened. I talked about the even temperament of my friendships and the tepid quality of my relationships. In other words, I told her about the things that caused me to get on a ship and blast away every several months.

"But why didn't you fit in, just like everyone else?" she asked, and I thought that I heard compassion in her voice.

And I told her something that I'd never shared with anyone else. "It has to do with the test, which I gave to Remir," I said. "You see, I always knew that there was something wrong with me. I was too impatient, too ... deviant. My desires were too intense in comparison to other people. I could see that. But I had no idea why. And then there was all this talk about outliers ... after the military warning. It rang a bell. I took the test, just for myself. I scored positive."

"Your program said that Earth needed people like this to make progress," she took off the mask and looked at me quizzically.

"Yes. But it's not a very good thing for me, Lita. There was a reason why Earth got rid of us ... I mean others like us in the past. My emotions are very strong, but the theory says that they are ... not normal. Apparently, I don't have a moral compass. I can believe it. I don't like authority. I can believe it too. I don't *feel* other people, they say, I can't *feel* what they are *feeling*, vicariously. But I can read people very well. I can pick up on the slightest hint when someone is in psychological pain, for example. I know how it hurts, because I have experienced it myself, and I don't want other people feel it, especially the ones I care about. And then I use logic to act ... to help. I am not a monster."

She got up, came over and lightly touched my hair as if confirming that I was real.

"I see," she said, "you and Remir ... no wonder. Let's run your test. I don't think ... but we might as well."

She didn't return to her spot and instead sat on the bed next to me.

"Lita," I looked up at her, "put this thing on again. And these hypnotic sequences can be unpleasant. I'm sorry."

"Give me your hand," she asked and covered her face with the mask. "We can start."

"Kir, turn on the assessment program," I said and changed my position on the floor so that I could see her well. I took her hand as she asked, and suddenly felt an almost unbearable desire to caress it. Stop it, I told myself. She also tensed, but it lasted for just a brief moment before she fell into the standard program trance.

I was watching her, trying to guess what was happening behind the emotions that gradually passed through her face. They were too subtle to interpret precisely, and the mask was in the way, but there were discernible flashes of a happy smile, a worry, a shade of anger. I thought that she was beautiful in all these states, even though beauty wasn't exactly the right word. There was something that eluded direct definition, making her expressions unique, infinitely complex, magnetic. I realized that I wasn't even thinking about the test behind her phantom experiences when Kir abruptly turned on the negative result indicator.

She stirred slightly, her hand still limp, and then I felt the hint of a squeeze as if she was thanking me.

"I'm sorry. You didn't pass," I said.

She lifted her arms, taking off the mask.

"So, I am not that special," she smiled, "but don't apologize."

I didn't detect a trace of sarcasm in her voice, or disappointment on her face.

"One pays a price for being special," she added calmly, "like Remir, you know."

Not surprising, I thought. She was in the front row of his self-destructing show.

"Nick, I haven't eaten since yesterday morning," she said, getting up. "I'm not even hungry, really, but I don't want to faint on you. Can we go out and get something? I saw a small place across the street when we pulled in. It will probably close soon, like everything else here."

I asked Kir to look it up and check the hours.

"It's still open," I said, glancing at his response, "we can make it if we hurry."

The sun had already lost its intensity, and the light breeze was pleasantly refreshing. Fortunately, the restaurant, which was too kind a word for this hole in the wall, had an outside seating area in the back. We chose one of the few plastic tables in the shade of the building and sat across from each other. An elderly couple in the opposite corner was finishing their meal, and, glancing at them, for some strange reason I thought that growing old together with someone might not be as weird as I'd always imagined.

Lita put her elbows on the tabletop and leaned forward, looking right through me.

"I'm not surprised that your test flagged Remir," she spoke as if simply continuing an old conversation. "All the things you said about yourself, like this crazy intensity, is true for him too, and also … I know that he is a real thing. Life is richer for him than for others. His filters don't block the world as strongly. That is why he can do his music. But when the filters are not thick enough life burns through. And then it's not fun … for anybody involved."

A woman in a uniform that had the same unique character in all shabby joints across the Mirror Worlds approached our table.

"We're closing for today, but if you order and pay, you can sit here as long as you want," she said, handing us a paper menu, its frayed pages covered with suspicious yellow splotches.

"Lita, can you choose for me, please?" I wasn't planning to touch local food anyway. Lita quickly asked for two of the day's specials. The waitress left and came back with two plates almost immediately, probably prompted by the desire to lock up shop and go home.

Lita didn't even look at the food.

"And it burns through a lot. Life burns him all the time," she continued, staring at the invisible point in the distance again. "So you ask why do I stay?" she addressed me, as if finally remembering my presence.

I didn't ask, but I nodded.

"Because I'm an addict. A weak-willed addict. People say that I'm a saint because I'm always there for him when he needs me. You see, they value me because they want more and more of what he does. So … whatever helps him keep going … whoever. And he does need me, every time when he feels like shit, when life pins him down. Frankly, I don't think he would have lasted this long if I wasn't around." An expression of pain crossed her face.

"But I'm not altruistic. It's just … when he is at his best, full of energy and charisma and light, and he aims it at me, it feels like nothing else. I get to taste life his way. Everything is brighter. His passion is so … intense while it lasts."

She was making a rope by twisting a napkin, and it was getting tighter and tighter.

"But then … he is somewhere else. With somebody else. You see – life to the fullest …"

I remembered the brunette at the bar.

"It hurts. But I'm always there when he comes back – because he does love me in a twisted sort of way."

And unexpectedly, inappropriately, irrationally, I felt the sting of jealousy. I didn't like it at all.

"But he didn't even call me before he didn't show up. I was there for him. I knew that he would drink after that interview. And I wanted him to at least do it with me, not in dingy bars, not to the point when somebody would have to drag him home the next morning. I felt like an idiot, standing there with this wine bottle. He knew what he was doing when he didn't show up. He screwed up our lives, my life, in a major way. And I wouldn't blame him, I would understand. But he didn't even bother to tell me before he did it. And these other women again…"

I gently took the napkin from her and held her hands in mine. She didn't pull away, and her fingers were trembling. I felt a swell of pity and tenderness and immediately noted that it wasn't a part of the job. I let go and sat back.

"Will you go with me?" I asked and quickly clarified, "I mean you and Remir, provided that he agrees?"

It took her a moment, but then her lost expression disappeared.

"It's funny," her voice acquired a lighter, ironic tone, "it always made me furious to think that I would spend the rest of my life here. So I always imagined a miracle."

Her face changed again, now turning cold and disdainful, "Nick, this place is rotten. I always knew it, even when I was growing up. Everything around me was a lie, an enormous farce. I was a kid, a teenager and I boiled with rage, but I knew better than to show it, even to my friends. You never knew who actually believed in what." She paused and looked down as if noticing something on the unevenly painted surface of the cheap plastic. "And then we grew up. And I saw how it all worked. Nick, they did give us a choice to play their game or not. Of course, they made the rules. And almost all of us did go along, even though the price to refuse wasn't very high. Our jobs, city permits. Not even jail time," now there was sad bitterness in her voice. "They corrupted us … me included. They made me *feel* ugly. So, yes, I want to go with you. This is my chance. Your place is free. You say so. And I believe you."

She raised her eyes, giving me a wan smile, "You showed up like a fairy tale prince to whisk me away from this misery."

I scrambled for an appropriately light response, but failed.

"Assuming that Remir is with the program," I replied in a pointedly businesslike tone, thinking that I sounded surprisingly dumb. "I'll make him the offer when he wakes up. Given the way things are here I hope he will agree."

"I don't think he has a choice now, after what he did," she said, shrugging her shoulders. "They will shut down his music. He has nothing keeping him here now."

I should have been elated – my goal was getting closer. But instead, I had a strange uneasy sensation in my chest. Jealousy wasn't a familiar emotion. "You don't seem to be angry at him."

"Well," she said, "you are like a painkiller."

I didn't like what was going on with my heart. It was in obvious conflict with my professional interests.

I noticed that she was very pale.

"Lita, what about your food?"

She looked at the cold coagulated substance on her plate and winced.

"I can give you my meal substitute if you'd like. Better than this anyway."

I handed her my nutrition bar, and she ate it without a comment. In the twilight, I noticed deep shadows under her eyes and realized how many hours she must have been awake.

"Do you know how he is doing? Can you check on him?" she asked.

"Kir is monitoring him all the time. He is getting better. He is asleep. Lita, you need to sleep too. Nothing will change until tomorrow."

Apparently, she was almost too weak to hold a conversation, so she just nodded in response. Fortunately, the hotel was just across the street, and we were back in the lobby in a few minutes.

"Would you like me to help you relax?" I said when we stopped in front of her door.

"You can do that?" she asked, and there was a note of awe in her voice again.

"Kir can," I answered honestly.

She leaned against the wall.

"Sure, let's make use of your superior technology."

Kir could have beamed the relaxation package remotely, but I put my hand on her forehand. It felt cool and smooth, and I had to resist the desire to gently stroke her face.

"Kir, go ahead with a basic sedative," I said softly. She sighed, and anxiety and tension disappeared from her eyes. I removed my hand and felt that she instinctively followed my hand as if trying to extend my touch.

"This was great. But ..." a shadow passed across her face. "It's scary. Nick, can you promise that you won't ever use your magic on me without asking me first?"

I nodded even though I wasn't sure that I could keep my promise. It was work, I reminded myself again.

"You'll sleep as long as your body needs. See you in the morning," I said and went to my room.

I slumped on the bed, threw uncomfortably hard pillows on the floor and decided that I didn't want to think about anything else today. Unfortunately, I couldn't order Kir to make me fall asleep – by design implants couldn't alter the psychological state of their hosts. It was annoying and unreasonable, but I dozed off before I could dwell on this for very long.

When I opened my eyes, it didn't feel as if any time had passed at all, but it was already the next morning. For a moment I stared at the wavy surface of the ceiling, trying to recall why I was here. And then I remembered everything, and the thought that Lita was nearby, only a few rooms away filled me with such a sharp sense of happiness that there was no way to deny the fact that I liked her. I liked her very much.

Hold on, I said to myself. This was really messing things up. It was Remir that I was after. I had to do whatever I could to get him to leave with me, and that included not hitting on his lover. Tomorrow he would wake up, and hence it was time to start working on the next steps of my detailed plan steps. More so, I reminded myself, was JJ's ominous warning, which meant that I needed to get off this planet as quickly as possible. I was trying to decide the best way to approach my upcoming conversation with Remir, when Kir sent an emergency signal.

"Nick, a change in the global Beta Blue situation affects your safety."

I moaned and shook my head.

"What now?" I sat up on the bed, focusing on the internal displays. A satellite feed showed a plume of smoke over the presidential grounds. "Kir, connect to cameras inside the palace," I said, applying considerable effort to snap out of shock.

"Nick, there are no cameras – as of one minute ago."

"Search for the closest feeds in the vicinity."

Kir was now showing me several screens, but I couldn't see anything except for white wisps of smoke. I thought that my Beta Blue operation had lost its original smoothness.

"Kir, what happened?"

"Remote demolition was triggered at 6:03 this morning."

"Trace it. Anything you can find."

The redundancy of the last sentence indicated my state of mind.

"Here is the most relevant recording, Nick. Time stamped just before the explosion."

According to their bios, which Kir pinned in the background of my vision, most people in a large boardroom belonged to the top military echelon, and the rest represented some high-ranking government officials. They were looking at a screen that showed the intact presidential building, its smooth curved surfaces glistening peacefully in the pink morning light. I thought that they were insane to allow surveillance in this room. But then again, they might not have been aware of the camera's existence. The Homeland Security minister who was at the head of the table picked up a small device from a tray in front of him and held it in the air.

"As you all know, the explosion will start only if everybody here activates this launch pad," he said in an understated commanding tone.

One after the other, they each touched the remote control as they passed it around the table. The room was very quiet. Suddenly, the building on the hilltop jolted and folded in on itself. In a moment, there was nothing where the structure had been except for a billow of smoke, which immediately started losing its shape in what appeared to be a strong breeze.

"Now, gentlemen, let's get to work," the Homeland Security chief got up from his seat. At that position the camera happened to point squarely at his long impenetrable face. "Follow your protocols and notify me in case of any issues. I am calling the media now."

"Kir, enough," I was whispering for some reason. "Tag this recording and show me the news."

Various channels were going through their usual routines, providing updates on weather and road conditions in cheerful morning voices. Abruptly, all screens simultaneously switched to an image of the burning remains of the presidential building.

"We are interrupting this program to bring you an emergency announcement," the news anchor spoke in a professionally calm, but slightly unsteady voice. "In an unprecedented act of violence by covert Earth agents, the president and his family were killed this morning in a targeted explosion. The total number of casualties remains unknown ..."

"Nick, check this out," said Kir, turning on video feeds from the city center. Sleek military assault helicopters were landing in the middle of the streets.

"A security breach was detected in the vicinity of the government district, and a temporary emergency executive council has been assembled to take all necessary actions to guarantee public safety," continued the commentator. "Citizens should remain calm and stay in their homes until special units perform an extended search for possible enemy infiltrators inside the city perimeter."

Kir's analysis indicated that my safety hadn't been directly affected yet. He warned, however, that the situation was too fluid to make a reliable prediction beyond the nearest future. Just as I was resetting the security parameters to compensate for any increased exposure risk, I was interrupted by a communication request.

"Nick ... it was Lita, and I remembered that I'd told her to use my mask to get in touch. Nick, can you hear me? What was that? It can't be ... your people?"

I didn't even reply, I just sent her the clip of the secret meeting tagged by Kir a moment ago and the live feed from the empty city streets where silver wasp-shaped vehicles were now positioned at regular intervals from one another.

"Nick..." When her voice came back after a short break it was so quiet that Kir had to activate amplification. "Nick, please come."

Her door was ajar, and I went in. She stood in the middle of the room with the mask on, but I could still see the expression of complete dread on her face.

"Nick," she said, "do you understand what this means?"

It meant a serious headache for me, but only after looking at her face did I realize what it meant for the people on Beta Blue.

She took a step forward, then another, and then she put her arms around me in a tight embrace as if looking for protection. Her face pressed against my chest, and I froze, the room and the voice of the news anchor from the video screen on the wall quickly fading into the background. Her grip relaxed slightly, but she didn't step back. She slowly tilted her head, raising her face until she was looking into my eyes. I removed her mask and dropped it to the floor.

I couldn't say that I didn't understand the ramifications of what I was about to do. It just no longer seemed important. Time slowed down and then sped up uncontrollably when my lips found hers, and she responded, stretching up. With quick jerk I pulled her even closer, causing her to lose her balance, and lowered her onto the floor. I took off my shirt, threw it aside, and in a moment was next to her, searching for her mouth again, tracing the curve of her throat with my lips. Her dress was in the way, and I had to let go of her for a moment, stripping off her clothes and getting rid of the rest of mine. There was nothing between us anymore, and that was a new level of raw intimacy, in which she was still a stranger to me. I covered her skin with rough brief kisses, slowing down only over her nipples until she moaned, and then I reached for her mouth again. She pulled herself towards me as if she wanted to fuse her body into mine, and I completed her motion with one impatient thrust, making our touch absolute, leaving nothing that could make us closer. Then everything went out of focus, except for her face, its perspective changing in rhythm with the movements of my body. It was getting harder and harder to fight growing swells of desire, but then she gasped, arching her back, and I convulsed in almost painful spasms.

"A fairy tale prince," she whispered and let go.

I rolled onto my back and for several moments lay still, as my heartbeat returned to normal. Then, thinking that she might be cold, I picked her up, carried her to the bed, and kneeled down on the floor next to her. She wrapped herself in the blanket and stroked my face.

"Nick, what are we going to do now?"

"It'll be fine." At that point I still believed that the situation would somehow untangle itself.

She propped herself up on her elbow and looked at the video screen on the wall. The same commentator was now reading a list of emergency rules and regulations.

She listened with painful concentration, and her face started to contort into the same expression of dread as before.

"Lita, you'll be safe," I said, trying to distract her. I was fully aware that my priorities on Beta Blue had changed.

"… during the times when the deadly fight is directly upon us, any participation in scientific or cultural activities without explicit government approval will be considered a punishable offense effective immediately." By now the news commentator had collected himself; his voice sounded firm, with a carefully measured note of scorn.

"They will kill him," she said flatly, "or he will kill himself."

Until now, I had been carefully avoiding any thoughts of Remir.

"He does have an option. He can go with me. He will be fine." It was true, but I stumbled over my words.

"Right," she nodded, "he has an option."

I got up, threw on my clothes, and sat in the chair.

"Kir, summarize the security situation."

"Nick, your personal safety is not a concern," he replied. "There are no special forces in Oren. The local police department hasn't received orders to search private residences or hotels. There's a planet-wide ban on being outside today, however. Citizens with valid reasons will be allowed on the streets starting tomorrow morning."

Lita was now leaning forward and looking at me with worried impatience and I remembered that she couldn't hear Kir.

"Kir, connect your audio to the TV speakers in Lita's room. Provide Lita and Remir's security status."

"Lita's safety is not a concern. Remir's safety is not an immediate concern," now Kir's voice accompanied images from the news translation.

Lita sat up, her face instantly paling.

"What does that mean – not an *immediate* concern?" she whispered.

"Kir, provide the details. Quantify timing," I asked.

"Remir's name is on the list of people to be detained. He is classified as category B. The arrests in this group are scheduled to start five days from now."

Lita tried to smile, but her lips couldn't quite take the proper shape. "He lucked out that you're here for him," she said finally.

I thought that she was most definitely right, but she rubbed her forehead with a pained expression, still looking distraught. The ambiguity of my presence in their lives was now part of the landscape. The good news was that the immediate plan seemed very straightforward.

"Lita, you will go to the hospital when he wakes up, but until then there's nothing for us to do but wait."

"How long will that be?"

I checked Kir's estimate.

"Twenty-three hours give or take," I said.

"Can't you wake him up earlier?" she asked anxiously, "With him being on that list ..."

"That would interfere with his recovery. We'll need to move fast once we leave the hospital, and his condition could slow us down." I anticipated her next question from the expression of increased worry on her face. "Kir is monitoring Remir's security situation. He will alert me if he detects any change in the arrest schedule, and I'll intervene if necessary. It's safer to wait."

She reached down, picked up the hotel robe and put it on. It was too big for her, the flaps hanging below her knees, the sleeves sliding down her arms. She started pacing around the room, her eyes glued to the floor.

"Fine," she said, "it makes sense. What doesn't make sense is that my life will never be the same in any possible way ..." she paused for a moment. "I'm not surprised that they will be going after him. Even the previous regime ..." she looked at the screen where images of the burning presidential palace taken from different perspectives replaced each other, "... even they never liked him. They didn't understand his music. It was too different. And it had an air of ... disobedience. He never received the stamp of official approval – no membership in the Composers Union. Can you imagine, they even threatened to charge him with a parasitic lifestyle?"

I knew that willfully unemployed citizens could be given prison time in accordance with the local constitution. The former authorities preferred to hold onto this card against Remir for a rainy day, however. He was too popular. Holding this axe over his head was a better tactic. All these shenanigans nicely fit the standard pattern of outlier-totalitarian dynamics, but I immediately realized that she was a real person involved in this mess.

"But they worked it out, made some trade-offs. Remir never made any political statements, and for the most part they let him be," her face had an expression of chronic worry now. "He knew that he was constantly walking on the edge, of course."

She looked at the screen where the Homeland Security minister was currently addressing the nation and muted it.

"No balance for him anymore. Terminal stop. What a striking finish," her voice didn't go up at the end of the sentence.

I stepped in front of her, stopped her pacing, and put my hands on her shoulders. "Lita," I waited until she raised her head and looked into my eyes. "There's nothing we can do now. Tomorrow you'll tell him about the offer, when he wakes up from the coma. Lita, we have almost twenty-four hours."

She stood still for a second and then pressed her forehand against my chest.

I deleted these hours from Kir's log. I wanted to ensure that I wouldn't be able to return to them. I knew that it would be much harder to fight those real memories. It would take time to fortify protective boundaries created by the accumulation of wounds and cuts acquired when I got too close. And I also knew that I would never forget this morning with its first hint of dawn in the window and the hollow feeling in my chest at the clear thought of losing her forever.

□　□　□

I checked on Remir just before he was supposed to regain full consciousness. As expected, he had completely recovered from his overdose.

"Time is up, Lita," I said, and she looked at me with an almost frightened expression.

When she was ready to go, I handed her a palm-sized piece of blue plastic.

"It's a copy of the recording from the boardroom, the same one that I sent you yesterday. You can decide if it will be helpful for him to see it. Don't worry; I'll erase it from the hospital camera. And it'll only work when you're holding it with your fingers this way," I showed her how to grip the plastic. "There's no danger of anyone knowing what it is even if you are searched."

She nodded and put the card in her bag.

"Nick, I have to ask you something," she said, avoiding my eyes. "Please don't monitor the room when I talk to him. I don't want you to ... watch us."

"Of course," I was sure that I wouldn't keep my promise. The stakes were too high, and after all I was still a professional. I gently squeezed her shoulders, pressing a microscopic surveillance chip into the fabric of her dress, "Go. It will be fine."

She went out, and I lay on the bed, putting my arm on my forehead.

"Kir, follow her," I said as soon as the door behind her clicked shut.

She was hurriedly walking along empty streets until a burly man in a local police uniform blocked her way. She told him about Remir, and he picked up his communication device. Kir intercepted the signal, and I heard the man's conversation with the hospital. Then he nodded and stepped aside, letting her go.

She entered the lobby, checked with reception and was let in. I watched as she approached Remir's unit and opened his door.

"Kir, delete my card from the camera images. And … block the feed from me."

Did I do it because she'd asked me, or because I didn't want to see what was happening inside that room? In any case, I knew that I had a problem. I wasn't behaving rationally anymore. Moreover, I was acting downright stupidly, because everything was quite simple. In a moment she would walk out, wait for his discharge, and then they would leave the hospital together. We would drive to Oren's outskirts and travel the remaining way to the shuttle on foot. Not much to it, really, and afterwards we would all have a comfortable flight home. And yes, I would handle it just fine.

Lita suddenly stepped out of the room into the hospital hallway and leaned against a wall as if trying to regain her balance. I had no idea what to make of her strange expression, but I didn't like it. She slowly walked along the corridor towards the exit, went down the hospital steps and crossed the small lawn where our mesh chairs still stood in the same position close to each other. All the while she wore the same expression of helpless disorientation. There definitely was some snag with Remir, and it was the last thing I needed. No more games, I decided.

"Kir, rewind your log to the moment when she entered his room and play the whole segment that I asked not to see," I said through clenched teeth.

Kir immediately showed me the interior of Remir's unit from the viewpoints of my surveillance chip on Lita's shoulder and the hospital camera under the ceiling. Remir, half-sitting in the reclined bed, started talking to Lita right away.

"I just heard the news. The whole thing is too weird. If I died on the way to the ER, then I am in a very peculiar type of hell. This explosion and …" he frowned, as if trying to clear the confusion in his head, "I told you about Nick, right?"

Lita pulled a chair over next to his bed and sat down with her back to the room's camera. I couldn't see her expression, but at least the microphone inside my chip on her dress worked.

"You did tell me. And no, you didn't die."

I didn't know what he read on her face, but he glanced aside.

"Lita, about that morning and … the night before …"

"Forget it," she said in an even tone, "the situation is worse than you think."

He looked at her with relief. I almost smiled.

"Is it? How do you know?"

"Nick gave me a comprehensive overview."

"You talked to him?" he raised his eyebrows.

She nodded, "He waited outside the hospital."

"Did he tell you what he wanted?"

"Remir, things have turned really nasty here, but because you passed this test of his, we can leave. We can move to Earth."

"Lita, wait. This Nick could be saying anything. Not that I care about our president, but who blew him up?"

"Check this out," she said and pulled out the card I gave her and held it so that he could see the recording.

As he watched his face became gloomier. When the clip ended, he took the card from Lita and slowly rotated it in his hands. Now, it again looked like just a piece of plain blue plastic.

"Fine. If this thing isn't manufactured, then it's definitely a military coup."

"It's real, Remir, and you will be arrested. Nick found you on the detention list."

"I see."

I was impressed – he didn't flinch.

"Well, then it will make sense to get the fuck out of here. I've had enough of this place anyway. Unless it's even worse on that … Earth. What do you think?"

"Remir, it's not worse. I trust him."

"Really? How come?"

"He showed me his planet. It felt right. I didn't see fear in people's eyes. It was so beautiful, too," she paused for a moment. "I don't think he made it up. I could tell because he mentioned these little details from his life, his childhood." Her voice suddenly got warmer, "For example, he showed me an education center – the one he went to. There was a girl he liked, and he walked on a beam between two buildings to get her attention. I saw the beam … their civilization is very advanced, obviously. Their technology is mind-boggling, but it isn't the most impressive part. Their world seems to be free and … humane."

Remir was watching her face and his eyes became harder and harder. Lita, be careful, I thought, knowing that it was already too late.

"They built new continents in the oceans, but they remained in harmony with nature. He showed me an artificial island where he spent his last vacation. He made friends with a bird there; he played a recording as it waited for him on his porch … to say good morning."

"Was there anything you didn't like?"

She still didn't see it coming.

"Well, people there don't seem to be too exciting. Nick is not typical."

"Lita, what happened between you and Nick?"

"What are you saying?" she said, her voice lacking even a shade of proper indignation.

I couldn't see her face, but his eyes narrowed as if blinded by a flashlight.

"Lita, I don't know. I'm going to think about all this."

She didn't move, and the pause was becoming abnormally long.

"Remir, you're on the list," she finally said, panic rising in her voice. "What is there to think about?"

"I understand. But, as I said, I need to think this through. They told me that I need to stay here another day in order to monitor my condition. Seems like a perfect arrangement."

She leaned forward to take his hand, but he lifted his arm before she could touch it, and brushed a strand of his hair from his forehead. She recoiled as if he had hit her.

"Lita, go away, please. We will talk tomorrow."

She stood, picked up her bag from the foot of his bed and made a step towards the door, and then abruptly turned back and gave him an awkward hug. He didn't respond, looking straight over her shoulder, at the opposite corner of the ceiling, almost directly into my eyes. Nonsense, I thought, he wouldn't know the camera's position. His arms remained motionless alongside his body, but when she started to straighten up, he suddenly stopped her, jerking his wires so sharply that the monitors simultaneously blinked. He pulled her close and held her in a tight embrace, so strong that I thought it must have hurt.

"Visitation time is over. Please vacate the recovery unit," a sterile voice announced from the intercom above the room entrance. Remir's grip grew even tighter before he let go and fell back onto the pillows.

"Kir, stop the recording," I said and moved to the chair and kept looking at the door until it opened.

Lita walked in and dropped her bag on the floor.

"He sensed something when I was talking to him," she said in a flat voice. "He has always been good at it."

Of course, he was, considering his Dark Triad score, I thought.

"He will know for sure when he sees us together," she continued, "and there's no way he will go with you then."

"But, Lita – he did understand that he would be arrested, didn't he?"

"He told me he needed … to think. They will keep him until tomorrow. His test results are fine, but his doctor is cautious because of his unexplained coma. So, he will stay there one more day and then, I don't know. It seems that we have killed him, Nick."

I didn't say anything. There was absolutely nothing I could say. It was my fault, as simple as that.

"Nick," she said not looking at me, "I need to be by myself, away from both of you. Can you please leave my room?" I got up and walked towards the door. I had no control over the situation at the moment.

"I'll contact you as soon as … I am able," she added.

I tried to keep my distance from her on my way out, but she unexpectedly came over, hugged me, and there was something in her hug that I didn't like. It felt like a farewell.

It was a farewell, I thought, crossing the hallway. The only way she could save Remir was to erase any memories of me.

I entered my room and sat down in the chair. Regardless of my psychological condition, I had to analyze the options and plan my actions. I was still a professional, I had to remind myself. But before focusing on the overview of the global Beta Blue situation, I quickly checked on Lita through the chip on her dress. She was curled up on the bed in a very still position. She wasn't sleeping as far as I could tell from her breathing. I switched my attention to the city.

The picture looked worse than my most pessimistic expectations. The streets were quiet, almost empty, with few people outside. The detention list was growing, as was the number of people that had already been picked up by inconspicuous military vehicles. I thought that if Remir refused to go with me, I would need to leave the planet immediately. The current conditions were too dangerous to look for another outlier. Remir would die in this scenario, and I will have effectively killed him. But then again, I could have chosen a different target in the first place. Remir died in that case too – shot in a basement, starved in a camp, or left in a cell with a noose to hang himself. But it wouldn't have been my fault.

Lita stirred on her bed. She got up and looked into the small refrigerator. It was empty with the exception of a lonely liquor bottle. She grabbed her bag and walked out of the room. I thought that any energy from my food bar had to be running out by now, and that she was probably going to get something to eat from a vending machine downstairs.

She got to the lobby and, as I expected, picked up some items from the automatic food dispenser. She stuffed them in her bag and returned to the elevator. The doors opened, but she glanced at the corner where a security camera was positioned in plain view and hesitated. Then she turned around, quickly walked towards the stairway and ran down the steps leading toward the garage. She must have guessed that I could jam the elevator, I thought, and darted to the door.

"Kir, bring the lift to my level," I exhaled, sprinting to the end of the corridor. The elevator doors were opening with dignified slowness, so I forcefully pushed them aside and jumped in.

"Skip all floors to the garage," I said. The car whirred and unhurriedly moved down, "Kir, make it go faster!"

"I can't override the speed, Nick," Kir replied immediately, "it's a hard setting."

Lita, on the other hand, didn't lose any time. She crossed the garage floor, got into her rental and without a moment of hesitation drove toward the exit. I attempted to take over the autopilot, but, not surprisingly, she was using manual mode. I called her through her car intercom.

"Lita," I spoke in my calmest voice, "you missed the news. Driving isn't permitted today. You'll be arrested."

"Hi, Nick," she said in an upbeat tone, "by the way, thanks for asking for my permission to talk. No, I didn't miss the news. I was planning to ask you for help – I knew you were watching me. Once I get outside, please tell Kir to cover me on my drive to the city. Have him delete my electronic trace and avoid checkpoints."

The elevator stopped just as her car approached the open garage exit. There were no gates for me to control. I had to find convincing words to make her stop and do it quickly.

"Lita, why the city – what are you doing? Wait …"

She drove out onto the empty street.

Kir's map showed a police car a few blocks away. It was slowly cruising in her direction.

"Lita, the police are coming. Get back to the garage. You have time."

She kept driving forward. There was no time to apply my negotiation skills.

"Alright, I'll do it. Turn on your autopilot." She did so immediately. "Kir, take over Lita's car. Drive away, avoid detection. Make a circle around Oren."

"Kir, change the direction to my city residence."

Kir, obviously, ignored her request.

"Nick, please, tell him."

For a second, I considered driving after her and physically intercepting her car, but I dropped the idea right away. I couldn't afford a chase and altercation in the open; it would be too much activity to hide.

"Lita, why the city? You need to be here so we can leave with Remir."

"I'll come back tomorrow. I'm sorry, Nick. But I need some distance between us, between me and Oren, and everything that has happened. Don't tell me that you don't understand."

Part of me understood, but the drive was unjustifiably dangerous, even with Kir taking all precautions.

"Lita, it's not safe. It's not worth it."

"Nick, please. Otherwise, I'll turn the autopilot off and drive there myself."

"You will be arrested."

"It'll give the situation an interesting spin, don't you think?"

I kept standing in the elevator, looking at the brightly lit garage wall through the open doors. For some reason, it seemed important to find a pattern in the shiny curves of its surface. Loss of control was a novel sensation.

"Lita, ok – I'll get you to the city," I said. "Kir, go ahead."

"Thank you, Nick. Goodbye. Please, don't contact me. Don't make me physically break the intercom."

She disconnected and turned the flexible arm of the internal camera to face the ceiling.

How did she manage to outmaneuver me? I asked myself riding the elevator back up to my room. There was a simple explanation. I stopped being a professional the moment she stopped being a part of work.

The next several hours I spent in the bed looking at the white car that was moving in the direction of the city. There was no physical military presence on the roads, and Kir was erasing her image from the highway surveillance system. A couple of times he had to drive the car down a detour to avoid manned checkpoints, and one time he slightly altered the flight path of a helicopter unit, but all in all it wasn't too bad.

Through my chip on Lita's shoulder I watched her face in the reflection of the glossy surface of the dashboard screens. She had the tense focused expression of someone who was trying to think through a hard problem under severe time pressure.

She reached the city border in the late evening. Fortunately, she lived away from the center, and her residential area was sparsely patrolled. Still, I felt that my neck muscles relaxed once she drove into her building's garage. She pulled into her spot and turned on the voice intercom.

"Thank you, Nick," she said.

"Don't mention it," I didn't even try to hide the sarcasm in my voice. I expected her to hang up, but she kept the line open.

"Nick," she said, "you've been watching me. I can feel it. I felt it on the way to the hospital. I felt it in the hotel. Please stop. We don't have a chance if you don't. I need to be alone." She paused for a moment and added, "Promise – if what happened between us mattered."

It felt like the air I was breathing instantly became too thin. Yes, it did matter – otherwise why would I be doing any of this? "Damn you, Lita."

"Thank you," she said. I zoomed the garage camera at her face, so close that I could see the reflection of fluorescent ceiling lights in her eyes and heard myself saying, "Kir, stop streaming her trace – unless, she is in physical danger."

Her image disappeared.

"Now, go away," I whispered and pressed my hands against my eyes so hard that irregular reddish spots appeared on the velvet blackness of my empty vision field.

I lay still for a while, then got up, went downstairs, bought a packet of sleeping pills from the vending machine and swallowed the double dose right there in the lobby. The desired effect kicked in shortly after I returned to my room. My eyes became heavy; I slumped onto the bed and fell into a dreamless void.

Two emergency alerts simultaneously woke me up.

"Nick, Lita's in a critically dangerous situation," Kir commented on the live feed he was streaming from the interior of the Media Center's computer hub.

The second line was a direct call from Lita. In spite of a residual fog from the tranquilizers, I immediately felt a bout of terror. Lita stood in the middle of a large room filled to the ceiling with server racks. She squeezed a random intercom handle in her hand and was waiting for Kir to connect me. She knew that he was monitoring all communication lines.

A young man with a work badge clipped to his sleeve was hunched over a central console several steps away.

"Lita, Nick is online," said Kir.

"You didn't follow me, Nick. Thank you," she smiled, but her voice suddenly broke down, "but … I don't have much time now."

Kir showed me a feed from the Media Center hallways. A group of armed people ran towards the door of the server room.

"Lita, what happened?" I whispered.

"Nick, I had to do this. This was the only way out. It's logical – you, of all people, should understand. If I disappear, Remir would never be sure what happened. But if he sees us together … I won't be able to pretend and he won't go then, Nick."

"Kir, play back the main events from her timeline since I fell asleep," I said, and short video clips started replacing each other in chronological sequence.

… *Lita disappearing into her apartment. Lita picking up a land-line phone…*

Now I was talking to her in real time and listening to her voice from Kir's recording simultaneously.

"Nick," she was saying through the live connection, "don't blame yourself, please. It's not just about Remir and you. You can't imagine how happy I am to show these pigs that they don't own all of us. I've been swallowing humiliation my entire life and now I am paying them back. It's my chance to stop feeling ugly, o stop being a coward. Being a coward is the worst thing to be."

...*"Doug, can we meet at the marina? Now. Yes, it's urgent. Don't forget your badge."*

I saw her living room through my microchip on her shoulder. The uniformed men were now on her floor.

"Nick, I hope I didn't cause a problem for you. You weren't the only one who had access to that camera, right?"

I saw my surveillance chip as it flew into the laundry chute together with her dress.

Now Kir was only showing me recordings from the street cameras.

... *Lita talking to a young man just outside of hearing range as they walked through the back doors of the Media Center reserved for technical support personnel. Lita removing a small personal camera from her pocket in the computer server room ... The young man uploading a copy of the file with the scene of the secret meeting that I given her on my device was incompatible with their technology ... The young man overriding the live news translation ... Lita introducing the recording... Men smashing the door with their machine guns.*

"But even if it does, can you forgive me?" I could see now that she was searching for signs of surveillance lenses on the walls trying to look into my eyes.

I felt lightheaded when I understood what she had done. Before returning to the hotel, she took a video of the recording while holding my card in front of her camera.

With a cold horror I realized that all the news channels were now transmitting my file.

"Goodbye, Nick. I want you to know ..."

The men crashed through the door.

She dropped the phone.

A tall man with the chevrons of the top security commander pushed her away and she hit a rack and slid to the floor. He waved pointing to the main server, and a series of machine gun rounds rattled through the room.

All news stations went dead.

"He just let me in. He doesn't know anything about it," she said from the floor.

"Sure," the tall commander glanced at the guy and calmly shot him in the head.

"But we definitely have a lot to discuss," he said, turning to Lita, "but let's first disable all local communication channels. We want some privacy from your Earth friend."

All of Kir's feeds from Media Center went blank.

"Kir, the main priority now is to keep her alive." I got up, moved the chair to the center and stood behind it squeezing the top of its arched back in my hands, "Can you trace her location?"

They succeeded in blinding me inside the building but using a satellite, Kir managed to catch a moment when they ushered Lita into an armored van from the Media Center's back door. The car rushed toward the highway, and in a moment it was joined by several identical vehicles.

"Kir, what is their destination?"

"Homeland Security headquarters."

"Show me the route."

The Homeland Security grounds were located roughly in the same direction as Oren, but much closer to the city.

I knew that I wouldn't be able to do anything once she disappeared inside the HS building. I was a headhunter; I wasn't trained or equipped for a rescue operation like that. And there was no way I could reach the motorcade in time with the local transportation options.

Local, I thought. If only I could use my shuttle. But it was deadlocked in the mountains per standard security rules.

Using *my* shuttle, I thought.

There was only one local contact code in Kir's memory, but it was all I needed.

"Kir, call JJ's line back."

"Please, respond," I wasn't addressing JJ; I was pleading with some nebulous force. I never expected myself to do something like that.

"Nick," JJ's face appeared on the communication screen, "we know what is happening. I'm sorry."

"JJ, I've a deal to offer you," I didn't want to waste time feeling relieved. "I'll give you access to Kir's memory, and you can delete all incriminating records. This whole thing never happened, I never met you. In exchange, I need a lift. I want to intercept Lita's convoy before it reaches Homeland Security headquarters."

His sympathetic expression immediately changed to a more natural look of extreme alertness.

"What if you're lying?" he suggested, but there was a definite interest in his demeanor.

"Who will believe a paranoid headhunter without proof?"

He didn't object to this. I tried to smile.

"Think about a potential bonus – if they kill me, it'll be cleaner for you."

"Accepted," he said immediately. He kept looking in my direction, but now he was obviously focused on some internal feed.

"I'll meet you there," he sent me a map and zoomed in on an image of a field covered with patches of short, yellow grass and random pieces of industrial garbage, right behind a row of dilapidated warehouses at the very edge of Oren. "In half an hour," he leaned back apparently preparing to turn off the line, but hesitated.

"Nick," he asked, and for the first time I could see genuine worry in his eyes, "are you sure? I don't understand ..."

I just nodded. I didn't want to say that I didn't really understand either.

His screen folded.

Now my brain worked in a maximally detached mode. JJ would get me to the motorcade. Let's assume that I could stop the convoy and free her. But where would we go? The whole planet would recognize her face from the news. Getting off Beta Blue was the only option. But I couldn't bring her to Earth. She wouldn't be allowed. She was a nobody. She could only come as a Mirror Worlds outlier's partner, a sweet bone that was thrown into their defection offers. My own Dark Triad was irrelevant.

"Kir," I said, "locate Remir."

Remir was sitting on a bench in the hospital garden, chewing on a grass straw. Even though he appeared to be a person with all the time in the world, I knew that he was waiting for me.

I walked along the eerily calm hotel halls. Employees hadn't shown up, and the guests were holed up in their rooms. For a moment, I imagined what it must have been like for them watching the board room meeting video. Funny, I thought, it wasn't supposed to be my war. How did I manage to get in the middle? I added this to the growing list of my moral and administrative issues and focused on the task at hand.

He didn't turn his head in my direction when I sat down on his bench.

"We need to save her. You have the technology," he said, spitting out the straw.

For a moment I was impressed how cool he was considering his impeccably astute guess about my affair with Lita. Then I understood. He wasn't jealous, he just simply didn't take me seriously. He was a Dark Triad, even without knowing what it was, and he had no way of understanding that other people could be wired differently. He assumed that I was a handsome emotional vial of temporary emotions, which she would discard after things returned to normal. He also didn't know that, despite the colossal difference between our DT scores, I was a Dark Triad too, whatever it meant in the context of the situation. The whole geometric construct was much deadlier than he understood, but his oblivion suited me perfectly.

"We need to get her off this planet. I will be needed as her ticket to Earth. You have the technology," he said.

"A motorcade is taking her from the city to Homeland Security headquarters. We will intercept them on their route," I said.

For the first time he turned his head towards me. "There's no way we'll get there in time."

"We will. Just trust me on that."

Now he definitely smiled sardonically. Obviously, he had his reasons for not considering me a person at the top of his trust list. But he didn't say anything.

"We will need to drive to a point where my Earth shuttle can pick us up."

We walked to the parking lot.

"Take this car," said Kir, pointing to a latest sports edition. "The owner just died from a heart attack."

"Why didn't his meds save him?" I asked out of mild curiosity getting inside the luxuriously comfortable vehicle.

"He was running a conference call from this car for a critical board meeting, and then it was too late," said Kir. "No reason."

Remir joined me in the car.

"Kir, drive to JJ's meeting point," I said

Remir didn't ask either about Kir or JJ.

The car rolled along the empty streets of Oren. On a map, I watched the complicated patterns of the route that Kir chose to avoid police patrols.

I glanced at Remir. He sat silently, looking straight ahead, and I knew that I didn't need to convince him to leave. He wouldn't have humiliated himself by running away with her lover, but he would also do anything to save Lita. Not too logical, but I suddenly thought that I would have done the same in his place.

Why was he so obsessed with her? I asked myself. Why didn't he discard her like any other romantic partner, as the theory predicted? Anyway, the word *Game* disappeared from my mental vocabulary very quickly after I'd met her. She wasn't standard *Game* material.

Not only did she recognize Remir for who he was – the Dark Triad monster. She understood his *Game,* and she played along on the same level. Like everyone else, she played off from the intensity of passion he created, and she found his fucked up soul perversely interesting.

And she could break boundaries. She had slapped the new authorities in their face, knowing what it would cost her. She didn't let Beta Blue just quietly slide to the next level of dehumanization. I didn't know anyone who had the guts to do what she had just done. It seemed that she ignored fear in the same way that I did when I went after something I really wanted. These thoughts were too complex and impractical now, but the warped dynamics of Remir's obsession with her became obvious. And, possibly, confusing signals from my heart became explainable too.

We continued in silence until the car reached the rows of abandoned warehouses and storage yards that created the town's boundary on the south. The road ended there, blocked by a massive steel barrier.

We got out and crossed an overgrown field to the first strip of desolate concrete structures and empty lots.

"We need to get to the other side," I told Remir. "I have a map of the fastest way."

He followed me through the labyrinth of passages between empty blocks, careful to stay away from unstable beams and torn mesh fences, and finally we emerged onto the field from JJ's image – a vast concrete wasteland covered with patches of short, yellow grass and random pieces of industrial garbage.

I looked around thinking that by now JJ should be here, and then a number popped into my communication frame. I adjusted my vision to that frequency and saw that we were standing right next to an Earth military shuttle. It hovered silently above the ground, its main door open.

"Remir, I need to temporarily induce unconsciousness. Kir, go ahead." The indignation in Remir's eyes was instantly replaced by a blank stare. I caught his body as he collapsed like a rag doll, dragged him inside the vehicle and placed him onto the backseat. I almost fell into the front chair next to JJ as the shuttle jerked forward before the door had time to close.

"Damn it, Nick," he said, "you didn't tell me anything about transporting your outlier …"

"Look at him. He's out cold."

"Still … I'll be in even deeper shit if anyone finds out," he shook his head.

The interior wasn't blocked so I restored my normal vision range. We were inside of a shuttle-type carrier, but it looked way more complicated compared to anything I had seen.

JJ was looking at me with deep interest and, as it appeared to me, some sympathy.

"Nick, I won't help you once I get you there. I can't risk any exposure."

It sounded almost like an apology.

"But we'll clean the traces. Your bosses won't know who posted the file. Your meeting with the convoy will look accidental. It'll help you with the claim of self-defense … if you make it."

I nodded. It was nice of him, but at this point I didn't really care about the administrative consequences. Self-defense conditions were defined very broadly in our contract. Otherwise, my agency would have had serious difficulties hiring anyone for my position.

"Where exactly would you like me to drop you off?"

Kir sent him the interception coordinates, and the shuttle steadied in that direction at the maximum speed.

I checked the countdown – we would get there with a few moments to spare. JJ sent me an outside image, and I saw the convoy turning off the highway onto a smaller road that wound around through a rolling plain, the last stretch to the Homeland Security grounds.

We landed on the road at a distance, which gave us several minutes before the motorcade would appear in view.

"Kir, remove all internal security," now it was my turn.

"Nick, there's an attempt to delete some of my memory files," informed Kir.

"Allow."

JJ nodded and unlocked the door. "Well ..." he said, "you should know that I will personally be upset if I pick up your TT."

"You know about TTs?"

"We know a lot about you. Your implant sends the Terminal Transmission before self-destructing after your death."

I restrained myself from asking how often they get such transmissions. Instead, I pulled Remir from his seat, dragged him outside and lowered him to the ground. When I straightened up and looked back, there was nothing except for the vast plains in all directions and the clear blue sky.

I waved goodbye. I knew that JJ was still close enough to see me.

Then I sat next to Remir's body on the crumbly grayish soil covered with the harsh yellow grass and shut my eyes, enjoying the gentle warmth of the mid-morning sun on my face.

The motorcade was still far enough away so the only audible sound was the peaceful chirping of cicadas. I almost laughed at this sign of the elaborate symmetry between the beginning of my journey on my artificial Pacific island and the final countdown on Beta Blue.

There was some time, but there wasn't too much of it. I glanced at Remir and told Kir to wake him up.

Remir stirred and opened his eyes. He lay still for a moment, then slowly raised his head and sat up.

"The cars will appear from that turn," I motioned to the road emerging from behind a low ridge, about a hundred meters away. "I'll stop them right there."

"How did we get here?" he was visibly disoriented, but not hostile. Apparently, the shock from the change of scenery had made him forget about his anger at the unceremonious way with which I knocked him out.

"Remir, forget about it. It's not important. Stay here, behind this bluff until I get back."

To his credit, he didn't ask what he was supposed to do if I didn't.

I started taking off my clothes until I was down to my briefs.

"They need to see that I'm not carrying anything," I explained to Remir who was watching me in puzzled silence, "and it will be easier to move."

I waited until the motorcade appeared from behind the bend and then told Kir to jam all car electronics and turn off all their surveillance sources, including their satellite feeds.

The vehicles were designed for a sudden system failure so they continued moving for a while, losing speed in a controlled way and stopping in the same formation.

I hoped that they would investigate and discuss their plan before they continued in manual mode. Indeed, people started emerging from their vehicles, looking with surprise at the dead communication devices in their hands and motioning in confusion.

"Now," I whispered and stepped onto the smooth surface of the road. With my hands above my head, I slowly walked towards the stalled vehicles. They noticed me when I was about eighty meters away. Kir needed another twenty.

They stopped talking and watched me. But none of them reached for their machine guns, their black barrels reflecting the sun with a nauseous oily glimmer.

That was the plan. I didn't expect them to shoot at a slow-moving empty-handed target until they found out what it was about.

"Come forward, slowly. Keep your hands over your head. Get on your knees in front of the officer," a PA system sounded very clear in the silent air. A person from the front vehicle walked towards me, his gun accurately pointed at my chest.

I looked at his face as we approached each other. He was very young, blond and light-skinned with a handful of freckles, and his blue eyes were fixed on me with unguarded curiosity.

It was not his fault. He had been brainwashed, I thought. Why do I need to think about this now? I asked myself. But I had to think about something, and it was better than focusing on the fact that there was nothing between my skin and the black muzzle of the guy's machine gun.

I was in range.

I could tell Kir to knock him down. But I didn't.

"Kill," I told Kir.

Pain exploded inside the guy's head so quickly that he didn't have time to wince, falling face down on the ground. I darted forward, zapping them down one by one as soon as they got in range, too quickly for them to react. It took several moments and then I stopped, relieved that it was over, that the worst part now was the knowledge that I would live with the memory of their still bodies scattered on the ground. And then another person got out of the car parked way back, in the rearguard. I didn't know why he had stayed inside, but it was too late. He was too far for Kir, and there wasn't enough time to duck from the line of his straight shot. During several very slow seconds, I thought about how I'd always wondered what would be the very last thing I ever saw before I died. It turned out to be a barren plain with sun-bleached yellow grass and a very bright summer sky.

Then I heard a rattle from behind. The man aiming at me fell on his knees and toppled sideways.

I turned and saw Remir standing over the first dead soldier holding his machine gun. He knew how to shoot, I thought with brief amazement.

We had very little time before Homeland Security would react to the loss of communication with the convoy.

"Kir, take over the car with Lita. Open the detention cell," I ordered, running to the van where she was locked in the windowless back compartment.

The back door rose up. Lita was there alone, sitting on a metal bench in the far corner. A translucent tape held her hands together and she awkwardly rested them on her lap. I resisted the urge to look at her face.

I heard approaching steps and twirled around. Remir stood right behind me holding a bared dagger that he had probably picked up from the same dead soldier. Once again, for a split moment I imagined how soft my skin would feel against the metal, but Remir jumped inside not looking at me and began cutting the band that tied Lita's wrists.

"Stay here and hold on tight. I'll need to drive this thing as fast as it can go," I closed the back doors and ran to the driver's seat. As the car began to turn, I felt soft bumps under the wheels. I recognized what it was, and I figured out that I had just discovered something about myself. I could've just as easily knocked all these soldiers out temporarily, but I had simply wanted to kill them. My cognitive emotional intelligence informed me that other people would experience an emotion of guilt at this moment. I wouldn't even know how that felt, in accurate accordance with the theory.

A reconnaissance motorcade left the gates of the Homeland Security headquarters and moved in our direction.

"Kir, jam their engines," I asked.

"Nick, I can't. They are all in manual mode."

Sure, I thought, someone guessed this part too.

"They are getting all their patrol cars ready," Kir was monitoring headquarters communication lines. "They realized that they can only rely on actual visuals." It wasn't surprising considering that Kir blocked all their feeds and satellite images.

They wouldn't know what happened until they got to the dead convoy. It gave us a relatively safe half-hour before they would identify the missing transportation van.

"Kir, interrupt all government electronic communications across Beta Blue," I ordered. "Let them take time driving around to pass the orders."

Kir sped up in the direction of my shuttle, which I left moored on the mountain slope above Oren. He used the shortest possible route, not bothering to avoid local police patrols. Without direct orders they wouldn't even think about stopping a vehicle adorned with high-ranking military insignia.

My only focus now was getting out of there as quickly as possible, and all complications between me and Remir and Lita were temporarily put on hold. But the two of them were there, locked in the back of the van, without any clue about what was going on. I turned off the portrait mode of the camera, and projected all Earth satellite footage onto the van screens.

"We're going to my shuttle," I used the audio, "it is parked in the mountains behind Oren."

Neither of them replied. I guessed that part of their reaction was pure aftershock, but it was also a reflection the simple fact that there wasn't another option for them. They couldn't fight *this* rip current, not without me anyway.

We all watched the aerial view of the motorcade now surrounding the stopped vehicles and dead bodies.

By now Kir had successfully jammed all communication lines on Beta Blue indiscriminately, so to report on the situation, one of the cars had to turn around and speed back to headquarters. Its top speed was almost twice that of our transportation van.

I told Kir to track it on the maps as the three of us watched two pulsating dots. One was moving towards Oren, the other towards Homeland Security headquarters, closing the distance with unnerving quickness. I always underestimated the level of excitement one can get from watching a chase. Of course, it helped that there were lives, mine included, at stake.

The reconnaissance car finally reached the base. I told myself to enjoy the last moments of relative calm as dozens upon dozens of high-speed attack vehicles burst out of the gates and spread out in all directions.

None of the silver wasps left the ground, though. There were too many critical electronics inside of them, and it was clear that I would simply crash them down. It was a relief. I didn't want to kill people, who had done nothing to me.

The good news was that this fleet was their only chance at stopping me. However, within a short time they would reach other bases and get additional vehicles on the road, and I was now a well-defined quarry. They acted in a very coordinated way despite the lack of electronic communications and were methodically setting up roadblocks slowly cutting off the number of usable routes.

We had been off the main roads for a while now playing hide and seek, weaving through the narrow back streets of provincial towns, ducking behind tall buildings, crossing unpaved patches of ground. The occasional regular police patrols, not clued in on the situation and totally confused by the lack of ability to communicate remotely, gave us the right of way with speedy politeness.

Finally, I started to relax – we were getting close to the point where I came down to the valley from the mountains. I silently thanked Kir. His judgment was impeccable as long as there was a solution to the posed problem.

Until there wasn't.

"Nick, we can't proceed without crossing a visual field of at least one of the military vehicles." It must have been my imagination that Kir sounded concerned. He wouldn't survive without me, but as far as I knew such considerations were not a part of his program.

"Turn off autopilot," I said.

We had to cross the familiar agriculture field, the one I'd walked through on my way to Oren, and I didn't need a satellite feed to recognize the sleek shape of an attack vehicle parked in the middle. I asked Kir to give me the weapon capabilities of this model.

I didn't share Kir's answer with Lita and Remir. They didn't need to know that this elegant-looking car carried missiles capable of penetrating the armor of our transporter as easily as a paper bag.

Calm down, I told myself. They can't use the lock-on feature in manual mode. So it was Kir and I fused together against their human reactions. Stop this bullshit, I said to myself. I had no chance of crossing a space so wide without being shot no matter how elaborate my escape zigzags were. These were not inexperienced shooters.

I looked around. We were hiding behind the wall of the last structure separating Oren from the rural area, next to an enormous parking lot for heavy agricultural machinery. Normally, they would be out working in the fields, but today they remained abandoned, idling in sleep mode, exactly as I had seen them on the night of my arrival.

The gates were locked with conventional metal bolts. I thought that I might as well make some use of our mighty armor and drove the military van straight through.

Inside the yard I stopped the car, jumped out and opened the back door. Lita and Remir had the same silent question in their eyes, but I didn't feel like explaining. I wasn't sure if it would work, but it was our only chance.

I had a very vague idea about what exactly these machines were supposed to do, but I had Kir check their maximum speed. It was unexpected luck, but those bulky caterpillar-like contraptions happened to have the ability to move relatively fast when not engaged in their primary harvesting activity.

I allowed the adrenalin to hit my brain, and the beat of blood in my temples became a cadence of music, celebrating the start of the most reckless adventure of my life.

"Lita," I said pointing to the rows of identical machines, "pick one."

She looked at me in confusion.

"Fine," I said, "I'll choose then. This one looks the coziest."

I walked to a random vehicle in the middle, climbed the ladder to the driver's seat of the wide cabin and motioned for Remir and Lita to get in. I didn't know how to operate it in manual mode, but I hoped I wouldn't need to.

"Kir," I said, "drive them out, slowly. Spread them over the field. Keep me away from the middle."

The metal giants around us suddenly came to life, folding their mechanical arms in preparation for movement.

Remir understood. He grabbed Lita's hand and helped her up into the cabin. It was a bit tight, and his shoulder pressed against mine, but we fit.

"Here we go," I whispered as we exited the gates in a line of peacefully humming combines.

It took us several minutes to get into the open.

The car in the middle of the field didn't move. The appearance of the harvesting machinery could have very well been the decision of law-abiding, but confused citizens to conduct business as usual.

The landscape looked idyllic – a gentle breeze sent waves across the golden wheat field, creating various shades of yellow under the bright afternoon sun. The cooling system didn't work in automatic mode and the mid-summer heat spread through the open windows, adding to a lazy atmosphere of carefree calmness.

The expanse to the base of the mountain steadily decreased as the line of harvesters slowly advanced across the field.

The distance to the assault vehicle was steadily decreasing as well. It still sat motionlessly, and I could already see the complicated system of radar, completely useless now, dark-tinted windows and a gun barrel sticking out from a slit that encircled a smooth bump on the roof. It was well out of Kir's bio-transmission range, unfortunately.

Suddenly, the barrel slowly rotated towards the closest combine – the soldiers in the vehicle had apparently started to suspect that something wasn't quite right.

A loud hissing sound ripped through the air, and the ground in front of the approaching machine exploded in a fountain of moist brown soil.

"Kir, stop it," I said. The combine obediently backed off, flashing its headlights in acknowledgement, and stood still. But the rest of the harvesters kept moving forward as if oblivious to the incident.

I sensed hesitation from the car operators. After a couple of minutes, another missile hit the ground in front of another combine. The machine backed off in a similar fashion and lifted its mechanical arms in a human gesture of surrender.

Soldiers in the car seemed thoroughly confused because for a couple of minutes again nothing happened. I smiled – the standard protocol of requesting an order from above was out of the question.

"Think for yourselves, my friends," I said through my teeth. "Sorry, you aren't used to this."

Remir looked at me sideways, but didn't comment.

Finally, the vehicle darted forward and came to a skidding stop in front of the first stalled combine. Two uniformed men jumped out and ran towards the cabin.

From a satellite feed, I saw a winding dirt road that led up from the valley in the general direction of my shuttle.

I allowed myself a glance at Lita. She was tightly gripping the handle of the side door, strands of her hair were drenched with sweat and stuck to her forehead. She had been biting her lips so hard that their color seemed to have been painted onto her white face.

She didn't notice my glance and kept staring straight ahead.

The shrill sound of an alarm pierced the air, and a flare exploded high above.

In satellite view, several identical vehicles in the nearby area left their current positions and picked up speed in our direction. I counted five of them, and each sent a flare up as they approached.

There was another loud hiss. A combine close to the middle of the line exploded and a sound of cascading metal parts reverberated through the air. The assault car was back in the center assuming the best shooting position.

"They figured it out. Showdown time," I said, closing the windows. "Kir, put all the harvesters at full speed in a random movement pattern. Keep at least two of them between me and the point of fire. Drive straight to the mountain road entrance, maximum speed."

The engine howled and the combine dashed forward, throwing us into the back of the seat. This mode was designed for relatively smooth surfaces, which the field definitely wasn't, and the machine convulsed in short spasms every time it hit bumps or shallow irrigation ditches along the way. The best I could do now was to continue holding onto the control bar that Kir had locked into still position; Remir was clutching it too.

For someone not directly involved, the overall scene must have looked comical; awkward bulky machines were running amok like a herd of terrified animals. The part that wasn't especially funny was that from time to time one of them would go up in a plume of smoke.

One of the ditches we encountered was deeper than the others, and the combine hit the ground hard. Lita was flung across the cabin. I grabbed her with one hand and pulled her toward the seat. Remir moved over and I squeezed her between us, giving her best access to the horizontal bar. Streaks of blood crossed her face, getting in her eyes and dripping down her chin.

She noticed my worried glance and said calmly, "Just a cut."

The machine coughed and growled like it was hurt, but continued forward.

The sound of an incoming missile was so loud that I involuntarily ducked, and the first of the two harvesters shielding us exploded, and shards of metal hit our cabin with a series of banging sounds. Kir immediately positioned a replacement, putting another combine in the line of fire.

I could already see the ramp to the dirt road that led up the mountain when the first of the reinforcement vehicles entered the scene. It pulled over to the first car, apparently for a short exchange, then quickly drove some distance away and joined the shooting. When the third car showed up, I already guessed that we'd lost anonymity by accumulating an obvious cluster of harvesters around us. Indeed, the cars stopped firing randomly and began to remove our remaining shields methodically, taking them down one by one.

"Kir, can we make it to the road?" I asked.

"No," he said.

The expression with which Remir was watching me changed. He couldn't hear Kir's answer, so my face must have given it away.

"The van," said Remir suddenly, "our van, the one we left behind."

I should've thought of it myself.

"Kir, drive the van, across the field, away from our harvester," I said.

Our getaway car appeared from behind the wall and sped to the mountain from a different angle.

It was perfect. They all darted after it, every single one of them.

"Lack of communications leads to inefficiency," I said, thinking that I would give Remir proper recognition for this later, after we made it to the shuttle.

Eventually, the van was surrounded, but we had already left the open field and started climbing the road up the mountain. A tall forest of trees formed a visual screen and gave us some precious moments to gain altitude.

Things in the valley were unfolding rapidly. After a brief inspection of our decoy, the assault cars began turning around. There was predictable confusion as they tried to communicate with the units that were just approaching the scene. Again, I had to give them credit for how quickly they regrouped. Someone obviously had been ordered to stop a combine that was disappearing into the forest because several cars took off towards our dirt road. The remaining group started shelling the mountain slope.

They couldn't see us clearly, but they guessed well – the sound of a missile impact was so deafening that only the fact that I was still alive convinced me that they had missed. All I could make out through the cracked windshield was a white blanket of dust. The combine careened, lost balance and stopped, perched on one side.

My door was pressed into the ground, Remir's was jammed, but he kicked it open, climbed out and pulled Lita out of the cabin. I followed, pausing for a moment to observe the surroundings from the raised part of the combine body. It was almost impossible to see anything through the thick cloud of dust, but it was obvious that there wasn't much of a road left in front of us. I looked down.

Lita and Remir waited for me on the ground, Lita wiping blood from her face with her blouse sleeve, Remir looking at her with a calm expression of someone fully convinced that this was nothing more than a bad dream.

Better not to think how much of a chance we have, I thought, jumping down.

"The shuttle is in this direction, not far," I waived to the right. "We can get there in twenty minutes if we run."

If I ran, I thought. These two were not in the best shape to begin with, and it was unclear how bad Lita's head injury was. But it didn't change anything. The multitude of options had been cut down to this last available one.

I took a straight course to the shuttle, not bothering to go around low shrubs and occasional rocky patches. Remir seemed to keep up, but Lita started lagging behind right away. I slowed, looked back and saw her fall down hard. We backtracked, and Remir helped her to her feet, but she stumbled again, barely taking another step. I stopped Remir as he bent to pick her up.

"It'll be faster if I do it," I said, getting her off the ground and draping her body over my shoulders.

A nearby blast shook the forest, and the bitter smell of burning trees started spreading through the air.

"Come on! Let's move!" I shouted and started running uphill.

A satellite feed showed the forest canopy punctuated with plumes of gray smoke. It seemed that they were randomly shooting grenade guns. I grinned, thinking that I'd never imagined being in an inferior position with respect to a Mirror World military. But here I was, in a forest foot chase.

I kept running, trying to ignore the sound of explosions and wincing when sharp low branches scratched my face. Lita's head was bobbing in rhythm with my movements, blocking my peripheral vision, but I could hear Remir's winded breathing just behind me. Finally, not too far ahead, I spotted the familiar clearing where I'd parked my shuttle, seemingly an eternity ago.

I heard indistinct shouts behind and sped up. The sight of the brownish ground jumping in front of my eyes suddenly gave way to the bright green of a flat meadow rimmed by the gray cliffs of a mountain range on its far side, with a blue patch of sky above it.

"Kir, adjust my eyes to the masking frequency," I exhaled in raspy whisper. All shapes immediately lost their sharpness, colors faded, but now I could make out the shimmering frame of my shuttle hovering above the far edge of the clearing. Way too high, I thought, and put all my remaining strength into the last dash across the open space.

The system acknowledged me only when I was several steps away, and the shuttle started slowly descending. Too slowly, I thought. Whoever designed it didn't think that anyone would be in a bit of a hurry. I glanced back, saw Remir appearing from the forest at the edge of the meadow and put Lita down for a moment. I jumped up, grabbing the bottom edge of the opening hatch and pulled myself inside even before the shuttle settled close to the ground. I tumbled in and was about to unfold the air stair when a shock wave knocked me off my feet and I fell backwards, smashing my head on the wall.

I probably had a mild concussion, because for the next several moments I lay still, staring at the smooth white ceiling with complete tranquility. Then my memory came back. I pulled myself up, clutching at the back of the nearest seat, and stumbled towards the light coming from the open hatch.

My vision was still adapted to the masking mode, and everything outside was fuzzy and colorless, but I recognized the two still shapes on the ground.

"Kir, return the normal frequency," I mouthed the words without a sound and jumped down. There was an eternity of free-fall until I landed and then three long leaps towards the two bodies. I noted that my senses had been strangely distorted; the red blotches on the grass seemed almost fluorescent despite the gray veil of smoke, and all outside sounds disappeared, drowned by the heavy slow beat of blood in my ears.

I would never know if Remir tried to shield her in the last moment or if he was just thrown in this direction randomly by the strength of the explosion, but his body lay across hers in an awkward pose. I grabbed his shoulders, turned him over, and his head lifelessly rolled backwards, revealing a blank face with open eyes staring into the distance.

"Nick, no sign of brain activity," I heard Kir's voice. "His condition is irreversible."

But I was not even listening to him. I was staring at Lita's white face her eyes shut by the led-colored lids.

The smoke burned my throat as I finally gasped for air.

"And ... is she ...?" I stopped as if I could postpone her death by not uttering the words.

"Lita is alive. But you need to stop the artery blood loss from her left arm instantaneously."

I needed to make a tourniquet, and I grabbed the side of Remir's shirt. It was very slippery, drenched in his blood. I moaned through clenched teeth, applying so much force that my fingers burned, but eventually ripped the fabric apart. I tied the strip of my makeshift tourniquet around her arm, and just as I finished, figures in gray uniforms started appearing at the edge of the meadow. For a second, I wondered why they were not shooting – I was as good a target as they could get – but then I realized that they couldn't see the shuttle and assumed that I was safely trapped against the cliff wall.

"Kir, release the air stair, prepare engines for immediate take-off," I whispered. I stood holding Lita's limp body in my arms, and slowly backed up until I felt the ladder behind me. Then I twirled around, pushed off the ground and jumped inside, barely touching the steps.

"Kir, go," I yelled even before I landed inside. The sharp acceleration threw us to the floor as the shuttle shot straight up into the air. I climbed to the pilot seat, not letting go of Lita.

Below, in the crosshairs of my missile lock, people in gray uniforms stood with an expression of pure shock on their faces. Remir's body was in the same position on the ground.

No, I thought, I was done there. I let go of the gun control and tightly held Lita's body against my chest.

A distorted perception of time was the first symptom that my emotions were eroding the wall of my professional conditioning and psychological self-defense. It was a short flight, but every minute stretched endlessly as Lita's blood kept slipping through my fingers. I asked Kir to display the parameters of her brain activity and watched the graphs on the screen become flatter and flatter.

I already felt cracks in my ability to function, but I was still behaving in maximum efficiency mode when the shuttle smoothly inserted itself inside the ship. I carried Lita to the emergency vat, carefully placed her in the inner tube and started the program. I didn't look at her face as the sides of the lid blended. Based on the state of her vitals, she might be dead or close to it.

I tried to focus on the next step, but apparently I had reached my limit. I held onto the smooth white shell of the vat and slowly slid down, leaving two red smudges on its surface.

I sat on the floor, my forehead pressed against the vat's curved wall, and my body started shaking.

I don't know how long it continued and I didn't check with Kir. I was letting go now, purging the memories of what had just happened – the bitter odor of burning forest, the ease with which Remir's head rolled backward, the surprised blue eyes of the soldier on the desert road.

"Nick, you need medical assistance," said Kir.

"What kind," I pushed the words out between the spasms in my throat.

"Minor cuts and scrapes. Psychological destabilization."

The body could wait, I thought. As far as my brain ... I somehow knew that I shouldn't interfere with what was going on, that it wasn't something that I wanted to numb.

I needed time to say goodbye to the person I used to be before I'd landed on Beta Blue.

When I felt that I could move, I pushed myself towards the wall, slumped against it and sat very still for a while. Finally, I managed to get up, holding onto the wall with my hands, still sticky from drying blood. I looked at the vat one more time, walked out of the room and locked the door behind me.

With slow precision, I went through the decontamination process and wound repair. I then stood under a hot shower, changed into light clean clothes and brushed my hair carefully to create as much mental distance as possible between the present and Beta Blue.

I settled into my favorite chair in the main cabin, dimmed the light and with relief noticed that I could think with calm accuracy.

I was faced with a peculiar problem; it didn't have a solution, but all the steps on the way were obvious.

I had to get Lita to an Earth medical facility as soon as possible. But it had to include a detour to another Mirror World. I had to find another outlier if I was going to be able to pay for medical services, which were prohibitively expensive because of their niche status. And I needed to do it fast, while the biomass could still hold back the deterioration process. I would skip safety stops and pilot the ship manually, but I still wouldn't know if I could make it home in time.

"Kir, find the closest inhabited sector," I asked.

"M-847, by a wide margin," said Kir.

I made a quick calculation. The total time of detour plus the return flight to Earth was roughly equal to the remaining full functional lifespan of the biomass.

I didn't have clearance for M-847.

I shrugged. I wouldn't have waited even if communication was theoretically possible. The violation of my professional rules was nothing in comparison to the crime of bringing a Mirror World commoner to Earth.

But my company would pay my commissions before firing me if I delivered an outlier. And Earth would provide Lita with emergency medical assistance if I had the money to pay. They would do it before addressing other issues, whichever way they chose to address them.

What the hell else was there to do, push out the vat with Lita's body into open space?

"Kir, tell me about M-847."

"Its local name is Y-3," said Kir. "The population size …"

"Let's go," I interrupted. It didn't matter. I had no other options.

PART III:

THE TASTE
OF
FREEDOM

Y-3

On a cold autumn day Hilgor was, as always, working in his small sparsely furnished study, a pure minimalist's dream if not for the piles of paper scattered on the floor. A sudden draft of strong wind drove rain in through the open window. Hilgor got up, closed it and lingered for a moment, absent-mindedly staring at the dimly illuminated street outside. Then he took a deep breath, returned to his desk and checked the time indicator at the corner of his computer screen. The clock was counting the last seconds until the vote submission deadline, and his fingers nervously tapped a cheerful rhythm on the edge of the table. Finally, the announcement section moved to the front, and the text with the decision lit up. Hilgor pushed the chair back, got up, turned around and kicked it so hard that it flew into the wall.

A black narrow muzzle appeared from behind the half-open door, and a large dog with long black hair made his way into the room. He looked up at the man with mild concern. Hilgor walked past the dog, grabbed his coat and opened the entrance door. He paused in the doorway and glanced at the leash lying on the floor. "Sorry, Riph," he said and left the apartment.

It was unfair to go to the park by himself, but Hilgor needed to process the latest event alone.

His eyes glued to the ground, he quickly walked along his usual route, entered the gates of the park and stepped under a sparse canopy of half-naked trees.

He circled the narrow wet paths long enough for water to creep in under his collar and penetrate through the inner layer of his clothes, but a feeling of defeat still sat like a briny lump inside his throat. A gust of cold wind made him shiver, but it was a welcome distraction from the helpless anger. For a moment, he was even able to see the irony – while the result of the vote was deeply insulting, it wasn't personal.

There was nobody to blame. Two centuries ago a nuclear war almost erased life on Y-3. The fight for survival taught people the value of efficiency; and with time optimization, it became a foundation for all ethical principles.

Unfortunately, its practical applications consistently destroyed Hilgor's work, and there wasn't much in his life beyond mathematics. Of course, there was Del, but it was a separate and complicated subject, and it wasn't something he was thinking about now. At the moment, he was consumed by a helpless rage against the major source of his permanent irritation – mandatory practice for all scientists to collaborate in assigned units and exchange their ideas anonymously. In theory, he agreed that associating personal identity to the research process could lower overall productivity. But that was the theory. In practice, this moronic vote had just crashed a beautiful structure that had already formed in his head. It was the bridge to a solution of a highly prized problem that his unit had been pursuing for almost a year. In the last couple of weeks, Hilgor had suddenly come to see how to assemble the right object from an unexpected combination of several seemingly unrelated branches.

A wave of anger rose again, and, not finding an outlet, almost choked him.

How could he have failed to convince them? It was so obvious that the approach they chose would lead to a dead end. But the unit had discarded Hilgor's idea, fearing that his construct would lose stability and disintegrate at the critical point. His intuition told him that wouldn't happen, but he couldn't translate this intangible feeling into a clear argument as of yet, and his inability to do so had determined the vote.

And the fact that his insights stood behind the most brilliant solutions his unit had ever produced couldn't even influence the decision. For everyone, except him, they were just anonymous thoughts of the collective mind.

He stopped in the middle of a wet trail, lifted his face to the bleak unfriendly sky and cursed. Even if he gave the slightest damn about offending anyone, there was nobody around. The weather and the late hour had emptied the park.

He resumed his brisk walk, ignoring the increasing rain. He would finish the problem anyway, he thought gloomily, even if nobody ever saw the solution. But then he thought that he would show it to Deait, his secret collaborator, which calmed him. Deait would appreciate it. Turning a sharp corner, Hilgor almost collided with a tall man standing in the middle of the path. Hilgor recoiled sharply, almost falling backwards, but he managed to regain his composure almost instantly. After all, he told himself, there was nothing unusual about this young man, except that he was also drenched; his dark hair stuck to his forehead and raindrops were dripping down his pale face.

"My name is Nick. You're right," said the man, "your idea is one of the biggest breakthroughs in several generations."

"What idea?" asked Hilgor suddenly feeling a tight knot in his stomach.

The stranger was looking at him with a placid encouraging smile. It flashed in Hilgor's mind that, in fact, there was something unusual in the man's appearance. He was taller than average, his facial features were impeccably balanced, and his posture was naturally graceful. It wasn't a common combination on Y-3.

"The one that was just voted down by your unit," said the stranger.

Hilgor tried to hold onto the shaken reality.

"How do you ..." he started, and then interrupted himself quickly, "*why* do you think so?" He cringed at revealing the degree of his vanity.

"I don't think. I know."

For a moment Hilgor thought that this must be a dream, but the cold rain was too real. He looked into the man's eyes and didn't find a hint of insanity or mockery. Hilgor instantly felt very uncomfortable in the twilight of the empty park.

The stranger took out a pink plastic envelope from his coat pocket and offered it to Hilgor.

"Take a look at this first. It'll help."

Hilgor put it inside his pocket without saying a word. The man turned around and began to walk away, then stopped for a moment before disappearing in the dusk and added, softly, "Hilgor, you'll be fine. There's no threat to you in this. You can even forget the whole thing if you choose to."

By the time Hilgor got home his clothes were as wet as if he had just taken a shower in them. The dog greeted him with a couple of excited barks, but, noticing something unusual, moved aside and settled down in a strategic corner to watch Hilgor's movements. The man's behavior was, indeed, a bit strange as far as Riph was concerned. Hilgor sat down on the couch without taking off his drenched coat. He looked at the wall for a while. Then he shook his head, stood up abruptly, threw the raincoat on the floor, turned on the lights and, whistling a cheerful tune, began to look for a dry change of clothes. In a moment, however, he dropped his dry pants back on the shelf, walked back to the raincoat, retrieved the pink envelope from the pocket and went to the study. Riph got up to follow him, looking with interest at the small puddles made by the water dripping from Hilgor's pants.

The dog pushed the study door open, lay down in the doorway and continued to monitor the proceedings. Hilgor sat in the chair in front of the computer and looked at the thin envelope lying on the desk. He wasn't whistling anymore. He officially admitted to himself that he was done pretending that the whole incident was a weird, but harmless joke. There wasn't a single innocent explanation for the stranger knowing about the recent developments in Hilgor's work.

He opened the envelope and took out an unmarked plastic circular device, a very outdated method of information exchange. He guessed that the stranger was using it to avoid an electronic trace. Hilgor held his breath as he stuck the small opaque circle to the sensor area and watched it melt into the surface. The monitor went black, flashed a couple of times and came back on. Hilgor stared at the screen in shock. The file must have reprogrammed his entire system to achieve this quality of resolution, subtle color variations and almost tangible textures of images.

And then he realized that a slowly rotating shape in the center of the screen was a representation of his construct. The object that had existed only in his mind was drawn with exact precision, leaving no possibility of a coincidence. It was beautiful, and it was stable at the critical point.

For the next several hours, Riph watched Hilgor's face lit by the soft glow of the computer screen. At some point, the dog let out a nervous yawn, got up, went closer and gently pushed the man's knee with his head. He had learned to read the slightest variations in Hilgor's moods over the years, but at this moment he wasn't able to tell if the thing that was making his master behave so strangely was threatening or exciting. Hilgor stared at Riph for a few seconds, and then suddenly realized that he had forgotten to walk him. "Sorry Riph. How disgraceful," he said guiltily as he got up from the chair.

When they went outside, dawn was quickly approaching, and only a faint hint of the rainstorm remained, replaced for the most part by the clarity of a crisp morning. Riph trotted along the familiar road to the park, periodically checking on Hilgor whose expression was still worrisomely enigmatic.

It would be a severe understatement to say that Hilgor was at a loss. The file was a collection of mathematical facts vastly surpassing anything that was known on Y-3. And indeed, just like the stranger said, Hilgor's construct stood out as one of the most influential results. With an odd feeling, Hilgor recognized his own ideas in somebody's solution and tried to imagine the unknown mathematician who had solved it years ago. It must have been long ago because there were layers and layers of complexity and abstraction piled on top of the landscape, which Hilgor recognized.

He had been absent-mindedly following Riph's lead, but then realized that they had come to the very location of the unusual encounter. He halted and froze, watching the dog gallop in the direction of the lonely figure sitting on a nearby bench.

With familiarity, Riph thrust his wet paws onto Nick's lap and tried to lick his face. It immediately changed the genre from mystery and suspense to a comedy of apologies, as Hilgor, who finally arrived at the scene, attempted to offer some help in cleaning the mud from the victim's clothes, simultaneously producing muted threats in Riph's direction. Unexpectedly, Nick laughed and patted the dog's neck.

"I never saw a dog when I was growing up," he said, comfortably taking Riph by the collar and guiding him off the bench. "I always wanted one, though."

He paused for a second and added, "I knew that you would eventually be here, but I'm glad that you came again so quickly. Please allow me to convince you that I pose no threat. I'm very sorry that you are probably understandably disquieted by my actions. I'm ready to answer any question you have, for as long as you want."

An image of the slowly rotating object flashed into Hilgor's mind, and the remains of the common sense that were feebly trying to stop him disappeared in the cool morning air.

"We can talk at my apartment," he said. "Riph, let's go home."

Hilgor whistled to the dog and headed to the park exit ignoring Riph's reproaching glance. Nick followed them, staying close behind. Soon they reached the main "alley," where a slightly wider path was divided down the middle by a strip of low shrubs. Riph suddenly stalled, obsessively sniffing something on the curbside. Hilgor slowed down, waiting. After a couple of impatient shouts from his master, Riph reluctantly tore himself from the engaging spot and moved on. Hilgor picked up speed and suddenly realized that Nick was waiting ahead of them, having already turned in the right direction at the fork of the path. Hilgor stopped several steps away and looked at Nick suspiciously.

"Yes, I know where you live. I've been tracking you," said Nick.

Hilgor promptly thought that he might regret getting into this adventure after all.

"Is it connected to my work?" he asked, not getting any closer.

Nick nodded hesitantly as if not completely sure about his answer.

An automatic cleaning machine rolled out from behind a sharp curve of the path. It moved at full speed on the opposite lane, vacuuming small debris from the ground. At the same time, Riph spotted a sleepy meerkat blinking at them from the other side. The dog gave out a yelp and darted in the animal's direction.

"In a sense, it's related ..." Nick stopped in mid-sentence. Hilgor followed his gaze and saw that Riph had jumped over the bush median and was on a direct line of impact with the cleaning machine.

Nick looked straight at the approaching vehicle.

"Kir, stop it," he said quickly.

The brakes screeched and the cleaning contraption came to a halt less than a step short of hitting the dog.

Hilgor exhaled and stared at Nick.

"What was that?" for some reason he was whispering.

"You should put his leash on," said Nick ignoring the question. "These things," he nodded toward the stopped machine, "have a bad reaction time. And your friend is not trustworthy."

They both looked at Riph. He was enthusiastically digging at the burrow in which the meerkat had discreetly retreated during the commotion.

"Riph, come back!" Hilgor's voice was threatening, but not perfectly steady.

Riph recognized Hilgor's tone and immediately left the meerkat in peace and trotted back with a look of insincere remorse.

Hilgor clipped the leash to Riph's collar.

"Let's go," he said to Nick, "and thank you." They didn't exchange another word until they walked into his apartment.

Hilgor's apartment, provided by the Scientific Guild, was unusually luxurious for Y-3; spacious and lit by natural light coming in through the large windows. The decor was up to Hilgor, however, and the resulting picture was somewhat incoherent.

The room reflected some spastic attempts to create an eye-pleasing environment. Hilgor didn't suffer from a lack of funds, but he had a short attention span for anything beyond his work; the furniture was limited to a minimal number of high-end objects. Some of the rather fancy-looking chairs around the elegant dining table were still wrapped in their transportation plastic sheets. A layer of dust betrayed the fact that they had been in this state for quite some time.

"Would you be interested in breakfast?" he asked awkwardly. "Coffee?"

Nick nodded and sat on one of the unpacked chairs. He looked around with curiosity while Hilgor rummaged in the pantry searching for something edible. Riph jumped onto a super elegant white couch in the middle of the room, sighed contently and closed his eyes. Finally, Hilgor brought out a plate of stale protein cakes and two cups of synthetic coffee and went back to the kitchen. Seizing this window of opportunity, Riph quietly appeared near the table and in one smooth bolt snatched a piece of food just as Hilgor returned to the room. The dog's front paw brushed against one of the cups and pushed it off the edge. Hilgor closed his eyes, expecting the sound of broken glass followed by the cry of a frightened dog, but nothing happened. When he looked again, he saw Nick holding the intact cup, still full of coffee and apparently caught the moment after it slid off the table. Hilgor stared speechlessly.

"It's genetic," said Nick, "many generations of perfecting human DNA material."

Hilgor admitted that no amount of exercise and training could have achieved this efficiency of movement. And Nick's face, with its clean bone structure, slightly prominent chin, elongated deep brown eyes and firm outline of the mouth, was another sign of impressive genetic craftsmanship.

And then there was the mysterious file, and saving Riph in the park.

"You aren't from here, or not from now," said Hilgor with complete conviction.

"Excellent analytical reasoning, but I wouldn't have expected any less from you." Nick put the cup on the table. "I'll answer your questions, as promised. But first, I need to run a test. We can do it the other way around, but depending on the result, your questions may change. It just will be more … efficient."

"What sort of test?" Hilgor immediately assumed a disappointed expression, "An intelligence test?"

Nick shook his head, "No," he said, "the score does correlate with some aspects of intelligence, as well as with other traits, Hilgor. But, in essence, it measures something we don't even fully understand ourselves."

He searched inside the inner pocket of his coat, pulled out a thin oblong box, put it on the table and slid the smooth lid open. On the black velvet background, Hilgor saw something that looked like a silver face mask.

"It doesn't take long, and there are only a few mildly unpleasant sensations," Nick hesitated for a moment and added, "not physically unpleasant, anyway."

"You said 'intelligence,'" Hilgor was staring at an invisible point on the table, "does it correlate with 'some aspects' of creativity, too?"

"The terminology around these topics is extremely sensitive, Hilgor. Let's say it measures your level of being 'drastically different' mentally from the majority of the population. In your case, it obviously has to do with your ability to develop new mathematical concepts."

Hilgor was going to ask him something else, but the words got stuck in his throat. Right in front of him, finally, was a chance to know the answer to the question that secretly tortured him every day of his life. A sober thought that the objectivity of this test was questionable passed through his mind, but everything about Nick was so fundamentally improbable that all kinds of things could be possible.

"How do I put this on?"

"Just like a pair of goggles," answered Nick, "I'll run a program that will induce a mild hypnotic state, sort of like daydreaming. The program will generate some interactive sequences. I don't know what they will be; they vary from person to person. It doesn't matter what you think or do. The sensors will capture your raw brain responses."

Hilgor slowly rotated the silver device in his hands as if trying to convince himself it was safe.

Finally, he took a deep breath and put it on.

Nick got up from the chair, walked across the room and stopped in front of the window. His eyes hardened as he looked at Hilgor with a new, detached expression and said, "Kir, start the assessment program."

Then the room disappeared from Hilgor's view and he now stood in a large crowd of people looking up at a whimsical arrangement of huge glass sculptures. Today was a big day, the opening ceremony. The intricate interweaving crystal shapes towered over him, reaching to the sky, reflecting sunlight in their subtle bends, scattering sparks on the admiring faces below. As the last scaffolding melted in the air, he felt a startling anticipation of disaster and then in a flash recognized a fatal flaw in the way the glass pieces were balanced. The audience burst into applause. It took a second before the waterfall of shattering glass started cascading down in slow motion. The picture froze and disappeared.

He was then sitting in his study looking at his computer screen. Apparently he had just been interrupted by something because he couldn't remember what he was doing right before this. He refocused on the screen and read the last sentence. It started coming back – he was in the middle of his personal project, one of those that his unit refused to pursue, and he was searching for the last missing component, a certain limiting condition. As usual, it took several minutes to reach the point of concentration when the study, the computer screen and the noise outside started fade into the background. He was approaching the boundaries of his other world, a space devoid of any physical characteristics except for some vague notion of density. He was steadily increasing his focus, forcing matter to condense into the object of his search, with only a small portion of his consciousness still dimly aware of the warmth of the table surface and the sound of dripping water outside. The picture froze and disappeared.

Almost blinded by the speed, he twisted the control bar of the air capsule just in time so as not to miss a sharp turn in the road. He had only one chance and almost no time left to reach the closing gates of a fortress looming in the distance. He knew that the elusive truth he had chased all his life was locked in there, inside the walls. He couldn't remember who had told him, and why he believed it, but it was too late to doubt it now. The timer was counting the remaining seconds; time was running out. He hit the accelerator hard and crashed into the shutting barriers at full speed. For a split second before everything went black, he felt an almost unbearable happiness at having caught a glimpse of the promised vision. It was worth the chase and even the crash.

The darkness disappeared abruptly. Hilgor was back in his apartment. He gasped and tore off the mask, driving away the sound of mangled metal.

"What happened?" he asked, his head still reeling.

Nick was looking out the window, hands in his pockets, his back to Hilgor. He seemed relaxed and even slightly bored.

He turned, and Hilgor forgot about the test. The sharpness of retreating pain in Nick's eyes was impossible to miss.

"Nick, are you … alright?"

"Yes, why?" Nick asked, immediately assuming his usual demeanor. "Now we can get to the point. I hope you'll handle it well – imagination was a big part of what we just tested. Here's the deal … my planet is called Earth," he paused briefly, carefully watching Hilgor, "and Y-3 used to be our colony, centuries ago."

"I see," said Hilgor calmly, "it adds up. We suspected that much. Except … we've been searching and have never found anyone. We assumed that the original civilization was extinct."

"No," said Nick, "it's doing just fine. But it cut off communication with Y-3, in both directions. And here's the most important part, Hilgor. You're invited to come to Earth. Your … let's call it *talent*, is exceptional."

Hilgor felt a sudden pressure in his chest, and then his heart turned several erratic somersaults, and the sound of triumphal music exploded in his head. His love wasn't unrequited. His mathematics loved him back and it was his ultimate award, victory and vindication. He knew that he wouldn't have the strength to doubt the test. He wanted to trust Nick.

A sudden sting of fear sobered him.

"Invited?" he asked and instinctively leaned back.

Nick raised his hands, "I am not planning to kidnap you," he said with a smile.

Hilgor glanced towards the door, but didn't move.

Nick nodded, "You're right, I could, theoretically. And you wouldn't be able to stop me," his tone was effortlessly affable.

They looked at each other in silence. Then Hilgor exhaled and let go of the chair that he had been clutching. Nick wasn't lying, and it was reassuring.

"Hilgor, applying any force is against the rules. It's up to you if you want to come with me or not. I'm only allowed to present you the offer. It's not a very hard choice, in my opinion. I don't know what would keep you in this post-apocalyptic hell in the first place. Earth is a very old civilization. We have things you can't even dream about. Medicine, comfort – you name it. But, Hilgor, there's something else," Nick paused, and all lightness disappeared from his voice, "something you'll find interesting. On Earth you can work by yourself on anything you want. Nobody will tell you what to do."

It was a calculated move, and Hilgor recognized it for what it was. But a sudden amazing, overpowering feeling flooded his head drowning out all signals of caution. He searched for a word, and it came to him easily because it was something that he had longed for all his life. It was the feeling of freedom. Nick was offering him a future in which the unit, the majority, his helplessness and humiliation would be gone forever. A future in which Y-3 would be gone forever … but he had no idea what Earth was like. He didn't know what he would be getting himself into though.

He looked at Nick, who was watching him from his position at the window, and admitted to himself that he knew nothing about Nick's motives either. "And what's in it for you?" he asked.

"I get paid if you go with me," answered Nick.

Well, that was simple, thought Hilgor.

"Why did your planet cut off communication? And … why are you back? What is it that you'll want from me at the end of the day?"

Nick shook his head, "There are answers to all of your questions, Hilgor. But it's a very long story. Right now, I suggest you get some rest. The test you just took is neurologically taxing, and this is all a lot to handle in one sitting. Get some sleep. Then put this on," he nodded towards the mask still lying on the table. "It works in an interactive mode and will give you all of the information you seek." He began walking toward the door, "We'll meet again whenever you're ready. Believe me, it's the most efficient way. I would prefer a shortcut myself," he said in an unexpected bitter tone.

"Wait!" Hilgor hurriedly stood up pushing away his chair, "How do we get in touch?"

"Just ask it to contact me," Nick gestured toward the mask. "Or post a note to your internal files and I'll be here."

"You can access my private data?"

"How do you think I found you, with your efficiency equalizer?"

Before leaving, he stopped next to Riph, leaned over and gently patted the dog's silky coat.

He had already opened the door when Hilgor asked, "Nick, who is Kir?"

Nick turned back, "My personal fairy – you'll find out," he said and left.

Hilgor watched the door close and took the mask from the table. He was about to put it on, but the room immediately started swimming. He tried to focus, but his head responded with a dull pain. Nick was right; he just simply couldn't take in anything else right now. He needed a break. A short break. It would be more … efficient.

Hilgor dropped the mask back on the table and collapsed onto the couch.

He was caught inside a glistening metallic net, hanging over a gray abyss, helpless and exposed. A dark shadow slowly appeared from the depths and wrapped its tentacles around his head. He screamed and woke up.

Riph stood next to the couch watching him perplexed.

"I'm fine. Sorry, I scared you," said Hilgor touching the dog's head. Riph sighed and settled down on the floor.

It was early evening and shades from individual objects had already disappeared in the homogeneous dimness, but Hilgor continued to lay with eyes open, not turning on the lights.

The unpleasant dream was annoyingly clinging to his memory. He had been too emotional recently, he told himself, and that wasn't going to help. He had to calm down. He focused and started recounting the latest events, from the first meeting in the park to Nick's departure. Everything seemed to fit; Nick came from another planet, more advanced scientifically and technologically; Hilgor passed some kind of test, proving his worth; Nick invited Hilgor to leave Y-3. However bizarre, it seemed logical.

But he knew the pieces that nicely clicked together didn't matter nearly as much as the ones that stuck out. Pages of good arguments were worth nothing against a single counterexample. And in this case, the discord had something to do with Nick. It was true, Nick's motives seemed simple – he was a hired headhunter. But something about him didn't match that picture; namely, that glimpse of extreme emotions on Nick's face. Of course, there was money on the table and probably a lot of it, but it wasn't just that. Something was off; Nick wasn't telling him the whole story. Hilgor's imagination immediately invoked a sinister scenario: Nick was using Hilgor as a pawn in some other game. And in that game, Nick's stakes were high.

Why did he care, Hilgor asked himself, about Nick's motives? Because nothing about Earth, except for the math file, was verifiable inside his own system of reference; even the test could have been a sham that exploited his secret vanity. The only way to be sure of anything was to trust Nick. But Hilgor didn't trust him, and that brought them to a stalemate.

He got up from the couch, turned on the lights and went to the table. The mask was peacefully glimmering in the same place where he had dropped it before going to sleep. Hilgor stood still, thinking. He couldn't take anything it told him as fact. Nevertheless, it wasn't completely useless. There could be some truth in its data, and he would try to watch for inconsistencies.

Hilgor took the mask in his hands. This time he studied it carefully, surprised by the warmth and lightness of the material. It didn't look threatening, but it would lie to him, he warned himself, just like Nick. Hilgor sighed and began to put it on.

The alarm on his wristband chimed. He started, glanced at the clock and carefully placed the mask back on the table.

In less than half an hour he was supposed to meet Del at a newly opened restaurant in the Inner Edge District. It was too late to cancel, and he didn't even want to think about Del's reaction if he simply didn't show up. Of course, her displeasure was insignificant in comparison with the gravity of recent events, but somehow it didn't feel that way.

He looked at the mask pensively. He imagined the information it held, and his heart skipped a beat. Then he imagined Del's upset face.

He started looking through mess in the room, collecting items of clothing suitable for an elegant dinner out.

In ten minutes he was sitting in his air capsule, gliding high up in the traffic grid. Below him the city looked like an enormous wrinkled sheet. There were no individual buildings, but rather the whole structure was a continuous mold, built for optimization of a complex combination of parameters. Not too far in front of him lay the dark body of a massive lake whose opposite shore was so far away it wasn't visible, even from this height. Enormous glowing towers of stacked greenhouses encircled the lakefront and went on and on for as far as the eye could see. His destination, the thin strip of land that housed the city's most exclusive restaurants and clubs, was on the other side, squeezed between the greenhouse high-rises and the water. The location blatantly violated the eco-efficiency law, so a constant air of impending doom and tragic ephemerality hung over the place, unquestionably adding to the ambience.

He looked at the rearview screen. The shimmering fabric of the city spread out from the lake like a fan and made a dead stop at the bright neon curve of the perimeter wall. Beyond that there was just darkness, dead contaminated desert, extending to the rest of the world – nothing else on Y-3 had survived the nuclear war.

He assumed that Nick's ship was probably parked somewhere out there, and his palms became cold and damp at the thought.

Hilgor arrived at the restaurant door two minutes before the reservation, and it gave him some feeling of satisfaction, a small victory over the chaos of the last day. Del was running late, which didn't surprise him in the least.

He sat down at a table and let go for a moment, staring at the black expanse of the lake, periodically punctuated by flashes of sea cow feeding stations in the distance. The reflected lights of the waterfront buildings glimmered peacefully on the low waves. Suddenly, they transformed into the image of the glistening net from his dream. His subconscious wasn't too subtle, he thought with a slight shiver.

At that moment, he heard Del's voice. She was approaching, passionately apologizing to the maître d', whose expression of politely contained scorn soon transformed into a look of sincere desire to help and serve. Then she guiltily glanced at Hilgor, and looking at the table, muttered an apology. He suspected that she was trying to catch a glimpse of her reflection in the table's surface at the same time.

It was an overture to their routine, in which they would fight for emotional and intellectual space, but this time Hilgor decided to give up without much struggle – he was glad to escape his own thoughts, at least temporarily. He sat back and looked at her inquisitively.

She explained how she had spilled something on her dress as she was about to leave and had to change. It didn't hold water, however, since Hilgor could see that her outfit, including the smallest detail, was too carefully arranged.

Del, as usual, had mixed the most outrageously impractical items with austere pieces of the traditional style. The result, for those in the know, was beautifully ironic. The upper part of her dress resembled the standard multi-purpose bodysuit of the old days. Soft gray material, designed for optimal thermo control and durability tightly embraced her arms, chest and waist. But at the hips it exploded with a haystack of fluorescent red and white ribbons. A magnificent red fur scarf was wrapped around her sculpted neck. High-wedged white boots were a direct insult to practicality, and the regulation black wristband with identification chips and radiation meter was studded with large pink stones. Changing her dress would have been equivalent to destroying a fragile collage with a hammer.

Nothing was said, but she knew that he didn't buy the stain excuse. She was just plain late. Hilgor had scored a point for free. Now he just had to maintain the advantage.

"Any news?" she asked, after quickly ordering a designer drug cocktail. "You didn't answer my calls all day."

He hesitated for just a second before answering, "No, just the usual stuff. Sorry, it was very busy. A lot of voting is going on in the unit. It's important as you know. Good ideas could get lost if we're not careful."

He smiled again, not very warmly, but she didn't notice, taking a tall white glass from the waiter's hand. As far as Hilgor could tell from the drink's name, it was a mix of mild hallucinogens and stimulants. Normally, he would comment on it, but today he just … let it go.

Del sipped the drink and closed her eyes. When she opened them, there was a glint of excitement that he hadn't noticed before.

"I need to go outside the Wall tonight. I have an order from an old customer."

Hilgor dropped some elaborate appetizer utensil, which he had been absent-mindedly twisting in his hands.

The waiter interrupted this promising beginning, bringing menus to the table. They were printed on real paper, which, together with all-human service, was supposed to emphasize the exclusive air of the place.

"Let's order first," she said quickly, "it's not as bad as you think."

Hilgor stared at the menu, unable to concentrate because of a wave of irritation. "We agreed," he said through clenched teeth.

"But look, there's nothing wrong with it. I go over the Wall, pick up a good piece, write a review and release it to the common market for purchase - it's perfectly legal."

"Right," said Hilgor, "and then you upgrade your boat or something like that a month later as usual. And nobody will ever suspect anything."

"Hard to prove," she said quickly.

"Useless," he muttered massaging the bridge of his nose. Then he looked up at her, "Del, fine, your agent license will be revoked, you know the price. But it's simply not safe behind the Wall. Look, I won't try to stop you from your shady business in the city. But forget about the Wall."

"It's not dangerous," she objected. "Don't be so paranoid. You just assume that it's bad there. But there's no official information about it. And I go there, I know that it is safe ... if you take precautions," she looked straight into his eyes. He was silent.

"Excuse me for a moment," she said and sighed with exasperation. "Order for me, when this grand waiter comes back, please. Anything is fine." She got up and headed to the restroom.

Watching her move, Hilgor was reminded of a creature with the body of a fragile deer and the eyes of a hungry mountain lion.

Hilgor had met Del two years ago in a swimming pool where she was unsuccessfully practicing platform dives. Later, they could never remember how exactly, she got involved in this temporary and uncharacteristic activity, but he had helped her that day and they had gone to dinner later. She had a fantastic body, natural joie de vivre and a sharp if slightly brittle intellect. Of course, they had looked up their compatibility data in the personality matching system and then decided to ignore the disappointing results, joking that a general disregard for the rules was at least something they had in common. In any case, neither morals nor common sense stood any chance in the beginning of their romance. She opened a door to a world he never knew existed, the exhilarating world where everything was bright and delightful and sensuous and where the air itself was permeated by the magic of her presence. It felt precisely like love was supposed to feel. It probably was love.

But things had not been going well recently, and sometimes he thought that there was nothing left between them except for constant tension and sparks of irritation. Hilgor's pet peeve was Del's perfect ability to destroy his inner universe by randomly bursting in with her unrestrained energy, noise and disorder. He had to pick up the pieces and glue them together after each of her unceremonious intrusions. She didn't care about the fragile objects in his mind. He wasn't sure she was even aware of them.

Hilgor suddenly noticed that their waiter had been patiently standing next to the table.

"Sorry," he said quickly, "two chef choices, please." The waiter quietly disappeared.

Hilgor couldn't explain why he didn't cut his losses and move on. Perversely, it could be due to the same thing that had bothered him in the first place. Del, with her brightness, her vibe of excitement, was the only outside entity that had successfully competed with his imaginary world. She was his connection to reality, and she persistently dragged him there, away from the company of his abstract creations. He thought that it was probably a good thing.

She returned and sat down with a collected expression indicating that she was ready for a fight. "You know that it's more than money for me," she paused and continued, "*do* you know, though? You have never been interested in what I do. You don't care what matters to me."

Now she was really upset, and her lower lip quivered. Usually, at this moment, Hilgor would explode with irritation, which would be followed by a bitter exchange and, ultimately, his lonely ride home.

This time, however, he imagined his empty apartment and the silver mask waiting for him on the table in the dark room. It abruptly sent the restaurant and Del and their fight to the background. Instead, a sequence of very vivid memories flashed through his mind: the cold rain in the empty park, the howling sound of the motor before the imaginary crash, the offer to move to Earth. And then he remembered his helpless thrashing inside the metal net, the dark shade ascending from the abyss and his scream filled with piercing terror.

He didn't want to go home. And he didn't want to be alone.

"I care about what you do," he said, taking Del's hand. "I can ride with you behind the Wall tonight if you want."

It wasn't clear if her face expressed disbelief or shock.

"I'm serious," he said before she had a chance to say anything. "But you're driving."

"Are you sure?" she checked his face for any signs of a trick, then sighed and looked away, trying to hide the fact that she was genuinely touched.

I am a lying bastard, thought Hilgor.

"We can even leave now, unless you are hungry," she said hurriedly, obviously worried that he might change his mind. He definitely wanted to get out of there too, away from the polite attention of all-human service.

"Let's go," he said.

They got up, ready to leave, when he hesitated.

"But your dress … it'll look strange there, won't it?"

"Strange – in that place?" she tried to hide a smile.

He shrugged, slightly embarrassed. He had never been outside the Wall. How would he know?

Within several minutes, Del's air capsule was taking them across the city towards the bright contour of the Wall. She gave him periodic glances trying to make sure he wasn't still angry with her.

"Hilgor, there's almost nothing new coming from the city anymore," Del was speaking almost pleadingly. "And even if something comes up, there are so many people watching that I have practically zero chance to hit it first."

It was hard to argue with that, but there was a fatal flaw in Del's logic.

"Why can't you just stick to your job description?" asked Hilgor almost rhetorically. They both knew why.

Del had the extremely bizarre and exotic profession of art critic in a society where art was at best ignored and at worst discouraged.

The rule, carried throughout the centuries, stated that everyone on Y-3 had to perform a useful duty in order to be allowed access to life-sustaining resources. Naturally, the profession of an artist wasn't included in the list of approved jobs.

Of course, independent pursuit of art wasn't illegal, even though it was dubious from a moral point of view. People could even release their work to the market, anonymously and at a nominal price. Officially, Del had an administrative position, enabling the logistics of the sales and writing brief reviews on the submitted pieces to help the public orient themselves in the confusing terrain of art artifacts.

"I would shoot myself if I had to stick to the job description," she said with complete conviction.

Of course she would, thought Hilgor. She was a hunter, a predator. She needed constant excitement and she got it in the murky art underworld that had its own rules, rewards and dangers.

She scanned incoming pieces for something promising and made purchases on behalf of one of her clients. On the surface this appeared to be an official sale, but it was followed by another transaction, when a satisfied client paid her the black market price. It was a profitable, albeit illegal gig, and Del was extremely good at choosing the right pieces.

"It's been too slow, recently," she said.

Hilgor knew what she meant. Unfortunately, part-time artists didn't release much, and only a fraction of it was valuable, so competition between buyers was fierce. Sometimes items would be snatched up in the seconds that it took for her to enter the payment information.

But there was another way. If artists didn't have access to the submission system, if they lived outside the Wall, Del, in her official capacity, had the right to release their work to the market herself. In this case, she would have to split the black market money with the artist, but she was the one who assigned the timing release.

"Who are you meeting?" asked Hilgor.

"I've been working with this woman for a while. I first noticed her stuff when she was still inside."

"When did she cross?"

Del thought for a second, "Maybe five years ago. Something like that. She hasn't been feeling well recently and she needs money to pay for tests."

"Is she good?"

"Very," the way Del said it; he knew that this artist was the real deal. It meant that Del had found something, both obvious and unexplainable, that had, in her words, some connection with ultimate beauty. He could never understand what she meant precisely, but he knew that this mattered to her the most, and that the money and the excitement of the hunt were mere by-products. Not that both weren't completely and undeniably enjoyable in their own right.

The Wall was now looming right in front of them, casting a bluish light on the city structures that stopped just short of it. It was made out of translucent material, designed to pass sunlight to the city during the day and illuminate a nearby area after dark. It was very tall, almost half a mile from its base to the top, and seemed very thin from a distance, almost fragile. Close up, however, it looked like a giant fortress of ice, its surface polished and smooth, except for the tunnel entry holes that led into its glowing interior.

Hilgor's eyes searched for guards, or barriers, or checkpoints at the entrances. But of course, he didn't find any. Everyone was free to go in either direction. The Wall was simply a gigantic shield built to block and reflect the contaminated winds and radiation from the outside.

Del pushed a button on her wristband, "It'll let us know if contamination levels get dangerously high. Ready?" She waited for his nod before sliding the capsule into the nearest tunnel. The tube turned out to be surprisingly long, but so straight that Hilgor could make out the dark circle of an exit in the distance.

Outside, as far as he could see in the faint glow, the bare low hills stretched out in all directions and finally disappeared into the darkness. Unpleasant-looking shadows of automated decontamination equipment created a regular pattern on the ground, making the scene reminiscent of a pre-war period graveyard.

The light was growing dimmer as their capsule flew forward, over the empty land, towards complete darkness. Hilgor was about to ask Del if she was lost when he noticed a faint light ahead. They were moving fast, and soon he could distinguish a cluster of white semi-spherical buildings, which resembled a flock of lost sheep.

"Where do they get energy? Clean water? And food?" Hilgor realized that he had never thought about life beyond the Wall.

"They buy it from the city." Del was making a wide turn getting closer to the buildings on the far side of the camp. "Some come with their savings. Some sell their work. It's cheap to live here."

The capsule came to a stop, and Del turned to Hilgor, "You can wait inside, or you can come with me. It won't take long." She checked her wristband, "We have about an hour – technically more; but better to be on the safe side."

Hilgor opened his door and stepped out onto the dry crumbly soil. He caught himself trying not to inhale the outside air. He pulled himself together and looked around.

They had parked near the last line of identical white structures. Behind them, to his right, there was an impenetrable darkness like nothing he could ever imagine. He shivered, picturing the enormity of the dead space, thousands and thousands of miles of plains, oceans and mountains. It was more disturbing than he'd expected, so he turned away quickly, relieved to see signs of life in the form of a small village. He was surprised that his memory offered him that archaic term, but it seemed like the perfect phrase for it. A couple hundred small portable homes of a standard round design were huddled together at the base of a low hill, like a herd of animals trying to conserve heat during a harsh storm. This was another image from the past, from some documentary about extinct bison that had walked Y-3 before the war.

Hilgor couldn't seem to locate a single source of illumination. In confusion, he raised his head and nearly lost his balance, struck by the totally alien sight of myriads of small white lights that almost covered the unfamiliar deep blackness of space. The city inside the Wall was too bright, and all he had ever witnessed was a handful of dim dots on a dull brownish background. It was impossible to believe that the limitless expanse above and that washed up tarp were the same sky; that he was still on Y-3. It took him a moment to connect the gorgeous cloud of diamond dust to the name from his astronomy lessons. "Milky Way," he whispered. He kept looking up, unable to tear his eyes from the stars, and surprisingly thought that he wouldn't have seen any of this had it not been for the mask in his living room. It was as if Nick had sent him a distant greeting, revealing a glimpse of the future in which this shimmering wonder was just the first gift.

Hilgor heard Del's footsteps receding, and reluctantly looked away from the sky and hurried after her, uneasily aware of the dead expanse of desert behind them.

At close range the buildings no longer looked white – they were grayish, encrusted in layers of dust, muddied by the rains. Del approached one of them, the nearest to their parked capsule, and knocked on the door. It glided aside, letting them in.

A young, thin woman in a gray anti-radiation suit stepped away from the doorway, inviting them inside. She was so pale that her dark eyes didn't seem to belong with the rest of her face, and her shaggy mane of brown hair looked almost black in stark contrast to the whiteness of her lifeless skin.

She motioned for him to enter, introducing herself in a quiet, slightly hoarse voice, "Reish. Come in."

Hilgor met her eyes, and she held his gaze for a moment before looking back at Del. It was long enough to exchange a token of recognition. And it was long enough for Hilgor to see desperate fear hidden just under the surface of her eyes.

Following her inside, Hilgor glanced around the mostly empty space, struck by its resemblance to his own apartment. There were at least two things in common: an obvious lack of any interest in making the place nice and an inconspicuous efficiency with regard to where things were situated. He immediately recognized the same underlying reason – she was also an incredible time miser. The time she spent with her imaginary objects and landscapes was so precious that she had tried to simplify everything in her external world, making it efficient and maintenance free.

"I remembered an old world when we landed – a village," he said.

"A trailer park would be a closer match," she said, "but it requires some time to define the difference."

On their way to the large table in the middle of the open space, they passed a simple open kitchen. On the other side, Hilgor saw an area that reminded him of a physics lab.

"Del, the latest, as promised. Want to see?" Reish motioned to the large, flat black screen on the table.

"I don't want to waste your time, Reish. You know he'll buy it anyway."

"I want to know what you think."

"Of course, then, I'd be honored."

Reish nodded, picked up two metal hairnets from the table and handed them to Del and Hilgor. Del put it over her hair in a standard gesture. Hilgor mechanically took the other one, and recalled Del talking about neuro-art, something she believed would eventually prove all other art forms inferior.

He didn't know much about it except the main concept, a long known neurological effect where stimulation of one sensory pathway triggered specific experiences in another. Modern technology could temporarily induce variations of this state, but they were not especially popular with the general public, being neither very interesting nor very pleasurable in and of themselves. Hilgor hesitated, but the image of the Milky Way flashed in his mind, and he sat down in the closest chair and followed Del's example.

"Give it ten seconds," said Del.

The screen lit up with an unfolding pattern of intricate shapes, which slowly shifted and changed color and brightness. He felt a vague sense of déjà vu, luring him to search for a fleeting memory of something beautiful that he knew had never happened. A whimsical whirl of tender blue sent him a wave of happiness, stronger and purer than anything he had ever experienced in real life. He wanted to linger there longer, but suddenly lost his equilibrium, blinded by an explosion of deep orange, the color of the sun, parched desert, thirst, love and jealousy. And then it occurred to him what Reish was doing – she had found a way to ignite a cross-activation between the visual cortex and the brain areas responsible for producing direct emotional responses. She had interweaved variations of fear, apprehension, hope, anticipation, love, happiness, rage and feelings that existed deep in his mind, but had never been acknowledged or even named. The prominent theme of passion and desire became more disturbing as the colors grew deeper, approaching an inky mark of a catastrophe, breaking the symmetry, offsetting the balance. Colliding with the black void, he felt the sharp agony of the end, an uncontrollable childish fear of the dark, but, to his shock, nothing horrible happened. He was falling through calm melancholy, lightness of acceptance. A bright white suddenly flashed with anger and faded, leaving behind the burn, the pain of loss. It was a farewell.

"It's over," he heard Del's voice, but he continued looking at the empty screen.

"What do you think?" asked Reish. She leaned forward from a reclining position in her chair, watching them with rapt attention. They both turned toward her and the moment she saw their faces, her eyes relaxed. She bit her lip, trying to hide a content smile.

"Reish, it is …" Del stammered, searching for words, but Reish no longer needed to hear them. She was satisfied.

Hilgor absent-mindedly watched the women confirm the details of the deal at the large table. They looked more like friends than business partners, and it was clear that this was a familiar transaction, following a standard script. Except at the very end, Reish's voice suddenly changed, switching to a suspiciously casual tone and Hilgor noticed that Del immediately tensed.

"Del, I need a favor."

"Yes?" Del also tried to sound casual.

"I want you to sell another piece, my early work – A-243."

"But why? You had planned to keep it …"

"I got the results. It's in the final stage. They say three maybe four months tops."

Hilgor glanced at Del and saw that her face froze.

"I want you to find it a good home. I want to know where it goes," Reish's voice had an uncharacteristic, almost commanding tone to it. Then, in her usual demeanor, she added, "Please, Del. Besides, I need the extra money. Illegal painkillers aren't cheap."

Del finally managed to collect herself. "How are you handling it?" she asked.

Now it was Reish's turn to look away. "I don't know," she said, hugging her shoulders with her arms. "I guess someone in my position might be angry. But to me it all just seems so pathetic. What did I expect?"

She walked away from the table and stopped in front of the curved wall, pressing her forehead against its porous surface. Impulsively, she hit it with her fist, and Hilgor winced, imagining the sharp pain in her hand.

"But I didn't expect it to be so fast!" Del turned back, and Hilgor saw tears in her eyes. "I'm afraid, Del. I'm disgusted by the thought of my dead body. And the ugliness of all that."

Del quickly stepped toward Reish and gave her a hug. There was a long pause, and then Reish gently freed herself from the embrace.

"Thank you," she said and walked to the nearest chair and sat on its soft leather arm. "You know, it's kind of funny … you would never guess what happens to you after you learn that you're about to die. All my life I was stealing time from reality to create worlds in my head. I don't do it anymore. I want to spend my remaining time here, in the real world. I don't know where the things in my head come from. But they're not from here. So, there's a chance they'll be there, where I'm heading. Not that I really believe in it, though. But this," she stroked the smooth surface of the leather chair and looked at her hand, "this will be gone."

The chime on Del's wristband interrupted the pause.

"I'm sorry," whispered Del. It sounded like an apology for everything, not just for their departure.

"No need, Del," now Reish seemed very calm. "We both know that in my five years here I did more than I did during my thirty inside. I had the luxury of time. I hoped it would be longer, but even this amount was worth it. I don't regret that I left. Now go."

She waved them a quick goodbye and closed the door.

They walked to their capsule without saying a word and continued to ride in silence until after they had passed back through the Wall.

Del looked straight ahead as if she needed all her concentration to navigate the city, but when they got near the bright windows of a tall residential complex, Hilgor saw that she was crying.

"Del," he called, but she didn't answer.

He wanted to make her talk. "What did Reish do when she lived inside?" he asked.

"She worked in the Meteorology Department. She maintained programs for anti-tornado missiles." Del was silent for a while. Then she added, "Someone needs to fight tornadoes."

After another pause she said, in a more normal voice, "I wish I could keep that early piece, A-243," she nodded towards the small black package. "She calls it *Not So Subtle Signs of Obsession*." She looked at Hilgor for the first time since they had left Reish and smiled, as if remembering something good. "It's one of her first after she discovered the technique … my favorite part is where she managed to capture this feeling … imagine, you're in love, secretly, desperately. You walk outside, and your heart skips a beat when you think you caught a glimpse of your lover's face in the crowd. And then, as you realize your mistake, the immediate feeling of simultaneous disappointment and relief."

"Why can't you buy it?" asked Hilgor.

"Its black market price will be too high for me. I need to offer her the highest bid," she said and after a pause added, "except that it doesn't matter anymore. Money won't help her much now."

Hilgor didn't say anything, silently agreeing – knowing that when Reish refused to work at any official job, she had lost her right to the decontaminated space inside the Wall, including access to the city's infrastructure and public services. With medicine and pharmacology being one of those services, there was no amount of money that could help her. She was outside the system. And besides, it was very likely that at this stage it was too late. Even the best doctors would probably not be able to do anything for her; cancer had been by far the largest killer in the city after the war, and generations of researchers had failed to find the cure.

"She has a following, a cult inside," Del's speech was tense, as if she were arguing. "By now it's unfashionable to have private exhibitions without her work."

They stopped at the entrance to Hilgor's complex.

"I'm sorry I ruined the evening," Del's voice suddenly fell flat, and her face lost its tension, appearing wan and lifeless. Hilgor waited; he knew her well enough to guess that it wasn't the end. In a moment she spoke again, now in a distant, unfamiliar tone, "You see, Hilgor, it's … it might sound cruel, but it's not even about her. It's about her work, everything she won't do now. This universe will never make up for this. It's as if God lost one of his voices, forever."

Hilgor had never heard her talk like this before. He stared at her in surprise, but she didn't notice, looking right through him. Finally, she tried to smile, still avoiding his eyes, "I need to go home. I'm a wreck now."

He touched her shoulder and got out of the capsule. She sped away, and he walked uphill to his apartment.

He opened the door, getting ready for the onslaught of paws, wet nose and rapid body checks. Without turning on the lights, he grabbed the leash and took the dog out.

As he walked along the familiar path to the park, his thoughts grew increasingly darker. Del's last words were unnecessary. He understood. Reish was an ally who had been fighting the same battle as he did, sacrificing everything to free up beautiful things locked inside the indifferent emptiness. They both weren't doing too well at the moment, Reish and he, and it wasn't clear who had fared worse

– she, dying, or he, with his hands tied and mouth gagged by the accurate machine of efficiency.

Riph disappeared into the bushes, probably catching the smell of a lone meerkat. Waiting for the dog, Hilgor looked up at the sky. It had its customary brownish color, with a slight hint of crimson closer to the rim and several faint blinking dots. And suddenly, he thought about the world that Nick had talked about. The world where, according to Nick, you didn't have to breathe poison to see the stars.

"Riph, let's go home," he called and turned back. It was time to ask questions.

He hurriedly walked to the apartment, rushed in through the door and turned on the lights. But instead of heading straight to the table he stopped, his eyes glued to a piece of paper that had apparently been pushed under the door during his absence. He looked around, confirming that the windows were shaded, and picked it up.

There was only one person who could've brought this, and yet, Hilgor's heart sank when he recognized the familiar handwriting.

It was a protocol break. When he had decided to work with Deait on their secret project, they had agreed to keep their communication anonymous and untraceable. This sudden letter, delivered to his home, couldn't mean anything good.

He started reading.

Dear Hilgor,

I made a decision. I won't work with you anymore. In fact, I'll stop doing math altogether. Let me try to explain. You know that I have to spend my most productive hours on my government assigned job. When I come home and try to pick up where I left off, I struggle. I can't switch so fast. It's better when I have some time off. By the second day it comes back. But when it does, my job – forget about the job – my whole life becomes irrelevant, gray, meaningless. It kills me to return to my usual life, to my work. I feel that I'm going crazy, my personality splits. Hilgor, I couldn't do it anymore, I had to choose. And I won't move outside the Wall. It's not worth it. Nothing is worth this slow suicide. And after all, I'm not even good enough. I suspected that, always … Bye, Hilgor.

Hilgor let the letter drop to the floor.

So it finally happened, he thought. He always knew it would only be a matter of time. Why now? What was the last straw?

Deait and Hilgor had been friends for a while, since school, in fact. They both equally hated the system. They talked about it all the time. They had gotten to know each other well. But it took Hilgor by total surprise when Deait called and told him that he'd just made a public statement and, ignoring the unit, posted his strikingly beautiful solution of a very old and difficult problem to the shared net. In his statement, Deait explained that the current science setup was flawed. He gave an example of his approach that was just voted down, and showed that ignoring his technique would create recession in this field for a while. And it was connected with the improvement of tornado forecast precision, which was catastrophically needed in Y-3 lite.

Hilgor had screamed at him that it was professional suicide, but it had been too late. Deait said that he couldn't see his ideas being killed anymore. Hilgor didn't like it either, but he knew that protesting was a useless gesture. The efficiency programs wouldn't be changed. Now … he was sure that Deait wasn't impulsive. He was even more positive that Deait would never want to attract any attention to himself. Deait openly challenged the rules of Y-3 for killing his work. He was lighthearted and cynical about many things in life, but … he couldn't be cynical in this one case.

But the system protected itself, and Deait suffered the consequences. He was kicked out of the Guild and had to take one of the regular, government-certified jobs. He was stubborn, so he kept doing math in his spare time, and he had nothing to lose anymore, so he continued posting his results in the public space. This was a luxury Hilgor couldn't afford even anonymously – it could be tracked. Working with Deait had enabled at least some of his work, their joint results, to get out to the world instead of collecting virtual dust in Hilgor's secret private files. So, that was the end. He had now lost Deait.

Hilgor blindly stared at the wall in front of him, trying to control the familiar helpless rage at the perfect efficiency with which they were caged. Moving behind the Wall? Deait refused to breathe poisoned air in exchange for freedom, but who could blame him? Whose fault was it that they had to make impossible choices?

Except that was no longer the case. He, Hilgor, of all people, had been given a way out.

No more wasting time, he doubled checked the doors and windows, sent all his communication devices to sleep and turned off the lights except for a small table lamp. He looked around the room, rejected the couch and dragged a black shabby armchair from his study.

He picked up the mask, sat down and put it on.

For a while, he could still see the room. Riph was looking at him suspiciously from his usual position at the door. And then there was nothing except for a wall of milky fog.

A soft female voice called his name and then said, "Hello. I am interactive software designed to give you access to information about Earth and to explain the goals of operation *Renaissance*. Before we begin, you can change your preferences. Speed of responses, gender ..."

A list of options appeared in front of his eyes.

"Default," interrupted Hilgor, "no, wait. Change the interaction mode to casual speech."

"Done. Do you want me to walk you through the tutorial, or do you prefer to direct me with questions?"

Hilgor thought for a second. Then he asked, "Is our interaction recorded or transmitted?"

"It's your personal experience. Earth privacy laws don't allow this sort of information to be disclosed."

Hilgor had to admit that this question was rather stupid, considering that he had no way to verify the response, but he decided to go with the simple theory that the program was telling the truth.

"Show me the night sky from Earth's livable area."

"Hilgor, there are no unlivable places on Earth. Be more specific."

Hilgor almost bit his tongue. Of course, there was no reason to assume that there was any correlation between the two planets. "Show me the sky from the equivalent of my geodesic position," Hilgor didn't know why it was important. But he needed to see it.

The curtain of fog lifted, revealing the expanse of the night sky. It was the same as the one he saw from Reish's place. And, of course, the Milky Way was there too.

Apparently, the program was smart enough not to wait too long. It said softly, "The subspaces containing our planets are exact clones, Hilgor. Earth and Y-3 are identical except for the slight climate and some minor geographical differences."

It did help. He was able to think again, albeit not very rationally.

"What is there, on Earth, in this place?" he was surprised at how steady his voice was.

"It's a nature preserve," and forests, meadows, green hills with huge grazing herds of deer and bison quickly flashed in front of his eyes.

"They are not extinct," he said.

"Excuse me?" asked the voice.

"Never mind … how is it called, my home lake, the closest of the five?"

"It kept its ancient name – Erie."

Hilgor took off the mask and circled around the room.

Riph lifted his head and hesitantly wagged his tail, but realizing that Hilgor wasn't paying any attention to him, went back to sleep.

Hilgor made two more laps, abruptly stopped and commanded himself to snap out of it. After all, the explanation was logically consistent. He took a deep breath and reached for the mask again.

This time it didn't seem strange or frightening, and he kept the feel of the old leather handle of the armchair as a reference point to reality. Hilgor asked, "What happened? Why didn't you send help here after the war?" He forgot that he was addressing the program.

"It was your internal war, Hilgor. By that time, the old world hadn't had any official contact with your planet for centuries. The Earth's population didn't even know it happened."

"And unofficial … contacts?"

"Well," said the voice almost reluctantly, "you can imagine, there were always security considerations."

At this point, Hilgor decided to give up the initiative in favor of comprehension.

"Go to lecture mode. One hour. Main fact level, no informational branches."

Hilgor opened his eyes and looked at the clock. It was 6:38 in the morning, exactly one hour since he set the mask down on his nightstand. He looked at it with a growing sense of respect. Whatever technology it operated, it kept its promises; it made Hilgor fall asleep instantaneously, and it tuned his brain to wake up exactly as specified. Incidentally, the quality of his sleep far exceeded anything he had ever managed to achieve by any natural or artificial aid.

Hilgor stretched and quickly rose to his feet. He had to step over Riph on his way to the kitchen, and the dog shifted with a sigh conveying that it was completely uncivilized to be disturbed at this hour.

Chewing on the tasteless breakfast biscuits, whose state of semi-staleness was frozen in time from the moment of creation, Hilgor went through a mental review of the information the program had provided last night; facts packaged in concise narratives, maps, charts, live footage, still images.

Hilgor stood in front of the window, finishing his second cup of designer caffeine drink. It was raining again, and the pale shade of the sky added to the drab grayness of the buildings, making the city even gloomier than usual.

Earth had just watched them die. They had offered no help. But by now, he knew the complete story and struggled to figure out whose moral side he was on, or even if there was a side.

He thought about the methods used on Earth to stop the virus epidemic. It was impossible to miss the familiar pattern. Mechanical efficiency of quarantine levels. Moral efficiency of not treating the sick to fund anti-virus research. Emotional efficiency of mass disposal of dead bodies.

Earth didn't seem like an evil super-civilization anymore.

Hilgor took the empty cup to the kitchen and stood for a while, staring at his distorted reflection in the surface of the water dispenser cylinder, and going over the main narrative points once again. He had to admit that as hard as he might, he couldn't pinpoint any inconsistencies in the story. It didn't mean that it was true, he reminded himself. But how was he supposed to find out for sure? It was a closed logical loop, and no one could help – it was on him to make the judgment call.

That meant that he had to jack up his mental capacity to the maximum level. And that, in turn, meant that he had to visit the transportation hub.

He threw on his waterproof cape and went outside.

After a short walk, he came to the familiar shape of the terminal building – a huge uneven dome adorned by giant tuba bells of aerial transport entrances.

Hilgor approached a ground gate, went in and headed straight to the dispatch machine. His destination was on one of the highest levels, hidden behind the dense web of crisscrossing walkways, and the system assigned him a personal transporter.

The automatic system carried Hilgor up several spiraling levels to the entrance of a small convenience station. There his temporary vessel slowed down, its handle folded in, the blue light faded and the platform blended with the floor surface.

Hilgor stepped inside the shop, made his way between the shelves with miscellaneous travel necessities, passed two small tables at the window and greeted the middle-aged guy in a security uniform behind the low counter. Despite the longevity of their acquaintance, Hilgor knew almost nothing about him except for the fact that he was washed up on this transit hub long ago under unclear circumstances. The man lazily rose from his seat and walked to a frosted glass door in the back. Hilgor followed him to the familiar windowless den through the rows of small airtight drawers along the walls.

Law enforcement turned a blind eye to the trade and consumption of illegal substances inside the terminal hub, a tribute to either the lenience of the authorities, or more likely, a calculated efficiency.

"What's your strongest today?" asked Hilgor.

The owner pulled out one of the drawers, and the pungent smell of roasted coffee beans filled the small room. The guy scooped some, and then opened the doors of a white cabinet in the corner, where an antique, pre-war metal apparatus was squarely sitting on a lower shelf. He played with the settings on the control panel, muttering something about unusual humidity. A thick smell hit Hilgor as the viscous, dark brown liquid started slowly half-pouring, half-dripping from a small nozzle into a white cup underneath. Hilgor took the cup from the guy, sipped the drink and nodded contently. The owner acknowledged with a dry smile. Hilgor beamed him the money and walked out of the back room. Both tables were empty; he sat at the closest one and slowly finished the espresso.

The business of growing natural coffee beans was illegal on Y-3. Greenhouse space was too precious, the synthetic version was chemically identical, and the actual difference was really just a question of faith. Hilgor felt the sharp bitter taste on his lips and sighed, enviously thinking of the vast fields of Earth's coffee plantations, flashed at him yesterday among other images. In a couple of minutes, the familiar sensation kicked in. All of the dusty and frosty windows in Hilgor's mind started opening, letting light into the dim corners. He savored the feeling, firmly convinced that the artificial version never created a result of the same purity.

Waiting for the full effect to take place, Hilgor watched people glide up and down the spiraling walkways behind the window of the convenience shop. There were three distinct categories: regular commuters in their invisible bubbles of transit trance, focused consumers and suppliers of the illegal trade shops and gawking thrill-seeking onlookers from all over the city. They all shared, however, the same sad signs of living on an island surrounded by a contaminated desert. Their faces were grayish, their eye shadows were deep, their bodies looked fragile.

Hilgor just shook his head at the sheer absurdity of the operation – "Renaissance." Contaminating the physically and mentally perfect population of Earth with genetically compromised people from technologically and scientifically inferior worlds sounded like a perverse joke.

Hilgor admitted that the bait to lure him to Earth worked perfectly; he couldn't turn away the gift of freedom dangling in front of him. He didn't want to end up like Deait, Reish or the senior members of the Guild with that extinguished look in their eyes. He couldn't just walk away from the offer. But he couldn't leave his entire life behind to plunge into the complete unknown either.

Hilgor rubbed his forehead in frustration. Brute mental force, even fueled by good coffee, didn't work. He impatiently tapped his fingers on the table. There must be something that could help, someone who would know the right answer. And suddenly, Hilgor realized who it was. He put the empty cup on the table and got up.

In several minutes, he was sitting on the hard plastic bench of an underground train.

Fewer and fewer people remained in his car as the train approached the end of the line, and by the final stop, Hilgor was alone. He stepped out on the austere platform and looked around. It had been twenty-three years since he had come here, but nothing seemed to have changed.

He headed to the main access tunnel and for a while walked inside the empty passageway. The sound of his steps echoed loudly against the concrete walls, bare and smooth except for the large engraved letters *Y-3*, a code name for one of the dozens of fallout shelters hastily built during the last years of the pre-nuclear crisis. Y-3 was the only place on the planet that had survived the war.

Generally, Y-3 rules didn't allow wasting space for memorials, but demolishing the Old City would have been perceived as sacrilege, a bad omen, an insult to the generations who brought life back to the surface, so, as the centuries passed, the place continued to retain its ambiguous status. Some people still came here to pay homage, and the Survivalist Church used it as a place of worship, but most of the time it was deserted.

Ghost city – he would have thought that it was haunted if he had believed in ghosts.

He passed through several open metal gates, now perpetually stuck in their previously airtight frames, and the tunnel opened onto a huge cavernous space, the first section of the underground living complex.

Hilgor rode the elevator down and walked on a street between identical buildings, stretched far from the floor to the ceiling.

His steps evenly punctuated the silence, echoing in the brightly lit rectangular canyons, but suddenly he heard a strange change in the pattern, as if an extra beat had been added to the hollow reverberating sound. A hot wave of fear flooded his mind as he twirled around.

There was nobody in sight as far as he could see along the straight mile-long passage. He stood motionless, holding his breath. Then he turned and continued walking, still not convinced that it was the fault of his disturbed imagination.

He kept nervously glancing over his shoulder all the way to the former animal grounds, but once inside, his attention switched to the task of not getting lost in the multilevel stacks of empty enclosures. Surprisingly, even after so many years, he remembered the way into this maze well enough that it didn't take long for him to find what he was looking for. With a churning feeling in his chest he recognized the cheetah, with its serious gaunt face and intense eyes, looking at him from a picture on the cage wall.

He never came here, even in his thoughts, since the day of his eleventh birthday. That memory was locked and buried as deeply as possible.

The visit to the Old City had been his father's present. Hilgor was fascinated by animals back then, by both the real living creatures that had survived the new climate conditions and by those that had become extinct.

That day, the two of them spent most of their time in the big cat area, touching the very stones where paws used to brush the ground, looking at the pictures, watching the information videos. Holding hands, they imagined, eyes closed, that these magnificent creatures, now gone forever, were still pacing the narrow pens.

Hilgor's mother couldn't join them that day. A space program lead, she was gone, as always, to the unknown and unfriendly world of missile tests, control center emergencies and production deadlines. His father was his best friend, his guide and a guard against anything bad that could ever happen in his life. Like everyone else, he had a job. He did routine technical maintenance on a section of the Wall, which he performed with mechanical accuracy. He didn't talk about it much.

That day, on Hilgor's birthday, in front of this very cage, Hilgor felt that something wasn't right. They were watching the footage of a running cheetah, a blur of black spots on yellow grass, its flexible body coiling and uncoiling like the flying tip of a lashing whip, its eyes locked on its doomed target. Cheetahs hadn't survived the underground years, and Hilgor recalled the sharp sorrow realizing that no miracle in the world would ever bring these fascinating sprinters back. He looked up at his father, searching for consolation, but choked on his words, feeling even more unsettled by the unfamiliar blank expression on his father's face.

"Why would they care to survive if they couldn't run anymore?" his father didn't seem to be addressing anyone, just looking at the screen with unseeing eyes. In a moment, as if awakened from a trance, he turned to Hilgor and tightly hugged his slender shoulders.

He committed suicide the next day by crashing his air capsule into the Wall at full speed.

Hilgor stood motionless, staring at the cheetah. He had his answer. He couldn't live the rest of his life knowing that he had been given a chance to break free and let it slip away.

Why would they care to survive if they couldn't run anymore?

He accessed his private files from his wristband and posted, "Meet you at my place."

The traffic was light, and it didn't take him long to get home. And of course, Nick was already there, leaning on the door of his apartment.

They walked inside and stopped in the middle of the living room, waiting for Riph to calm down and settle in the corner.

Hilgor didn't need Nick's surprised look to understand that he was projecting a completely different person now. Hilgor finally realized that for the first time in his life, he had the power to call the shots that really mattered. Feelings of confusion, creeping fear and desperate desire to stay in control were gone without a trace, as if they had been swept away by a magic spell.

"I have more questions," he said firmly.

Nick simply nodded in response and sank into the couch.

With slight irritation, Hilgor realized that the intended interrogation wouldn't go as planned. There was nothing he could do about the irrational fact that he liked Nick.

As if on cue, but probably just concerned by the tension in Hilgor's voice, Riph got up, jumped on the couch and put his head on Nick's lap.

Traitor, thought Hilgor, you aren't making it easier for me. He sighed and continued, "How did you find me?"

"My programs determined that your unit was producing incomparably superior results. I went through everyone's private files, all eighty-five people. You were the only one who had just math, tons of unpublished personal math research in your secret files. It was an aberration. I have learned to pay attention to aberrations. So, I was right …"

"Speaking of aberrations, what about Deait?" asked Hilgor. "His mathematical output is outstanding; your program should have caught it."

"Nothing about him. He didn't pass the test."

Of course, thought Hilgor. I am not even good enough.

"But, Nick, Deait is good for real. Your program made an error."

"Hilgor," said Nick patiently, "I doubt it made an error. Remember, we don't know what this program is looking for exactly. Your math talent is clearly connected. But maybe by itself it's not sufficient? You have other things in your personality. And don't look smug. Let me ask you this question – is Deait a good person?"

"He is one of the nicest people I know."

"Well, don't take this as an offense, but let me inform you that I have been doing this for a while. And from my subjective experience, this program only chooses charming, self-centered assholes of different degrees …" Nick paused. "Trust me, there is an active political debate on Earth right now about all of this, but you and I have practical matters to attend to – Del."

"From the tutorial I learned that I could bring a partner," said Hilgor.

"It's the law. You can bring her."

Nick gently removed Riph's head from his lap, got up from the couch and walked to the window. Without asking permission he pushed the window wide open. "There's one more thing," he said, turning around.

Here we go, thought Hilgor.

"I need to get your waiver. My ship is in inadequate condition. I am required to have a functioning medical emergency vat on-board. If an outlier happens to get seriously sick during the several weeks en route, the vat would temporarily stop the body's metabolism until we make it to Earth," Nick stopped and looked away as if he didn't want Hilgor to see his face. "The vat is currently not available. It's occupied. My previous job didn't go well." With a noticeable effort he met Hilgor's eyes, "You have the right to refuse the trip. Once I get in touch with Earth, I will pass your information on to another headhunter."

"Wait," Hilgor shook his head, "didn't go well ... how? What's going on Nick?"

Nick wanted to say something, but his voice broke. Layers and layers of self-control started melting from his face, revealing pain, anxiety and desperation.

"A person on-board is dying. The vat's biomass is nearing its expiration. I am in a hurry, Hilgor," he said.

And with that, the whole picture finally fell into place. Except ... "Nick, why didn't you go directly to Earth?"

Nick winced as if something had physically hurt him.

"It's personal, complicated. I need a lot of money, but the person in the vat won't help. I promise that it has nothing to do with your situation. I can explain later."

Nothing nefarious, thought Hilgor. People are being people, space cloning phenomenon aside.

"I don't care about the vat. I'll sign whatever official waiver you need. I just need to talk to Del. Everything else will be fast," he said, and for some reason it felt good to see that the signs of pain on Nick's face had lost intensity.

Hilgor was about to head for the door, when he quickly stopped in his tracks. "Oh, wait," he realized that the program hadn't mentioned a critical subject. Nick's face tensed.

"Riph?" Hilgor's voice sounded scared.

"He's no problem," Nick smiled, "he is no threat to their genetics."

"I hoped so ..." Hilgor said with relief. "I'll be back soon. She's smart." A strange expression passed over his face, "And for better or worse, she is decisive."

After he left the apartment, Nick sank back on the couch, rested his head on its high back, put his hand on Riph's head and closed his eyes.

Del was on her way to meet one of her clients when she received Hilgor's call. She turned back immediately, not asking why the urgency, and told Hilgor to wait in her office.

As Hilgor entered the large windowless room, its walls began to glow with a dim ghoulish light. He looked around, located the remote control and pointed it at the floor. A section slowly opened up, and an armchair unfolded from inside. It was a compromise, a pathetic symbol of their relationship. She refused to let a utilitarian object distort her design; and he refused to sit on any of her furniture.

Generally speaking, Hilgor was capable of putting up with unpleasant surroundings, but this was different. A subtle perversity that was a trademark of Del's personality emerged in all aspects of her natural habitat. He winced and sat in the chair trying not to look at her desk. An unsuspecting visitor would question their sanity before realizing that it was stretched in one direction by the same almost undetectable angle. It was just one of the items, which she carefully selected over time from the public art pool. Her hobby was to pick works that balanced on a thin line and ultimately fell to the side of just not making it, most likely unbeknownst to their creators. She called her collection a shrine to a confused mediocrity and, unlike Hilgor, found it delightful.

The door flung open and Del entered the room making Hilgor think of a speedboat leaving a strong wake. She was apparently very busy today, so she had forgone her usual style in favor of a simple black dress. She gave Hilgor a quick nod, walked behind her surrealistic desk and sat in the chair. Imagining the level of craziness of what he was about to tell her, he shifted in his chair uncomfortably and firmly squeezed the armrests. He stammered a little, not sure how to start.

"We need to talk," he said finally.

"Obviously," she agreed cheerfully, "otherwise you wouldn't have called me here with such urgency."

"Right," he got up and started circling the room, navigating his way among the piles of miscellaneous artsy objects strewn across the floor.

During the next ten minutes, he listed the events of the last forty-eight hours and laid out the essential facts connected with Nick's offer. From time to time he lifted his head, checking her reaction. Her expression went through several stages, none of which he expected. At first, she appeared confused. Then for a time she became intensely attentive. And finally, she looked sad and, strangely, relieved.

He stopped and repeated the last question, "So, will you go?"

She leaned back and looked at him silently for a while. Then she said, in an unusually pensive voice, "How funny, it's not what I thought it would be. But it's even better."

She picked up a pen from the table and started absent-mindedly twisting it in her hands. "I thought you called to break up with me," she explained.

Now he looked at her in confusion.

"Hilgor, we needed to talk a long time ago," she spoke very softly, "I'm glad that we've been forced to, finally."

Without the mask of her usual flamboyant eccentricity, her face became unguarded and, surprisingly, tender.

"I'm happy for you. You should go. It's a crazy story, but you know ... this is why I stuck around for so long even though I knew it wasn't working. What's the term they use – anti-conformity index? I'm an expert in guessing it." There was sadness in her smile, "Hilgor, I won't go with you. The whole thing about us is wrong. We're ... a different species."

Now she spoke very calmly, as if delivering a long prepared speech, "We are not happy, let's face it. I am not happy. You spend the best of yourself on your work, it burns all your passion; I get the leftovers."

Hilgor tried to say something to protest, but she interrupted.

"I would have preferred to compete with another woman – at least it would be fair," she suddenly sounded bitter, but then forced herself back to an even tone. "I know you want me around, but I don't want to serve as your bridge to the outside world. My life here, at least, has some real meaning."

He wasn't surprised, really. He knew it was true. There wasn't much to say, but too much at stake, so he awkwardly ventured into the field of a foreign vocabulary. "Del, do you love me?"

"Define love. Do you love me?"

She was staring at the desk as if she just discovered something interesting on its surface.

He went to her and put his palms on the table, leaning forward, and tried to look into her eyes.

"Del, listen. I understand. But you don't have to stay with me there. Earth is a better place. They are way ahead of us; their planet is not sick; their medicine can fix anything. Why do you care about this poisonous world?"

"There are some things in this world I care about," she almost whispered, but held his gaze.

"What? Your art? Don't be stupid."

"Yes, my art," she said firmly, "and … I'm healthy. I don't need their medicine …" she interrupted herself, struck by an unexpected thought. "Their medicine … it fixes everything?" she asked with sudden hope in her voice.

Hilgor nodded, thinking about the information provided by Nick's program.

"Until what stage?"

"Any stage, I think, as long as the person is still alive." Then he corrected himself, "It depends on the definition of death, of course. I learned that the one we use is too simplistic."

"Reish," she said, "you can save Reish." She got up abruptly, pushing back her chair and looked straight into his eyes, "She should live, Hilgor." Intensity was returning to her face, which was regaining its usual hypnotic power. "She doesn't own what she has. And this Universe is not so rich to squander it like that."

He remembered the pale face, the bare room and the whirl of blue happiness in his heart. "But, Del …" he said helplessly.

"Hilgor, I'm not going. I'm sorry."

He made a move to get around the desk to give her a hug, but she stepped back so quickly that she knocked down the chair behind her.

"Just go, Hilgor. Really. I'll let her know. Just pick her up."

He walked to the exit. He had already half-opened the door when he remembered something.

"Can you spread the gossip that I have moved behind the Wall – as a protest against their stupid communal rules?"

"Feels good to give a farewell kick?" she smirked.

"There's that. But really, they don't track people there, so they will believe it. It's simpler this way." A random thought that Deait would guess the truth passed through his mind.

"Will do. Good luck! Trust me; we're going to be happier this way," now she was smiling, her face relaxed and radiant as she watched him going through the door.

He almost belicved her, but giving her a farewell glance, he recognized a funny-looking spiky ball that she was squeezing in her hand. She had taken it home from his office desk at some point, a three-dimensional model of an object he had tried to build. He remembered that she found the shape amusing and he also recalled that the spikes were very sharp.

The door closed softly. He stared at it in silence for a few moments, and then immediately reached for the doorknob. And at the same time, he heard a click – she must have used a remote to lock it from the inside. He turned around and walked to the elevator.

When Hilgor returned home, the dog and the man were still in the same position on the couch, with Nick's hand still on Riph's head. Riph barked once and jumped down. Hilgor gave him a brief pat and walked straight to the far corner where he had left his armchair the night before. He didn't turn on the lights even though it was beginning to get dark.

"She is not going," said Hilgor in an even voice, sitting back in the armchair, "and she is right."

"Did you expect her to go?" Nick's face was hardly visible in the remains of the gray light.

"I don't know. I never know with her. Although I should say – I knew, I guess." Hilgor shivered, only now noticing the bitter cold in the room. He walked to the window and shut it.

"She is right. This feeling of making things out of nothingness is so … addictive. I rush there the moment I feel that I have any energy. And I stay there until I'm empty," he paused and added, "it's not fair to her."

He began pacing the room along a silver patch on the floor created by the streetlight.

The silence lasted so long that Hilgor decided that this odd conversation was over. Then Nick said in a casual, almost indifferent tone, "Can you live without her? I mean, live a normal life, not bending in pain every time when you remember that she's gone?" His voice sounded strange, as if he was asking both Hilgor and himself at the same time, and for some reason, Hilgor felt embarrassed by the meek ambiguity of his response,

"I don't know. I guess I'll find out."

Nick didn't comment. Instead, he switched to a matter-of-fact tone, "Shall we go?"

Hilgor touched the wall, turning on the bright strips of the overhead light. "Nick," he said firmly, "I have one condition. There's this woman, behind the Wall. I want to bring her instead."

"That's not an option, Hilgor. We have strict protocols on who is allowed to …"

"How will they know we're not together? We'll pretend."

Nick shook his head, "But Hilgor, its illegal, forget about unethical. Listen, I'm sorry …"

"It's my condition. And she is dying, Nick."

For a while Nick just stared at him in silence. Then he sighed and nodded.

Hilgor sat at the table and jotted down a list of the remaining items. There wasn't much left. He made a quick pass around the apartment and threw a few necessities into a small bag. Then he returned to Nick and somewhat sheepishly pointed to the bulky shape in the corner of the living room. "This is the last thing. I really want to take it."

Nick looked at the worn leather armchair, so old that its original black color had turned into some undetermined shade of dark gray.

"Of course, it'll look amazing on Earth. Are you sure that you don't need anything else?" he asked with an impulsive grin. He walked to the heavy recliner and easily slid it across the floor to the exit.

Hilgor picked up Riph's leash and abruptly stopped.

"Sorry, one more thing. It won't take long. Let me throw something in their faces. As a revenge for Deait. They will get oh so mad at me in the same way, and rush to punish me in the same way, but this time they will be robbed of this pleasure. Plus, I don't mind if people know that it was me who proved Zongi's conjecture – it feels good from many angles."

He returned to his computer and moved all his private research files to the public domain, signing them with his full name.

The chair shifted precariously on the floor in the back as the air capsule crossed the city at the highest allowed speed. Night traffic was very light, and Nick turned the corners with exact precision. The Wall was quickly approaching, exploding in size, as they got closer.

"How do you know …" started Hilgor.

"… Where we need to go?" Nick finished the sentence not taking his eyes off the road.

Hilgor nodded, suddenly remembering the steps behind him in the empty passage of the underground city.

"Do you think I could afford to lose you? I've been shadowing you for the last two days."

Once they passed through the Wall, Nick told Kir to override the capsule's safety settings. The engine whined at an unfamiliar pitch, and Hilgor felt his body pressed into the back of his seat. He had no idea that a standard passenger capsule was capable of generating such speed. By the time they approached the cluster of white structures at the foot of the hill, Hilgor's palms were damp, and his heart was firmly stuck in his throat.

Nick landed the capsule exactly in front of Reish's house. Hilgor jumped out before it came to a full stop and hurriedly walked toward the entrance. The door opened, and he stepped inside. Riph sat up, looked at Nick and whined softly.

"You don't like it here, puppy? Can't blame you," Nick leaned back, turning off the engine. "It's cool, Riph. You and me; we both just need a little patience now." He was in the middle of the last sentence when the door slid aside again, and the bright yellow light from inside was cast on a rectangular patch of dry soil between the house and the capsule. In a couple of minutes, Hilgor walked out the door, dragging a heavy oblong container. In another moment, the silhouette of a young woman appeared in the doorway. She was hastily stuffing pieces of clothing into a bag that hung over her shoulder.

"Nick, I'm going to fasten this box and the chair. It's all of her work. Not that I doubt your driving ..." Hilgor opened the cargo door.

The woman was now quickly walking to the capsule. And all of a sudden she stumbled on the uneven ground and awkwardly fell.

Nick saw her trip, and time stopped and jumped back. As once before, Nick pushed the capsule door open, jumped down, ran the same three long steps through heavy smoke and fell on his knees. He lifted her head from the ground and looked into her pale face. Struggling to sit up, she said, apologetically, "I'm sorry, I got dizzy." Only then did reality come flooding back. He slowly let go of the girl. He looked at his hands; there was no blood on them. The gray shapes of houses in the dark, the outline of bare hills in the distance and Hilgor's worried face slowly came into focus. Nick stood up, helped Reish to her feet and walked back to the capsule, trying to make the smell of the burning forest in his head go away, to the past, to the place he didn't want to remember.

He climbed into the driver's chair and started the engine.

"Reish, what about your drafts, the unfinished pieces?" asked Hilgor from the cargo compartment.

But she just shook her head, reclining in the passenger seat.

"Let's get out of here."

PART IV:

THE
OBSESSION

EARTH

Nick had been up for so many hours that he had to resort to ever-larger doses of stimulants to keep the ship on course, and his mind eventually began to rebel by creating periodic glitches – for example, he suddenly noticed that he had been staring at the navigation screens for who knows how long without making any sense of the data. He needed a break, and he was lucky that all of the system indicators were green at the moment, except, of course, the status of the biomass that was keeping Lita alive. That light was stale red, and the expiration time kept oscillating between three days and three hours. The sensor was slightly off like every other monitor on the ship, but it was clear that the biomass wouldn't last much longer.

They were on the fastest possible route home from Y-3, and he had already sent an emergency request for an ambulance. There was nothing else he could do to speed things up, and it was better not to think about the red indicator.

He tried to picture Lita's face. He hadn't seen her, locked inside the vat, since they left Beta Blue. He liked to imagine that she was sleeping, dreaming of something good. He told himself not to check her vitals again. They wouldn't have changed, frozen in time, as long as the biomass held up.

He checked. They hadn't changed. But his palms got clammy.

He got up, swiped the navigation screens to the background of his vision, and walked out into the corridor. He was going to the medical wing again. He would just stand in that room, brightly lit and empty except for the smooth white cask in the corner, until one of the navigation indicators showed signs of instability, and then he would have to go back to work.

He had to pass through a common area on his way, and he really hoped it would be empty this time. But Hilgor was there, slowly pacing back and forth, his head slightly tilted, indicating that he was fully immersed in his work. Nick tried to quietly slip by, but Hilgor abruptly stopped and peered at Nick with keen intensity.

"How is it going?" he asked, and something in his voice suggested that it wasn't a rhetorical question. "You are spending all your time in the control room. Nick, you almost don't sleep."

Nick casually leaned against the wall. "I know, I haven't been around much these past few days," he said in an upbeat tone. "Don't take it personally. I just need to keep a closer eye on the ship's systems."

"What's wrong with the ship, Nick?" Hilgor asked quickly.

Nick hesitated for a moment. He hadn't mentioned to his passengers that he had skipped a safety stop after crossing the Y-3 Mirror Sector boundary, and that the ship's autopilot had been progressively failing as a result. But it was becoming too hard to maintain the illusion of business as usual, and they were at the end of their journey anyway.

"There was a glitch in the navigation system, and I've had to intervene manually. But we are almost home. Another two days if I don't get us lost," Nick forgot to smile, and Hilgor looked at him with genuine concern.

"We'll be alright, Hilgor," Nick said calmly. "I just need to stay awake a little bit longer."

It indeed took another forty-eight hours before Kir alerted Nick that their ship was entering Earth's traffic control range.

"Just in time, Kir," Nick exhaled sharply, leaning back in his chair. By that time, he was so tired that he had to repeat every task in his head several times before he dared to act on it. "Pass the controls to the Dispatch Center, specify Headhunter HQ as the destination. Check on the ambulance status."

"Our route confirmation has been received. The ambulance is on the way," Kir replied.

Nick shut his eyes and for one split second fell into a black nothingness. He woke with a jolt, grabbed a patch from his pocket and slapped it on his wrist.

"Nick, the accumulation of stimulants in your system exceeds the maximum safe dose by 5.71 times. The probability of heart failure …" started Kir, but Nick dismissed the message with a wave of his hand.

His focus returned, and he switched all his attention on the expanding image of the emergency medical transporter. It was moving at top speed, and in a few seconds was mooring nearby.

"Kir, release the sick bay module," said Nick, and a large oblong object detached from his ship. It floated toward the ambulance, which quickly sucked it into the cargo area and darted away.

"Goodbye," said Nick. There was nothing else he could do, but, unsurprisingly, there was no sense of relief. She was still dying, and everything now hinged on the question of whether or not her condition was recoverable by Earth's medical technology. For a moment, he imagined receiving the news that she was not going to make it, and it made him lightheaded.

"Kir, prepare for arrival," he said, and pushing himself up from his chair, he left the cabin.

His passengers had been waiting in the common room; their belongings, including the bulky holder with Reish's work and Hilgor's shabby armchair, were neatly lined up against the wall. Hilgor seemed to be appropriately wound up for the occasion, but Reish looked too sick to care.

"Welcome to Earth. Kir, display the external camera feed on the main screen," said Nick and briefly glanced at the images that spanned the wall.

All newcomers from the Mirror Worlds reacted to the constellations of Orbit's floating structures in the same way, and Reish and Hilgor weren't exceptions; awe on their faces put a brief smile on Nick's face.

The ship was instantly cleared for landing and zoomed past the enormous formations of the Orbit belt, beginning its rapid descent towards Earth's capital city.

Berlin was another sight that caused people to hold their breaths. Practical considerations played a minimal role in its architecture, and the artistic freedom had turned the city into a gigantic sculpture. It was overwhelmingly gorgeous, and even those who weren't particularly appreciative of spatial aesthetics were still affected by its mere scale and complexity.

The dramatic view of the skyline gave way to the sight of individual buildings, and the ship entered the canyons of the inner districts. Reish gasped and tightly gripped her knees as they joined a chaotic swarm of flying objects, whizzing by so fast that it was impossible to make out their exact shapes or sizes.

"Don't you worry, traffic control hasn't failed in centuries," said Nick reassuringly, but it didn't seem to convince her, and she remained stiffly frozen in the same awkward posture until they finally stopped in the shade of a tall angular building. The gates promptly opened, letting them inside the internal parking dock.

"Nick, you can disembark now," said Kir.

The arrival area had been thoughtfully designed to reduce newcomers' anxiety by conveying an enthusiastic message of universal welcome, but Nick stepped off the jet bridge with a bad feeling. He didn't expect an especially friendly greeting this time.

An outlier intake team immediately surrounded his passengers, cutting him off, and he suddenly found himself standing alone. He looked around the intimately familiar hall in slight confusion. Not that he anticipated an armed squad to arrest him on the spot, but he nevertheless assumed that someone would confront him right away. The authorities already knew about his misdemeanors – he had sent his report a while ago, right after he crossed the Mirror Wall, and transmissions could reach Earth. He had crafted his statement very carefully and omitted everything that should be skipped, including the exact nature of his relationship with Lita, but he did give a detailed account of his first meeting with Remir, and the last scene when Remir was shot. He hoped to prove that bringing Lita was an accident and not a predetermined action on his part. He had no illusions, however, that despite his careful editing, the Beta Blue story looked rather bad. And, of course, on top of everything else there was his unsanctioned detour to Y-3.

He started to think that he would be notified of disciplinary actions remotely and hesitantly moved towards the exit when a woman in a government uniform suddenly stepped in front of him, blocking his way.

"Elisabeth," she said curtly, without a veneer of custom cordiality, and beamed Kir her credentials. Her title made Nick blink – under different circumstances he would have been flattered by the personal attention of such high-ranking official. And she most likely was a Dark Triad – there was no other reason her name was so non-Commonwealth sounding. Of course, she could have been an outlier's partner, but Nick recognized the eyes.

"We saw your report," she looked at Nick with mild distaste, as if he was still covered with dirt and blood. "Did you keep the raw metrics from Remir Autran's test?"

Nick nodded. He had filed the encrypted file in Kir's memory back then, following the standard protocol of outlier assessment; he didn't know that he wouldn't need it.

"Excellent. Send it to me," she said.

"Sure. What's it for?"

"It doesn't concern the Headhunter Association," she said affably. It's none of your business, said her eyes.

Nick shrugged, "Kir, share Remir Autran's file."

Strange, he thought, why would the government be interested in a dead outlier? But he didn't have a chance to dwell on the subject.

"We have decided not to press legal charges against you for bringing a Mirror World commoner to Earth, but your professional license has been revoked," continued Elisabeth with an impenetrable expression. "Alya, connect him to the Headhunter Association," her tone softened slightly as she addressed her implant.

"They'll process your termination," explained Elisabeth, "and then I'll walk you out of the building."

An incoming call request flashed in Nick's vision.

"Kir, accept," said Nick. He didn't have any doubt that this was coming. A communication window opened up, and the face of a vaguely familiar company administrator showed up on the screen.

"I regret to inform you that we've cancelled your contract," the video connection was one-sided, and the man was looking slightly above Nick's eyes. "I assume you don't need an explanation."

"No, not really," Nick was glad that they had spared him the disciplinary lecture. "I get it."

"Please relinquish all headhunter-specific programs."

Nick was ready for that too, but he nevertheless felt a tight knot in his stomach.

"Right away, please," added the administrator uncomfortably. He clearly was not enjoying this task.

Not a big deal, Nick told himself firmly, headhunters weren't allowed to use their software at home anyway. "Kir, provide access to the proprietary programs," he said in a calm tone. This mess wasn't the company representative's fault.

The man exhaled and nodded.

"I am starting the delete sequence. After that the outlier's award will be transferred to your bank account, and we are officially separated," he said, and an explosion of warnings flashed on Nick's internal screens.

"Nick, I've been downgraded to civilian status," Kir's voice was accompanied by the soft but persistent sound of system failure alarms. "The following capabilities have been lost: Mirror edge navigation, neuro-transmission …"

The list of deleted programs was long, and waiting for Kir to finish, Nick glanced at Elisabeth, who was standing a couple of steps away. Her icy expression didn't make him feel any better, but he forgot all about it the moment Kir sent him an urgent contact request from the Emergency Medical Center. Nick propped himself against the wall and closed his eyes.

"Don't die," he said aloud, "please, don't die."

He then mentally stepped off the edge of the cliff by ordering Kir to accept the call.

A composed woman in a hospital uniform appeared on the communication screen. "Thank you for choosing our services," she said in a professionally dispassionate voice. "We sincerely apologize for the delay in contacting you, but the medical team just finished evaluating the patient's condition. The damage is significant, especially to her brain tissues. We ..."

"Will she live?" Nick pushed the words out almost without sound, but the woman understood.

"Yes," she said with a sudden glimpse of genuine compassion, "her physical and cognitive functions will be fully restored. We have already started the treatment, and we're expecting your payment immediately," she returned to her impersonal tone. "Do you have any questions?"

The sickly sensation in Nick's chest began to regress, leaving behind a nauseous residue, but his mind had already returned to its logical self, dismissing the dull heartache as an unhelpful distraction.

"When can I talk to her?"

"The full regeneration process could take up to three months, and she will have to remain in an induced coma for the duration of the treatment."

Nick cleared his throat. It sounded like an eternity, but it didn't matter; nothing really mattered except for the fact that in the end Lita would walk out of the hospital alive.

"It's alright," he said, "thank you. I am sending the money right away."

He glanced at the bill and beamed the amount, only slightly registering that the transfer almost emptied his bank account.

"Hello? Excuse me!" Elisabeth waved, attracting his attention. "By the way, it's very noble of you to spend so much on a Mirror

World acquaintance." Elisabeth turned her head back, "Especially considering that she won't even get a chance to thank you for it."

"Why's that?" he stopped, feeling a funny sensation in his stomach.

"I assume you know the laws," the woman turned around so smoothly as if she was expecting it. "The woman will be deported to her home M-237 right after her hospital discharge. We are already violating the rules by letting her stay on Earth for the duration of her treatment."

Nick stared at Elisabeth's face. Her words just hung in the air, not making any sense, but everything became a notch too bright.

"For security reasons we won't wake her up until her delivery to the originating point. She won't know she ever left. It'll spare her an unnecessary psychological shock as well."

"But wait …" Nick's mind finally switched on, and the whole thing sank in, "she will be killed there, for sure, by the military. You said you've seen my report."

"She doesn't have a relation to a living outlier."

"But there must be …" Nick was desperately trying to contain a rising panic, "just give me a moment …" He couldn't follow Lita to M-237, not without his border navigation software.

"I am listening," Elisabeth's expression remained politely restrained, but there was a hint of annoyance in her voice.

"You don't have to return her to M-237," Nick said hurriedly. "Please, just drop us off anywhere outside the Commonwealth."

"Us?" her eyes fixated on his face with sudden interest. "And just why are you so wound up about this? First world guilt? For a head-hunter, seriously?" Now she was looking at him with unmistakable sarcasm, "Are you sure you didn't miss something important in your report?"

Nick knew that his panicked silence wasn't making things better, but his mind went hopelessly blank. Thankfully, she didn't want to waste her time.

"Follow me to the exit," she said, turning, and Nick fought a momentary desire to grab her shoulders and give her a strong shake. It wasn't a good idea, obviously, and instead he walked slightly ahead of her in an awkward crablike sidestep.

"Please just leave us on an empty mirror world ... or a quarantined sector," Nick tried to suppress a treacherous trembling in his voice. "I'm a professional, we will blend, and you can forget about us forever ..."

Elisabeth gave him a quick dismissive glance. "You know that we don't do this," she didn't even try to sound sympathetic.

"You can't just apply a general policy in this case. It'll be a murder, you understand this, right?" Passing employees turned their heads in his direction, and Nick realized that he was shouting.

Elisabeth went through the exit doors, not breaking her stride. Without taking his eyes from her face, Nick stepped to the street backwards and bumped into a vehicle parked right at the entrance.

"Let me give you a piece of advice, Nick," Elisabeth stopped, and for the first time her eyes acknowledged him as more than a background nuisance. "Stop the hysterics and drop this thing. If somebody gets curious enough to look into the details of this mess you could lose a lot more than your license." She easily got around him, lightly jumped into the hovering flyer, and shut the hatch in his face.

He made a step out of pedestrian traffic, and stopped. At first, his thoughts were surprisingly detached. Apparently, immigration laws were brutally unforgiving, and the authorities didn't hesitate to send a ship across the Universe to avoid a precedent. He heard an annoyed exclamation, raised his eyes and saw that he was still a nuisance on a busy pathway. He muttered an apology, cut across the sidewalk and sat down on a bench inside a small green area. The last Beta Blue memories flashed through his mind – Lita, wiping the blood from her face next to overturned combine; the bitter smell of burning forest; two motionless bodies on the meadow grass.

He imagined how Lita would wake up in that place, and her last memories would be of Nick jumping up and grabbing something invisible in the air, Remir running towards her, and then the explosion. She would be disoriented, but not immediately scared. That would come later, when she realized that she had nowhere to go. The government would be excited to see her again.

The scene with the Beta Blue officer pushing Lita against the wall in the media control room unfolded in Nick's head, and his mind went haywire. He got up and started walking in a random direction, blindly staring at the ground.

In a brief moment of relative coherence, he told himself that there was nothing personal in his situation, and that the laws were designed to be fair to all of the ordinary people dying in military coups, wars and epidemics across the quarantined Mirror Worlds. It just so happened that they were going to kill Lita right after she survived.

The control room sequence flashed through his mind again. She would die on Beta Blue, but she wouldn't die quickly. By trying to save her, he had made it much worse. She would have been better off if he had left her bleeding to death on that meadow. This last thought was unbearable. He was not going to let that happen.

"Kir, I need a flyer," he said walking towards the holographic wall that shielded the pedestrian zone from the traffic zone. A generic city transporter pulled over to the boarding strip almost immediately. "To the Trauma Center," said Nick as he stepped inside. He had to see Lita even if her face still looked dead. He couldn't afford to give up hope, not as long as she was still alive.

The plaza in front of the medical complex was in use for a temporary art installation, which was common in open public spaces across the city. Nick had to work his way through the exhibition artifacts and their admiring crowds. But he instantly slowed as he walked into the almost deliberately disorienting hospital lobby. Large painted glass windows threw a veil of intricate patterns on the ornate furniture; oddly wrought elevator pillars cast complex shapes on the mosaic floor; tall wall mirrors multiplied every object under all possible angles.

Startled, Nick recognized himself in the surrounding reflections, and momentarily thought that his disheveled appearance looked ridiculous in the dreamlike place. He shook his head, dismissing the optical illusions, and established that he was the only visitor here, a definite sign of the truly niche status of emergency treatment services. But his presence hadn't gone unnoticed; a call was coming into his visual field.

Kir accepted the connection, and a young man behind a virtual counter gave Nick a look that projected bedside manners so earnestly that it was almost endearing.

"Welcome to our medical facility. Can you give your consent to use our cameras to establish two-way video interaction?"

"Sure ... a wounded woman was just admitted here, from one of the Mirror Worlds ..."

"One moment," the hospital representative glanced aside. "I see," he said right away, focusing on Nick with almost unprofessional curiosity. "And you are ..."

Nick beamed him his ID, and the guy immediately nodded, "I thought so. You called the emergency transport. Congratulations, that was very close. How can we help you?"

"I want to visit her."

"I am truly sorry, but that won't be possible," the man's face displayed sincere regret. "She is being kept inside a sealed regeneration chamber. But the good news is that she'll be completely fine by the end of the treatment."

Nick didn't move. Focus on breathing, he told himself, at least until this scratchy feeling in my throat goes away.

"The patient ..." he finally managed to say, "she was wearing a necklace, a silver chain with a pendant. May I borrow that?"

"I'm sorry, we're unable to release any belongings without a patient's permission. Everything she was wearing is safely secured in our storage locker. She can pick her things up when she leaves."

A stinging sensation in Nick's eyes signaled a warning that he was starting to lose his grip.

"Thanks. Nothing else then," he said through half-clenched teeth.

The man instantly disconnected, extinguishing his smile just a split second too early.

Nick raised his hands to his face and firmly pressed them against his eyelids. Bright fluorescent spots floated across his vision, and he blinked hard, trying to make them go away, but instead they changed into the red blotches on the meadow grass, and suddenly he was there again. The smell of burning trees was suffocating, and there were two bodies on the ground. He turned Remir over, but it wasn't Remir, the body was too light. The head lifelessly rolled backwards, and Lita's eyes blindly stared into the sky from her dead face. Nick gasped for air, and the smoke scorched his throat.

"Nick," Kir's voice was coming from far away, muffled and irrelevant. "You are experiencing psychological destabilization."

Nick sharply exhaled, realizing that it had been a distorted flashback.

He was on Earth, in the hospital lobby, and Lita wasn't dead on Beta Blue. She was still alive, somewhere in this building, but all the same she didn't quite belong to the world of the living from the logical point of view.

"It is recommended that you rest for at least ..." continued Kir, and then a beam of bright sunlight burst into the room, and a strangely recognizable silhouette appeared in the doorway.

"Kir, wait," whispered Nick, instinctively stepping behind the closest elevator pillar. There was absolutely nothing Elisabeth should be doing in this medical center.

Unlike Nick, she didn't hesitate at the entrance, and she didn't check in with the virtual hospital staff either. Instead, she confidently approached an unmarked section of the wall, which suddenly parted, revealing the plain doors of a hidden elevator. They obediently opened too, letting her in.

Nick thought that the chance that he had accidentally run into Elisabeth in Lita's hospital was equal to zero. He froze, trying to merge with a fancy lobby's pillar.

After a few minutes, Elisabeth reemerged, and she looked all excited now, her face glowing with immense satisfaction.

He didn't dare move until she disappeared behind the lobby doors, and when he finally followed her outside, she was almost lost in the thick crowd of the exhibition. He sped up, using the slowly milling people as cover, and noticed that she had started speaking as she walked.

"Kir, lip captioning," he asked.

"No capacity."

"Damn it," Nick winced. The program was a part of his lost headhunter package.

Elisabeth's flyer was parked on the pedestrian side of the holographic divider, completely blocking access to several pieces of art installations, but she apparently didn't give the slightest damn about public convenience. She kept talking as she walked, and Nick thought that it was rather sloppy on her part. He guessed that she hadn't expected to be watched, and decided that he could risk getting closer. Hurriedly working his way through the crowd, he managed to cut almost all of the distance between them, close enough to make out her sentence – "… these dimwits would sic secret services on me if they knew …"

Suddenly he was too close – he even accidentally brushed up against her shoulder, and he broke into a cold sweat, convinced that he would surely be discovered now. But she didn't notice him at all, preoccupied by her conversation. "I have material, and it's … well, you should see it for yourself. I will be leaving for Earth3 right away. Register my trip as a routine inspection …" and then her flyer door closed and she took off.

Nick stepped back into the crowd and watched her flyer pass over the exhibition area and disappear behind the holographic wall into the traffic zone. Important favors could be traded for important secrets, he thought calmly.

"Kir, what's my ship's status?" he asked.

"All repairs have been completed. Full functionality has been restored."

"Good. Let's go pick it up. We are going to Earth3, Kir."

His rented flyer had the lowest traffic priority, and the navigation system assigned to it had the most circuitous back route to a public hangar where Nick's ship had been towed from Headhunter headquarters.

"Kir, let's not panic about the lead time we are giving Elisabeth. Let's use the time wisely. Run the fastest options to get to Earth3."

Kir summarized the available options as precisely one.

Apparently, there was no setup for private ships to cross the border into the Earth3 Mirror Sector. It was a provincial Mirror Earth in a remote corner of the Commonwealth, solely used as a manufacturing hub, and there was not enough tourist traffic to justify the transit operation. In particular, the Mirror Border towing service, a fleet of "tugs" with navigation software, wasn't available. However, professional cargo transports, constantly shuffling back and forth between the two worlds offered to ferry passenger ships across the Mirror borders for a modest fee. The next one was leaving Earth in several hours. Nick checked his bank balance. The remaining chunk of his payment was still enough, even if barely, for a one-way toll.

He told Kir to take care of the logistics, and his ship took off towards the mega-transporters loading zone on Orbit.

Watching Earth's surface become farther and farther away, Nick thought that it was funny how the difference between no hope at all and having a smidge of an improbable chance that it wasn't over yet, made such an unreasonably huge difference in his mental condition. He still could fight. She wasn't dead.

Earth3 was a very strange place. Headhunters knew much more about it than the general population because in addition to being a standard "offshore" manufacturing center, it had a strange reputation of being the Dark Triads' "special" place. There was no official record of it, but Nick knew that most of his former outlier clients had visited it for some time. Some even stayed there, their government stipend making them independent of employment concerns. He didn't know more than that, and Kir's search didn't bring up more either. Whatever it was, it wasn't official.

"I guess we'll find out, Kir," said Nick. "Take over." He was dead tired and hadn't slept since he manually navigated the ship from Y-3. He stumbled to bed and fell asleep almost immediately.

EARTH3

Watching the approaching blue sphere through the external cameras, Nick suddenly had a weird feeling that he was about to start a regular headhunter mission on a Mirror colony; unlike any Commonwealth planet he had ever visited in the past, this place had neither orbit structures nor the glowing light grids of the densely populated cities. At that moment, however, a dispatcher from Earth3 requested his ship credentials, and the illusion was over.

The check-in process happened to be a mere formality here, so Nick received landing permission and full access to the infospace without the slightest delay.

"Okay, Kir," he said, "Time to find out where Elisabeth is and what she is up to, which, let's face it, will be somewhat challenging given your handicapped condition."

His casual chatter with Kir was a part of the mental technique he had developed in order to block any thoughts of Lita. By the end of this trip, he had become rather good at it, learning not to cringe at his phony cheerful tone. It worked just fine, except that it always required a certain amount of background effort, never allowing him to fully relax.

"Your civilian limitations are a real pain, Kir, but there is nothing we can do about it, is there? So let's focus on the bright side. And the bright side, of course, is that she's picked quite the planet for our purposes – the locals here don't give a damn about the precious Commonwealth Criminal Code. Well, it's going to play in our favor quite a bit because those pesky privacy laws can be circumvented. Otherwise, how are we going to find our Elisabeth friend? Of course, that does come with some drawbacks – this place seems just a bit unsafe, doesn't it? But getting back to the bright side, we have a rather non-trivial chance of digging something up. Anyway, let's land, for starters."

"Nick, non-commercial parking is located inside the main residential campus."

"Sure. Let's go straight into the center of things."

The ship started descending towards the eastern coastline of the North American continent, and Nick again focused on the external camera feed. It was late in the evening there, and the skies were clear, giving him an unobstructed view of the ground, which looked like a torn sheet of polka dot fabric from his current altitude. Identical bright spots uniformly stretched across the flat surface, endlessly expanding to the west and abruptly stopping at the rugged edge of the dark ocean. The only thing that broke the uncanny symmetry of their monotonous pattern was Nick's destination, a huge irregular patch of lights slightly inland from the shore, the so-called Hub, from which every industrial unit on the planet was remotely managed.

Nick refocused on the cyberspace and it definitely looked strange; publicly available data was completely sterile, even by Earth's conservative standards, Security walls were all over the place, and Nick was locked out of everything except for a handful of government portals.

"Ok, Kir, boots on the ground it is then," he whispered. He expected that it would be a bit harder than his usual missions.

As the ship dropped elevation, the dots began to resolve into unexpectedly formidable aggregations of plants and shipping facilities, and the Hub turned into a dense concentration of urban structures.

Nick expanded the external view, and Kir highlighted a constellation of egg-shaped hangars on the inner edge of the Hub. As they got close, one of the roofs folded, letting the ship in, and Nick got up from his seat.

"We've arrived at the destination," informed Kir. The ship was already hovering next to one of the holding cells attached to the wall of the giant underground lot. Nick gave the system his credentials, and the round gates opened, accepting his ship. "And remember, Kir – a positive attitude is the only helpful mode of operation. Kir, release the shuttle," he said. "Let's go cruising."

The shuttle flew at a relatively low altitude, and, looking at the rows upon rows of simple identical buildings, Nick was reminded of Y-3. The resemblance, however, faded as the cityscape abruptly changed, showing feeble but recognizable attempts at replicating Earth's architecture.

"Hold on. Let's see what we have here," said Nick.

The area directly below doubtlessly was a local center of some sort. Despite the late hour, there were a good number of people outside, and the streets seemed rather lively, due in part to the festive glow of their fluorescent surfaces.

"Drop me off here," said Nick. Kir landed the shuttle in a parking lot just off the busiest intersection, and Nick got out.

A mild fragrance in the air hinted at the existence of a blooming garden nearby, reminding Nick that it was early spring in this part of the world. But his first look around confirmed that the scent had to have been artificial; every patch of exposed ground was monolithically covered by the same illuminating material.

He assumed a sullenly preoccupied look, joined the pedestrian flow and began meticulously checking the area, street after street. Admittedly, this task was trivial in comparison to the challenges of his Mirror colony infiltrations. Here, at least in most places, he easily recognized the functional purpose of Commonwealth-like places. But there were differences still. Individual outfits of those in the crowd were nondescript. The paranoia about accidentally brushing against someone's personal space seemed to be less intense. Even more notably, not a single person seemed to carry the expression of unshakable confidence in the unconditional benevolence of life that so much annoyed Nick back home. All in all, he had to admit that he felt quite comfortable here in spite of the place's shady reputation.

Suddenly recognizing the logo of his favorite Berlin hangout, he slowed and took a closer look through the windows. It was just a rough imitation of the real thing, but he still felt a nostalgic tug at his heart. He thought that stopping in wouldn't be a total waste of time – it was a perfect way to initiate a direct contact, and then take it from there.

The interior, indeed, was rather approximately replicated, but the atmosphere was surprisingly right. Some people were comfortably seated at tables watching entertainment programs via synchronized inputs, and others gathered in open spaces chatting over drinks while busy waiters scurried between the groups with their orders. Just like the original bar on Earth, somewhat loud music blared in the room, boldly competing with the internal audio feeds of the patrons.

As Nick made his way to the bar area, nobody paid attention to his appearance, and it felt like a welcome contrast with the usual challenge of blending with the physically inferior inhabitants of the cut-off planets.

Nick sat down at the counter several stools away from the next person and glanced at the virtual menu, promptly beamed to him by a passing server. He didn't recognize anything and simply asked for the first drink on the list.

Several people turned in his direction.

Of course, it was his accent, thought Nick, annoyed at his blunder. Linguistic programs made his pronunciation impeccable on quarantined colonies, but thinking that the entire Commonwealth shared the same language, he forgot about the local dialects, and it hadn't occurred to him that he would need to make an adjustment.

People returned to their conversations.

A young woman, sitting alone in the corner got up, and the very moment she started walking in his direction he knew that she was from Earth; she moved with that unique smooth rhythm in her stride as she glided through the crowd without ever touching another person.

She stopped a couple of steps away, tilted her head and looked at him with lively interest. Her overall appearance was a typical product of standard DNA filtering, but at the same time she wasn't bland, by any means. Her bone structure carried a hint of Northern European ancestry, and it created a piquant dissonance with the golden hue of her brown eyes and the olive tone of her skin. But of course, he guessed, these could simply have been a nod to the latest fashion trend, just like the rich chocolate color of her luxurious hair.

"May I?" he noticed that she hadn't bothered to change her accent either.

He was in luck, he told himself, she was a shortcut. Nothing would be lost in the cross-cultural translation.

"Most certainly," Nick nodded towards the bar chair next to him.

"Eve," she said, sitting down, and upon closer inspection her impeccable gentility became even more obvious. Her clothes and make-up were designed to blend in, and they did, except that their exaggerated simplicity referenced something edgy, he just didn't have a clue what. He fully appreciated, however, that she projected Earth's chic full blast. A typical girl next door from home, he thought, except ... there was no belief in the benevolence of life in her eyes.

"Nick," he gave her the charming smile prepared for such occasions.

"You just arrived, you're brand new here. Welcome," she put her drink on the counter and changed angles to get a better look at him.

He noted that the bar stools were positioned a bit too close by Earth's standards, but she didn't bother to slide her chair back.

"What are you doing here, Nick?" she asked, studying him with open curiosity.

"Just visiting," he shrugged vaguely, "taking a break between jobs and decided to take a look around."

"Sure," she said, not concealing the soft irony in her voice, "only … good reasons never bring people from Earth to this place … with the exception of the Dark Triads, of course. Those do whatever they please, and visiting this shithole is for some reason one of their favorites."

Her looks eliminated any chance that she was an outlier from a Mirror World. But she still could be a rare case of Earth-born Dark Triad, like himself.

"Don't want to talk to strangers about yourself, do you? I am not with the police, Nick. Expats never work for the police. But you don't know that yet, so you won't believe me. Fair enough. You'll learn a lot of things soon. It's different here."

The bartender showed up with his drink and put the glass on the counter.

"On me," she said, giving the waiter a quick nod, and then turned back to Nick. "Please indulge me – I don't get to talk to someone so fresh from Earth very often."

"How did you know that I just got here?"

"Trust me, I can tell … and it's not just your accent. But don't worry – you'll blend in, in no time … if you want. I would know, I've been here for a while. This place is a lot of fun, no doubt about that," she glanced at him, and for some reason an image of a slow-circling hawk flashed across Nick's mind. "But I miss people from Earth. The men, especially," she smiled lightly, rotating the glass stem in her hand. "These guys," she nodded towards the room, "are lacking a certain – sophistication." She leaned back and gazed at him without any ambiguity.

Nick quickly looked away, breaking eye contact. What's wrong, he immediately asked himself with irritation. She was a great information source, and he should've automatically tried to connect with her. But he was sick of his manipulating women. She was right – ordinary people with normal lives didn't end up on Earth3. Maybe she also desired something strange, just like he did, and, who knows, maybe even due to the same genetic flaw. Maybe she was like him.

She kept looking at him, lightly tapping her fingers on the glass stem, and then she smiled and her armor of cool perfection shattered, and he recognized the type right away. She was a fragile warrior, both sensitive and cynical, a proud soul that wouldn't be caught dead wearing her heart on her sleeve. In this way, she was exactly like him and that was why she was able to see through his veneer of light nonchalance. With a dizzying feeling he thought that it was an absolute miracle that she even existed, let alone that she happened to be right here, close enough to touch.

He reached toward her hand, and she let go of her drink, responding, and something snapped inside his chest. A bandage lifted from his eyes, revealing a dazzling world, filled with delight and pain he had never known, and she was smiling at him from the center of it. He took her hand in his, and, suddenly losing control, he began stroking it insatiably, desperately, as if trying to convince himself that it wasn't a dream. His frenzied caress seemed to be more than his heart could handle, but it still wasn't enough. He stood up and said, "Let's go."

"Yes," she replied, not taking her eyes away from his face. "Let's get out of here."

They left the bar without saying a word and joined the thick pedestrian flow outside. She walked a step ahead of him showing the way; he followed not asking any questions.

It was impossible, and he was afraid to jinx it, but he knew that from now on they would be together forever, or, at least, for as long as he was alive, because he wouldn't let any force in this universe take her away. For a moment he imagined her gone, and blood rushed from his head, making him lightheaded. Wait, he told himself, he'd had that exact same feeling before – at the thought of losing Lita.

The fog in his brain abruptly lifted as if Lita's name had flipped some sort of switch. He was on Earth3 because he had gone rogue; he had put everything on the line, and he was doing it for Lita. But at the same time, there was no mistake about his deep, true, absolute love for the woman walking in front of him on the unfamiliar street of this tucked away world. It wasn't adding up. Something was very wrong, and he had to figure it out fast, and somehow he knew that he shouldn't let her notice his confusion. He'd met her in the bar, he told himself, and something must've happened during that conversation. He concentrated so hard that the street went out of focus, and then the mental image of her fingers tapping the glass shocked him by its unexpected familiarity.

It was something he had done on his Mirror World missions when he wanted to secretly send Kir a prerecorded command. And then it came to him in a flash; she must have launched a bio-transmission that was affecting his brain. Blood fled from his head again, and this time it was a sign of fear, which had a genuine chill about it

... but then again, there was no way to know. He couldn't trust any of his reactions anymore.

She was still walking slightly ahead of him, her face invisible at this angle. He glanced at their reflections in the window they were passing and caught a glimpse of her profile, and his heart instantly responded with a splash of impossible tenderness, drowning the fear – but the knowledge was there now. This feeling wasn't real, he thought, it was a symptom of a mental injury.

"Eve," he called, slowing down at a random shop entrance, "let's drop in here; I want to buy a drink."

She stopped and abruptly turned around. Careful, don't change your body language, he warned himself, and made a calculated step in her direction. There was an instant explosion of butterflies in his gut, and then a sudden wave of desire knocked down any remains of self-control like a sandcastle. He pictured pushing her against the wall, running his hands down her back, over her thighs, up her ribs, and made another, this time, involuntary step forward almost closing the distance between them. Some nagging voice in the back of his mind told him to stand back, and he deeply inhaled, clearing his head. She noticed and tensed, searching his face with increasing suspicion. Don't fight it, a rational thought went though his mind, ride this wave just like in a rip current. He gasped and let go with blind abandon, tightly squeezing her head in his hands, impatiently prying her obedient lips open, thrusting and writhing his tongue inside her responsive mouth. The street disappeared in a scorching haze, and melting sensations began spreading all over his body, but then she gently freed herself from his arms. He stepped back, slowly sobering, and saw her satisfied smile.

"Of course," she said, "we are blocking the way, Nick." She took his hand and pulled him inside the store.

They walked in, passing a booth with a bored store clerk at the door, and Nick let go of her hand shifting to the lead position. His pulse slowed slightly once he was no longer looking at her, and he managed to focus on the scene inside. Straight aisles stretched from the entrance in a funny spoke-like fashion, which, as he guessed, had a very specific purpose. Electronic surveillance hadn't been allowed on the Commonwealth for centuries, but this layout allowed a single store clerk to keep an eye on the entire customer crowd, which was very sparse at this particular moment.

Nick located the drink section, and slowly moved along its shelves, pretending to examine the rows of bottles, and carefully watching Eve's reflection in the mirrored panel that sealed the aisle on the other side. They finally reached the last rack with her just a step behind him, and then he quickly reversed their positions trapping her in the dead end. Her eyes widened in surprise, but this maneuver put him too dangerously close to her once again. He suddenly realized that the whole thing was pathologically inverted, and that, in fact, he was the one who was trapped in this store. He clenched his fists in frustration because he couldn't strip off her clothes right there in the aisle, lean her against these shelves, ignoring the cascade of dropping bottles, push apart her strong thighs with his hands, and, falling down on his knees, covering that tender slit between her open legs with his burning mouth. He shook his head, gasping for breath, and helplessly tried to remember why he was torturing both of them, wasting time in this random place, while they would have already been alone, away from all these people, from that watchful clerk at the door. Because he was being manipulated into something, reminded a sober voice in his head. Nick swallowed hard and looked aside to avoid facing her straight on, but it didn't help. Why did any of this matter if he would gladly do anything she wanted anyway, and all the logic in the word gave him an approving nod. That's exactly it, you stupid idiot, the rational part of his mind shouted in panic – she is dangerous precisely because of that.

"What are you using to induce … this?" he asked hoarsely, still looking past her. It seemed that his mind had regained some control the moment he openly dropped the pretense, and he sharply exhaled, clutching at the edge of his returning sanity.

It suddenly felt safe to face her again, and he saw that she had appreciated the change in the situation immediately.

"How did you … guess?" there was genuine surprise in her voice, and her eyes instantly became narrow and alert. "You're good for a greenhorn; I have to give you that."

He realized that he no longer liked having her physically close. Good, he thought, it meant that the obfuscation spell was largely gone. He didn't back off, however, staring at her with a hard smile.

"Ok, fine, it was just an amplifier," she said quickly. "It only amplified your natural feelings towards me. I just liked you … and it makes sex wonderful. It's not a big deal, just not very ethical."

"You're using mild terminology here, Eve. Owning bio-transmission software is a pretty serious crime, we both know that."

She looked over his shoulder at the security guard at the entrance.

"Don't make a scene, Nick. This program doesn't work long term. It's probably wearing off now that you are fighting it. Calm down."

"Don't you practice anything else on me," he said through clenched teeth. An image of the dead soldiers scattered along his way to Lita's van on the empty Beta Blue road flashed through his mind, and beads of cold sweat broke out on his forehead. Relax, he ordered himself, she wasn't about to attract attention by using something like that here ... but he wouldn't have time to stop her if she decided to go for it. He looked at his face in the reflective panel behind her back and saw the sheer dread in his eyes. Damn this bitch, his rage steadily rising, he should kill her for making him feel like this.

She blinked and suddenly looked genuinely frightened. "I can't," she quickly stepped backwards, bumping into the wall. "Trust me, I wouldn't want to amplify your current emotions, and it's really the only program I use. Just for fun, I swear. Just let me pass."

"I'm going to pretend that I believe you," he said in an even tone.

Her eyes quickly surveyed the geometry of their position, but he was standing right in the middle of the aisle, not allowing her to pass him without creating a noticeable commotion.

He nodded, seeing her realization. "Now ... help me, and we'll keep this small incident between us." Nick glanced past her at the reflection of the entry area in the mirrored surface and noticed that the guard was looking in their direction. "I have some questions. Where did you get this – amplifier?" Nick stretched his arm towards the closest shelf, keeping his eyes glued to her face, and grabbed a random bottle from the stack. She understood and quickly did the same.

"They are sold on the Darknet, all kinds of things like this."

"How do you get in?"

"I didn't buy it there, actually I bought it from a dealer. Normal people don't enter the Darknet. It's not safe."

"Who can show me how to get in?"

"Don't do it," a frightened expression crossed her face again. "I went once, long ago, out of curiosity … a friend had given me the access software. It's bad … even for Earth3. I also heard that somebody who had gone there disappeared for good. Nobody would know, or care. The police just leave Darknet alone, mostly."

"Do you still have your friend's program?"

"I do, but …"

"You really care about my safety, do you?" Nick couldn't contain a sarcastic smile. "Just send it to me, and I'll forget all about our – adventure."

"Nick, whatever you suspect about me, I actually just liked you."

"Listen, I don't give a damn about your real intentions. Just send it, now."

"Darknet is bad news. I'm telling you, Nick," she shook her head and muttered something under her breath.

"Nick, you've just received a copy of unlicensed software," informed Kir. "It appears to be an access portal to an encrypted network."

"Accept," said Nick.

The guard was now openly staring at them. Nick figured that time was up, and stepped aside, letting her pass.

He caught a faint whiff of her perfume as she went by, and his heart made a wild somersault. He stood still, watching her lithe body move in an effortlessly graceful stride towards the exit, and felt a lump in his throat, thinking that he would never see her again. The doors opened, and she walked out without a parting glance in his direction.

He bit his lip and counted to ten.

When he went outside, she was gone.

He walked a short way from the storefront and then stopped to collect his thoughts, pressing his back firmly against a nearby wall. He still didn't fully trust himself, so he tested his condition by running a kaleidoscope of recent images through his head: the dull glow of desire in Eve's half-closed eyes, her parted lips red and puffy from his kisses, the yielding curve of her breast under his hand – but the feelings elicited by these flashes were becoming more and more elusive, like memories of a quickly disappearing dream, until they had vanished completely.

He shivered and couldn't help a nervous giggle at the irony; the tables had turned, and he would finally get to appreciate a neuro-transmission program from the other side. It was an unpleasant feeling indeed, especially considering the fact that, according to Eve, he had been broadcasting his newbie status rather openly. An amplifier wasn't a big thing in itself, but it meant that other, much more dangerous programs were likely to be around as well. He again remembered the still bodies on the deserted Beta Blue road, and looked at the passing locals with a lot more respect. He was an easy mark, an obvious sitting duck here, and he needed to get the hell out of neuro-transmission range as soon as possible.

All that being said, his progress was good, he told himself encouragingly. The Darknet was a solid lead, and the next step was clear.

"Kir, show me the list of temporary public accommodations," Nick asked, and reviewed the available options. He checked the amount of his remaining money and told Kir to pay for a one-night stay at the nearest place he could afford. The description of the so-called "guest house" conformed to the true definition of basic, but it was located just a couple of blocks away.

The building curiously reminded him of Y-3 by its pure practicality. No imagination had been applied; the stairs led into a straight corridor with identical shutter gates squarely facing each other. One of its frames flashed, showing the availability, and the door lifted as Nick approached.

The room also reminded Nick of Y-3 with the no-frills efficiency of its actions; the moment he walked inside, the ceiling lit up and packages with disposable bedding rolled down from a chute in the wall onto a simple cot below.

Delaying the beginning of the unpleasant task, Nick slightly rattled the single chair at the modest table in the corner as if checking its sturdiness and sat down.

The initial steps were reassuring in their safe simplicity. First, he moved his remaining money to a bank vault that required his physical presence to initiate a reverse transfer. Then he wrapped Elisabeth's picture into a cocoon of maximum strength encryptions, tagged it with a "Help Wanted" label, and positioned it in the most conspicuous place inside Kir's shell. He was about to initiate Eve's program, but a sharp spasm twisted his stomach, making him double over in his chair. Once the pain let go, he slowly straightened, and admitted that he was afraid.

Earth didn't have a Darknet, at least not to his knowledge, so he had no idea what to expect. But there was something particularly dreadful about diving into this virtual underworld, even without assigning any serious weight to Eve's semi-hysterical warnings. It felt like being pushed out, blinded and unarmed, into the center of an abandoned amphitheater, whose steep rows shrouded in the darkness were filled by the most dangerous people on this planet. He was fine with the gangs of criminals gathering here to run their illegal businesses, but his blood curdled at the thought of bored freaks with sadistic tendencies lurking in this crowd.

But he had to find Elisabeth, and Darknet was the only crack that Nick had managed to discover in the Commonwealth's façade of wholesomeness. In theory, there were probably less dangerous ways to go about his search, but he didn't have time – the departure date of Lita's ship for Beta Blue was steadily approaching.

"Kir, run the Darknet program," he said, sitting back in the chair.

"Warning, my security can be compromised," there was a programmed concern in Kir's voice. "Are you sure you want me to proceed?"

"I am offering you as bait, Kir," Nick said. Then he switched into his usual mode of nonchalant banter, "It must be an unpleasant feeling for you, I get it … well, ok, I know you can't feel. Just trust me then, it doesn't feel so good. Yes, go ahead."

The room disappeared in a flash, and wildly enhanced colors and sounds rushed at Nick from all directions, changing their brightness and volume as they whooshed past at incomprehensible speeds.

"Nick, the software you loaded is out of date and unable to communicate with the current interface," Nick barely managed to make out Kir's words through the screeching noise.

"It's alright, just keep me logged in," said Nick.

Kir began to reply, but his voice was abruptly cut off and the program jammed all of Nick's personal feeds. He leaned forward and grasped the edge of the desk, hoping to maintain at least a spatial point of reference, but the notion of up or down jerked away, and he felt as if he was clutching a small dinghy being kicked around in a psychedelic version of raging surf. His ability to track time was gone; it seemed that he had been out there for eternity, but it might just as well have been seconds, there was no way to tell. Rolling waves of nausea hit him one after another, and he kept fighting them off until he couldn't hold the urge to vomit any longer.

"Kir, close the portal," he croaked, his voice inaudible in the howling cacophony of the program-produced noise, and then it seemed like he suddenly went deaf and colorblind, met with the silence and monochrome lighting of the hotel room. Nick dashed to the toilet, barely managing to reach it in time, and threw up. His head wouldn't stop spinning, and he kept retching in painful spasms, bending over the basin gripping its slippery edges for support. Once his sickness subsided he tried to get up, but an even stronger wave of dizziness hit him again, and he blacked out.

He opened his eyes, but didn't immediately move, trying to figure out why he was laying on the cold tile of an unfamiliar bathroom. His memory gradually returned, but he had no idea how long he had been out.

"Kir, how long was I unconscious?" his voice was so hoarse that he hardly recognized it.

"Three hours sixteen minutes," said Kir. "Your vitals are still not back to normal, but your current condition isn't dangerous."

Nick slowly hoisted himself up, grabbing onto the adjacent sink, splashed cold water over his face and stumbled back towards the desk, his legs shaking and his throat stinging with leftover vomit. The ground was treacherously heaving up and down under his feet, and he had to move carefully, making slow but steady progress across the room. All of a sudden, the floor and the ceiling swapped locations in several fast sequences. Nick fell backwards, hitting his head on the soft edge of the bed, and heard a distinct giggling. He tried to get up, but another flip threw him onto the floor again.

"Kir, power off," he whispered.

"Access denied. You are not an authorized user," answered Kir in his usual voice.

The room made a couple of more orientational changes and then stopped in merciful alignment with gravity.

Nick lay face down for several seconds, and then, not daring to stand, he began crawling towards the chair. Once he was close, he got to his knees, holding onto a leg of the table, and yanked himself up with an abrupt jerk. His butt barely managed to touch the seat when his vision was sharply replaced by complete darkness. He grabbed the edge of the table once again and peered into the pitch-black void, trying to make something out, and yet, he missed the exact instant when a faint pinkish glow flickered in the far distance. The light teasingly danced in the background, slowly dissolving into blurry letters, until, as if assuming sudden seriousness, it jumped ahead, and the blood-red words "*I know what you want*" clearly formed in front of Nick's eyes. They hovered there for a moment and then disappeared in a festive explosion, accompanied by the excited clapping of an invisible audience, while a still image of Elisabeth in 17th-century dress slowly developed in their place.

The room abruptly came back, and Nick heard a light knock on the door.

He got up gingerly, firmly holding onto the back of the chair, and coughed, clearing his throat. The knock, however, was just a courtesy heads up because the door opened without his permission, and a stranger confidently walked in. The guy was short and scrawny, a giveaway of his Mirror World origins, and he seemed relatively young, though his bad skin and skewed facial proportions made it hard to guess his exact age. He gave Nick a friendly smile, went straight to the cot and settled down on it in a relaxed cross-legged pose, casually leaning against the wall.

"Am I right Nick?" There was a distinct lisp in his voice. "It's a rhetorical question, by the way."

Nick still stood very upright, squeezing the top of the chair as if he needed something to prop him up.

"Please, make yourself comfortable," said the man, inviting Nick to sit with a hospitable gesture, "we need to talk."

Nick rotated his chair to face the bed and lowered himself onto the seat, noticing that his body obeyed with a minor delay. Nothing like that had happened to him before, and he wondered if it was a side effect of Kir being taken over or just the pure emotional shock from the most humiliating experience of his life.

"We'll need to communicate," the guy continued, viewing Nick with light amusement, "so let's say my name is … Johan. It's not real, obviously, but I like it better than the pretentious abomination my parents gave me to make up for my physical shortcomings. As you can guess, I know way more than your name. To be precise, I know as much as your implant has in its recordings – in brushstrokes, of course. I didn't take time to peruse all of your data, but I get the gist."

For a moment he watched Nick dispassionately, apparently letting his words sink in.

"There are a couple of gaps, but I figured out why you deleted that content," he said finally, his face brightening with a salacious grin. "You obviously took care to dispose of some sex sequences, but only with just that one woman from M-237. It's fortunate that you didn't bother to delete the rest – that would've been a real pity. Pleasure to watch, I swear to God. Excellent passion quality and kinky to boot. This could bring some serious money on the porn market for sure. Rare material – those Mirror World chicks are way more fun than the cold-blooded fishes here in the Commonwealth. You used the opportunity well, my resourceful traveler. And I must give you credit – I mean, you sure do know how to make them squeal," he licked his lips and winked at Nick.

The sense of violation was so sickening that Nick almost moaned. But this was what Nick had wanted; he had come here looking for someone who could do exactly that.

"Relax, my sex monster, I'm just kidding. It's not my trade … I had to confirm that you weren't with the police – which is why I was digging into your data. I had to understand your current plight, too – very romantic, my friend, very romantic. However, even considering the sentimentality of your motivation, you don't seem like a naïve moron, and I imagine that you were fully aware of what you were getting yourself into by coming to Earth3. By the way, good job with the hustler."

"Was she?" Nick hoped that he was in control of his voice.

"What did you think? Don't overestimate your charm, darling. Earth3 is the wrong place for that. She is a crook, for sure, but small time, not even a Dark Triad, lucky for you. She normally asks her marks to transfer their money to a fake honeymoon account, and then she vanishes, naturally. Fully respectable business, but the poor thing didn't know that she was wasting her time with you – you are as broke as a church mouse. But, in all seriousness, you did get lucky. It could have been much worse. You just don't walk around here without a neuro-transmission shield, buddy."

"What's here on Earth3 for the Dark Triads?"

"You mean, for us, right, Nick? But, to be fair, it's mostly for Mirror World folks, not Earth natives like you, Nick. It's not advertised, but laws aren't applied as strictly here as long as we don't cause trouble outside the sector. It's our safe space. It isn't a Dark Triad outlier's fault that they were born with the need for high risk, is it? It's unfair to apply common laws to us. We have a disability. So, it's an unofficial compromise. The Commonwealth lets us be, and we know to stay keep to ourselves. What happens here stays here."

Based on his knowledge of his former clients, Nick had thought that it would be wise to keep an eye on the Dark Triad travelers after they left this place. But Earth's ethics wouldn't allow it, and in any case, it wasn't his problem.

Johan shifted his position, sticking the bedding package between his lower back and the wall for added comfort.

"Anyway, I don't think I need to further advertise my services – I trust that you appreciate the teaser. In brief, I can hack the implant of your mysterious Elisabeth, and you can steal whatever blackmail material you hope to find to trade for your girlfriend," he said in a more serious voice.

Nick felt his face muscles relax slightly. The guy wasn't a nutcase, and he got Nick's request precisely right.

"There is a price of course. And, as I said, you're pretty destitute, my desperate Romeo. But you got lucky … again. I don't need any money – for me, money's easy enough to get. I care about something else altogether. I am a freelance scientist, you see, and I want to run an illegal experiment on a human brain – your brain – in this case."

"What sort of experiment?"

"My research is of no imminent importance to you, my curious friend. Not to mention that it wouldn't be all too wise for me to share much detail with you in case we are unable to strike a deal. The only things that you should be worried about right now, for our bargaining purposes, are the potential side effects for your mind."

Nick silently agreed, but he suddenly noticed a glaring glitch in this setup.

"Why bother about my consent when you are in range? Why not stun me with a neuro-assault transmission, which I'm sure you own, and just do whatever you want?"

"Well, let's see," Johan rolled his eyes to the ceiling, "maybe because I oppose violence as a solution … or, maybe," he winked, "because I need your cooperation."

"Lucky me …" Nick croaked. "So, what are the side effects, then?"

"Memory damage," Johan quickly said in a clear voice, his lisp momentarily gone.

"How bad?"

"You see, that question is one of the main reasons for my test. Worst case it turns you into a drooling idiot."

Nick's mouth went dry.

"But that's very unlikely, based on my research," Johan paused. "What's up? Lost your courage?"

Nick imagined Lita strapped to a chair in the investigation room of the military headquarters on Beta Blue, and the rest became irrelevant.

"I'll do it," he said simply.

There was something rather out of character in Johan's eyes now.

"Now lucky me …" he said with unexpected relief. "It has taken me fucking ages. Everyone else has bowed out at this point. You see, after hearing the price all my aspiring customers realized that their needs weren't as dire as they had thought," he winced, as if remembering something annoying. "But we seem to have an understanding, so let's go ahead and visit my workshop. We both happen to be impatient, for our corresponding reasons, my courageous friend." He then jumped up from the cot, "By the way, I blocked you from other hacker attacks. Not sharing you with other vermin here," he spoke in a very lighthearted tone again, carefully studying Nick's face from the corner of his eye. "I gave you a neuro-transmission shield as well. No need to thank me, I am a selfish bastard. I need your brain intact." He headed to the door, "Just so you know, we'll be taking your flyer; mostly to cover my tracks, but for nostalgic reasons too. You see, my headhunter used that same exact model as yours all those years ago."

"Kir ..." Nick started and broke off at the sight of Johan's grin.

"Kir, bring down the shuttle," said Johan. "To be clear, my genetically superior accomplice, I will maintain control of your implant to guarantee my safety. You are so much stronger than me. Handpicked genes and all that," Johan gave Nick an innocent smile, and stepped out of the room.

The shuttle was already waiting at the building exit, and Johan promptly settled in the host chair, inviting Nick to follow.

"Kir, take us ... right here," Johan said touching a point in the air. "It's not too far, just over an hour." The shuttle gently rose into the air, stabilized at a low altitude, and began to glide in the specified direction.

"Now, since our deal is underway, let me explain your exact role," Johan dropped his clowning manner and looked at Nick with an intensity that was freakishly similar to Hilgor's trademark expression. Of course, thought Nick, this piercing investigative look was a known feature of all Dark Triad people.

"Fortunately, your former profession, and your genetic fuck up makes the whole thing easier. It would've been a drag to drill certain things through the thick skulls of your compatriots. For example, why am I risking prison instead of hanging out with the outliers? Or, why do I work in this shithole instead of enjoying Earth's best research facilities. But you … you've met people like me – in fact, you are one of us. We tend to be obsessed, as you know. We don't take 'no' for an answer. I came up with an idea back home, and it has been consuming me. But our technology was a joke. It was frustrating as hell. So when one of your colleagues made me the offer, I didn't think twice."

Nick glanced out the window, trying to get a sense of direction, but the identical architecture made it hard to track their flight path without Kir's help.

"Your science was amazing indeed … I guess my home world deserved what it got, thrown back to the Stone Age because of that epidemic of yours, which I trust we had nothing to do with. Oh, well," Johan's smile wasn't even remotely nice. "Technology wasn't the only thing Earth stole from us by the way. I read a lot of ancient literature once I got here. You know, it was worth it to come just for that, really. But I'm digressing … I was given the best technical resources, and I caught up quickly. I became the best hacker in the Commonwealth, and I still am by a long shot. Sorry, I'm not one for false modesty," he said picking up on Nick's skeptical expression. "I can run circles around the rest of them and do whatever I want in cyberspace without anyone ever noticing. But, you see, that's exactly what's wrong! Nobody should be able to be the best, Nick! The scale is infinite in both directions – of all people, you should know that.

Sooner or later, someone better will come along from one of the closed Mirror clones – perpetual rat race, and never an end in sight."

He was talking quicker now; his lisp worsened, making his speech harder to follow, and Nick had to lean forward so as not to miss anything from this pressured rant.

"But there is a solution, Nick. You see, if the data are saved directly into brain cells, it'll be impossible to hack the host. Just imagine, your living body becomes the only key. Nobody would ever be able to steal information from anyone else, not even under physical threat – activation of brain fear centers would automatically block data transfer. That was the dream I had at home, and, imagine, your biotechnology was almost there. It took me some time, but I designed data exchanges between brain tissues and implant chips – but only theoretically. I needed to have it verified, which is where I got stuck. Brain simulators were too simplistic – test files kept becoming corrupted," Johan's face was now twitching in a vaguely unpleasant way, and there was a disturbing glimmer in his widely open eyes. "I was sure my program would work just fine on a live brain ... with some possible host memory damage in the early versions. But, of course, experiments on humans were out of the question. I could have tried to beg for an animal subject as an exception, but it wasn't worth it because I wouldn't have been able to measure the exact extent of memory loss. It was a dead end, and I was told to let it go." Johan's smile was almost vicious now, "But you see, your people brought us to Earth, and they didn't really get who we were. And we are rather tenacious when it comes to chasing our dreams. I had no patience for Earth's humanitarian bullshit."

He was right, thought Nick. This is exactly what made him different too.

"I told them to go fuck themselves and threw their cybersecurity chief title in their faces," Johan's face twisted into a contemptuous grimace. "I moved to Earth3. Remember, authorities don't bother us here. So I built a makeshift lab, and started searching for people like you, who had nothing to lose. I needed to see how my program works on a live brain, so that I could fix the remaining bugs. Making the download repeatable is trivial, just a final touch. Then I'll return to Earth and demo it on myself, for all these morons to see." Johan was looking past Nick, and his voice was harsh and derisive as if he was engaged in the old fight with some obstinate and hostile audience. "Nobody would object to me using my own brain as a test bed. One thing you got right on your sterile world is the freedom to fuck up your own body."

The shuttle made a wide turn and started descending towards an isolated patch of abandoned industrial grounds. Nick never expected to see a real slum inside Commonwealth's boundaries, but the landscape below fully qualified. Johan caught his surprised look and chuckled.

"This plant exceeded its functional lifespan a long time ago, and it wasn't economical to upgrade it or even to knock it down. They just rebuilt the factory in a new location, leaving this behind. These leftovers work great as squatting quarters for the most ambitious segment of our population. We like it, and the police don't bother nosing around."

The shuttle landed on a small plaza hidden between silent manufacturing structures, all of them marked by a somber air of dilapidation.

"So here is the exact deal, Nick," said Johan, his eyes clear and serious again. "I'll connect you to Elisabeth's implant. In return, I'll upload my file to Kir's memory, transfer it to your brain and then download it back to Kir. You'll trigger these processes by creating certain mental images. Then we'll check the extent of your memory loss. Listen, don't prepare a hanging rope just yet," he added, watching Nick's face. "You know what, maybe I nailed it. Maybe there isn't going to be any damage at all. I am very good, Nick – and I am not exactly a monster. I would've tested it on myself long ago, but how would I work on the tweaks if my memory got messed up?"

Nick shrugged his shoulders. Memory loss wouldn't exactly be helpful in his case either, but there wasn't another option on the table.

"Fine," he nodded, "let's go."

The moon was almost full, and the sharp black shadows of twisted pipes on the rooftops ominously stretched across the plaza making the place look positively haunted. Nick wondered about the purpose of this former factory, but immediately regretted taking his eyes off the ground as he narrowly avoided stumbling over a deep crack in the crumbling surface. He cursed, picked up speed and caught up with Johan, who was waiting for him in front of the most preserved building.

They walked inside together, but once the door completely shut behind them, Nick abruptly stopped, unable to see a thing in the complete darkness. Quiet wet sobs were coming from all directions, and he felt unnerved, imagining a host of damned souls floating in the pitch-black space.

"My apologies," said Johan. "Kir, turn on his night vision. Here you go."

Nick's eyes instantly adjusted, and he realized that they were standing inside a large industrial hall, filled with dozens of bio-chemical vats of some sort. They were empty, their once transparent walls smeared with flaking splotches of dried-up fluids from inside. However, some sagging conduits still held small amounts of a bubbling liquid, and the soft gurgling was what produced that unsettling ghostly crying. Johan paid no attention to this industrial cemetery, confidently making his way through, and Nick followed him, squeamishly dodging the furry grime of low hanging pipes. They walked past the gaping doors of non-working elevators, down several flights of rotting stairs, and out into a long straight tunnel, which, surprisingly, wasn't as dark as the floor above the ground – its cracking paint was covered with frayed illuminating strips, glued on probably half a century ago, but still giving off some faded glow.

Johan stopped, took a napkin from his pocket, wrapped it around his finger and traced a signature on the surface of a seemingly random section of the wall. A bulky panel slid away, and bright daylight burst through the hidden door, making Nick freeze – the surgically clean interior was in such contrast with the sordid underground passage, that he suspected that Johan had once again messed with his optic feed.

He touched a curve of the polished doorframe, and a firm correlation between his visual and tactile senses gave him some reasonable reassurance that his vision was unaltered, and the room wasn't an apparition. He walked in, and his eyes instantly stopped on the workbench in the center. It was covered with unfamiliar lifelike objects: clumps of spiderlike devices weaving invisible webs in meditating movements, swarms of fitfully breathing ellipsoids glimmering in the artificial daylight, slowly pulsating spheres hanging in the air without any visible support. Nick managed not to let his imagination run wild regarding the purpose of these things, but just then his gaze fell on an exposed human brain that sat on a surgical tray.

He gasped and almost jumped at the sound of laughter that suddenly came from behind him.

"Don't freak out, it's just this useless shit-for-brains simulator. You get to keep yours, I promise," Johan patted his shoulder. With some effort Nick unglued his eyes from the two wrinkled hemispheres, and took a closer look at the rest of the room.

As he'd already noticed, there wasn't a lot to see – just a solid closet half-built into the wall and a well-worn gray armchair that vaguely reminded Nick of Hilgor's attachment object.

"Please, make yourself comfortable, so that we can start," Johan gestured towards the seat.

"We should begin with Elisabeth," said Nick, taking a step back in order to face Johan straight on. "I have to insist. If a sufficiently large chunk of my memory is wiped out, I won't even know why I'm here, and there is no particular reason to believe that you'll help me to sort it out. I want to search Elisabeth's memory before you fuck up my brain." He sat down and dropped the tension in his voice, "I promise that I'll cooperate once I get what I need."

Johan leaned against the workbench, not too subtly enjoying their reversed height disparity.

"Well, actually, you can't leave this place without my help so I believe in your honesty. Also, and don't get me wrong … my neuro-assault capabilities are absolutely unnecessary in our situation, but I have deactivated your neuro-defense shield, just to be clear. But yes, we can start with Elisabeth," Johan lightly touched something invisible in the air, and his eyes refocused on his internal screens.

Nick silently watched him, and imagined a scenario in which Elisabeth had changed her mind about her travel plans and never came to Earth3. One step at a time, he told himself … and never mind that each of them could bring him to a solid wall. "Will it take you long to hack her implant?" he asked.

"It depends. But to put things in perspective, Nick, for everyone but me … and everyone includes the government … it takes more than an hour to crack even the most basic citizen chip."

"I see," said Nick, "and how are you so sure?"

"How do you think? I keep track of all hacking software out there for my safety … I coded half of them in the first place. You're in a completely different league with me, my lucky cyber criminal," Johan flashed Nick a bright smile, continuing to move his fingers over his virtual controls. "My break-in program is an order of magnitude faster and completely untraceable. Still, your Elisabeth is a big shot, so her implant security is going to be reinforced. But I would be shocked, frankly, if I couldn't crack it in a blink."

All of a sudden, he stopped, and nodded contently. "She is on Earth3. She's been staying in a private corporation, standard embryo genetic enhancement plant. They make DNA adjustments for skin sun protection, to be precise."

Nick unclasped his hands, and for a moment pressed his cold palms against his temples.

"What would she …" he interrupted himself, and his voice trailed off.

"Okay, Nick, let's find out," Johan's eyes glittered with childlike excitement, his fingers started moving faster, and his smile turned into a ferocious scowl. But then he froze with an astonished grimace.

"Oh …" he said, and Nick didn't like the sound of that at all.

Johan crossed his arms over his chest and thoughtfully peered at something in space. "She is using the president's personal cybershield, which I helped them to design before I quit," he said finally. "I wonder how your friend managed to get her hands on it. It's going to be hard, Nick – I did a hell of a job on that one. But don't you worry, I happen to enjoy a good challenge. Makes our petty crime more fun, doesn't it? Relax, my amateur sleuth, and let me focus now. Feel free to walk around, by the way, lest your butt starts hurting. Just don't break anything."

Johan began pacing the room, periodically swearing under his breath, his eyes focused on some invisible point in the distance, his fingers dancing in the air in front of him.

Nick shuffled around the workbench for a while, but eventually returned to the chair, closed his eyes and forced himself to relax. It was a mistake. His memory, not distracted by some urgent task, instantly rushed towards the very place that Nick was trying to avoid, knocked down the protective dam and flooded his mind with the flashbacks, each of them reminding him of various ways in which he killed Lita. He killed her in several steps, and this thought felt like a jagged rod turning inside Nick's heart. He'd had many chances to get out of her life, never to return, before it was too late. He could have done it right after he felt that unexpected, inappropriate, irrational sting of jealousy in that small open restaurant in Oren when Remir was in the hospital, and she told him her story. That sting and the swell of pity were loud and clear warnings that she had stopped being a part of his work. He should've started looking for another outlier if only he'd had had the decency of being honest with himself back then.

And then there was that exact moment when he pushed both of them past the point of no return. He remembered how she called him after the coup, and gave him that desperate hug in her room … and how, instead of freeing himself from her arms, stepping back into the corridor and getting the hell off that world, he took the mask from her face and dropped it to the floor.

"Got you, motherfucker!" the delight in Johan's voice was beyond mere jubilance.

Nick opened his eyes, and saw Johan pacing back and forth in front of his chair, rubbing his hands and glowing with satisfaction.

"It wasn't easy, but it still didn't take me too long, did it?" Johan abruptly stopped, noticing the absent expression on Nick's face. "What's wrong, my dude?" he asked with concern. "You are all set! I'll connect you to her implant, and you can dig there to your heart's content. Meanwhile I'll prepare for my test, but will wait for your green light before I start."

Nick shut down his Beta Blue memories, and acknowledged Johan's words with a slight nod.

"Listen, you look like you need a prayer, comrade," said Johan, refocusing on his internal screens. "Are you a believer in something, by any chance? Probably not, our Dark Triad lot is a cynical one. I am no help with that either – blind faith goes against my scientific principles on top of my natural skepticism. But I will be happy to stand in for your guardian angel," he paused. "Okay, I just gave you minimum control over Kir – just to view and copy her implant memory recording. No other functionality yet, sorry. But welcome to everything she has ever heard and seen, because, imagine that, you are in luck again – her overconfident highness has never erased anything. How very arrogant of her. She trusted her golden shield, you see, but as we have just proved, destroying records is the only way to keep them a secret … at least until my program hits the market. I am sending you her implant access link, just follow …"

There was no blackout or even the slightest shift in Nick's perception, but Johan was suddenly standing in a different place, staring into space, and a triumphant smile was twisting his features into a grotesque grimace.

"The file transfers worked perfectly, just as I expected! Both upload and retrieve functions were flawless, Nick!"

Nick shook his head, trying to orient himself, and Johan's gleeful expression immediately dimmed.

"Wait, now with your memory loss. Tell me you recognize who I am. Come on, Nick. What's the last thing you remember?"

"You connected me to Elisabeth ..."

"Excellent!" Johan's face lightened in relief. "Only a few hours of memory damage! Not a big deal at all! Easy to fix. That and the quick change to make the export function repeatable, and I am ready for my long overdue fame and vengeance! You can't even imagine the magnitude of what just happened! I'm a ..."

"Stop for a second," Nick interrupted hoarsely, "did I find anything in her recording?"

"Oh, you're good. I almost had to pour a bucket of water on your head to calm you down. You said that you found more than you had hoped, that you could trade your stolen information for anything at all."

Nick got up and took a blind step forward, squeezing his eyes as if the room's artificial sunlight was suddenly too bright. "I told you ..." he said flatly, "that I could trade this recording for Lita, did I?"

"You said you could trade it for anything. What's wrong? I haven't seen you go pale before, pal."

Calm down and sober up, Nick ordered himself – it wasn't the happy ending yet, he was far from being done. "What was it about?" he asked.

"No idea. I didn't pay attention, my euphoric friend. Some project she was involved in. I don't care all that much about your business, to be honest – I have my own things to be excited about. But don't worry about your trivial memory loss – you can watch your precious recording as many times as you want now that you have it in Kir's memory, can't you? But hold on a minute before you start … there is something special I brought from Earth just for this very occasion." Johan rushed to the closet. "It had to wait for a while, you know …" he opened the door and reached deep inside one of the shelves. "Twentieth century's red wine, imagine!" he said as he lifted the bottle into the air. "Now we need glasses and something to open it – something sharp!" Johan continued to go through the contents of his cabinet, but Nick couldn't wait any longer.

"Sorry, Johan, I need to see what I got. Kir, play the last download."

"Impatient … fine," Johan glanced at Nick over his shoulder, "just don't forget to pay attention to your taste buds while you are watching."

Nick removed everything but the recording playback from his vision, leaving audio as the only connection to the room.

"Kir, find the most relevant data," he said and the camera immediately started moving at eye level along an empty corridor with steel-colored walls.

"This wine must be excellent," Johan went on in the background. "Your compatriots have lost the pleasure of thinking, but they have preserved the traditions of drinking quite well."

The footage was jerky, jumping up and down in rhythm with a fast walk. It was very quiet, the silence broken only by the sound of Johan rummaging in the closet.

"Now, damn it, what can we use for an opener? All this junk around, but …"

The hallway on the screen made a sharp turn and came to a dead end in the form of a massive closed door with a smooth metallic surface. The perception of movement stopped, and Elisabeth's face stared at Nick from the reflection.

Her face didn't change in response to a loud explosion of glass shattering against something hard, and Nick guessed that the sound had come from the non-virtual room. He swiped the playback down and saw Johan standing in an expanding pool of wine. He was staring into the distance with an expression that instantly made Nick's heart go numb.

"What now …" Nick whispered.

"It can't be …" for some reason Johan was whispering too, and then he turned to Nick with a look of total disbelief. "My security alerts just went berserk. They noticed my hack of that bitch's data … and they just unleashed the hunt. Holy shit, it's fucking massive!"

Nick was suddenly back in the chair, with Johan's face looming right over him, his hands tightly squeezing Nick's shoulders. His expression was enough to make Nick guess that their situation wasn't good, and a quick glance around the room confirmed this assumption.

The workbench was covered with mangled shards; all the funny delicate objects were gone. A sturdy metal pipe was perched against the wall.

"Listen to me," said Johan, "you had one more memory loss. Some major shit happened, and we need to get the fuck out of here quickly. What's the last thing you remember?"

"You said something about a cyber raid …"

"Good, you remember that much," Johan let go of Nick, and picked up a half-full garbage bag from the floor. "They detected her security breach, there is something funky about your Elisabeth. For some reason, they used the best government resources to watch her perimeter. My fuck up, I admit, I should've been more careful, should have crawled deeper, but, damn it, I was too impatient … and I didn't expect *that*. The crackdown is fucking insane too. Have you heard of the Cyber Delta Force? They are only deployed if there is a direct threat to the Commonwealth's safety. Imagine, they are all now looking for the origin of this particular break in."

Johan moved around the tables in quick jerky steps, hastily sweeping the remaining debris into the trash sack. "I lost them in the net, but they'll trace the physical origin of her security breach to this lab location. I have to get rid of the hardware quickly and lay low for a while." Johan snapped the bag closed and wiped the sweat from his forehead. "You don't have to worry. You have nothing on you – I wiped all recordings made on Earth3 from Kir's memory."

"Wait," Nick said this very quietly, mildly surprised that the light in the room had suddenly become brighter, "you did what?"

For a split second everything turned into a silent blur, and then bolts of searing pain shot through his brain. His fingers let go of something unpleasantly warm and slender, and he collapsed onto the floor, screaming.

"Kir, cut his optic signal! Don't move you moron or I'll shut down your moronic brain!" Johan's voice thundered inside Nick's skull, making the pain intolerable, but Nick understood.

He froze, face down, squeezing his head in his hands and moaning through clenched teeth. The pain abruptly stopped, and the red veil in front of his eyes changed to total blackness. He heard a fit of a wheezing cough and realized that Johan was also lying on the floor nearby.

Then there was the sound of awkward scrambling, and Johan's cracked voice interrupted by uneven gasps came directly from above, "Calm down, you psycho … I don't have time for this … you have your file, you do."

"How?" Nick's lips felt leaden, too heavy to move.

"Before wiping Kir clean I saved your stolen recording to your brain using my program. This is how you got the second memory gap, my ungrateful co-conspirator. But you need to know how to get it out, don't you – which won't happen if you harm me. Are you following?"

Nick swallowed and nodded.

"Fine, now get up, but don't come close. Kir, return his vision."

The room came back, and Johan was now standing at its far end still clutching at his throat.

"You could have killed me, you superhuman imbecile. You almost blew it."

"Why did you bother to save my file? Why didn't you just fry my brain?" asked Nick, getting back to his feet.

"Maybe because I have a soft heart, and I'm a sucker for love stories. Or maybe it's because I would have had to deal with your body and a homicide investigation on my back in addition to everything else. I told you, there was an agreement – no homicides here. I would get in hot water with our people in addition to the Commonwealth's police. Not to mention that it's gross and I've never done it. Now, it is time to leave!"

"Wait … my memory gap started when I was about to watch the recording. I need to download it now to find out how I should handle this cluster fuck."

"I am afraid, it's not wise, my clueless one," in spite of genuine anxiety in Johan's eyes, he managed to maintain his mocking expression. "The transfer from the brain works reliably only once in the beta version. I told you, I left it as the final touch to fix before the release, which is apparently being postponed for now," his grin was rather nasty. "I wouldn't export your recording to Kir just yet – I'm sure your local Cyber Delta Force will decide to take a peek into your implant before they let you enter Earth's infospace. They are not complete idiots, my friend, and by the time you get home they'll connect the dots between your dead outlier, Elisabeth and your presence on Earth3 while this shit started happening."

"But I have no clue about that file, Johan! How can I … let me download it. I'll just give it a quick look, and then you can write it back to my brain and wipe out Kir again!"

"Considering your former occupation, I didn't expect you to turn into an idiot under stress. Didn't you see this, my brilliant idea generator?" Johan shook his garbage bag. "All my state of the art equipment is here. Not to mention that we don't have much time before a swat team shows up."

"How could I even have believed you?" The setback was so devastating that Nick started shouting in Johan's face, "There is no file! You are lying to me to make me go back to Earth, to get me out of your hair!"

"You have to believe my word, buddy. Makes it thrilling, doesn't it? But then again, you have every right to assume I'm lying and give up … though I expected a stronger spirit from you, my failing Orpheus. In any case, I don't have time to argue."

Johan picked up the bag and started quickly making his way to the exit. He was right, thought Nick, and there was no time to waste, but for some reason he kept standing still, silently admiring the shape of the red trace left by the wine-soaked trash bag; it was a perfect curve as Johan dragged it across the room, keeping a maximum distance from Nick. Nick bit his lip so hard that it shocked him into reality. It was shitty, all around, but it was the only reality he had.

"Johan … wait … how do I get the file out … assuming it's there?"

"Glad that your brain is back on. I don't like quitters," Johan stopped and rested the garbage bag on the floor. "When you are ready, close your eyes, and concentrate on your favorite color. Your brain waves will trigger an export to Kir." He paused and then said in the same harsh voice, which he had used to argue with his invisible nemeses earlier, "To answer your question – why I even gave a damn. As you rightly guessed, I don't care about your romantic story, but …" his face suddenly lost all its mocking plasticity, changing into a ferocious scowl of a small predator. "They fucked up my work, and I get a bit touchy when it comes to that subject. I even hold grudges, irrationally enough. It's my extreme pleasure to help you fuck them, using whatever shit bomb you happen to have in your recording. So that's why I am helping. I just gave Kir the security breach detector that I designed for myself. Watch for the red light in the corner of your vision field. If it's blinking, it means they are breaking in; if it's solid then it means that Kir has been hacked. These radars have been around, but mine is different – these fucktards won't notice its presence even if your implant has already been taken over completely." He caught his breath. "And don't waste time getting your money from the vault. I transferred more than enough into your account – just get the fuck out of this sector as soon as you can." Suddenly Johan jerked his head aside, as if hearing something through his internal channels; and his mouth twitched in the closest approximation of real fear that Nick had seen on his face. "How charming… they just dropped the idea of a raid. They already figured that it's not in the city, so they are planning to blow up a whole plant once they zero in on the exact location. This cuts my time to get the fuck out of here to … well, not to a lot. Have to leave now," he made a step toward the exit.

Nick involuntary lurched towards the door too, but Johan sharply turned in his direction. "No," he said, "don't move!"

Nick instantly stopped, remembering the exploding pain in his head, and Johan dashed out. The hatch shut behind his back and its outlines gradually blended with the wall.

Nick clenched his fists, but Johan's disembodied voice came through right away, "Don't panic, once I reach my getaway flyer I'll open the door and return Kir's controls. Now, so long and let's hope we won't see each other again."

Nick forced himself to stand absolutely still until he saw a widening crack of the opening hatch.

It was almost noon, and there were no shadows to hide from the direct heat of the sun, but Nick covered the distance between the building and his shuttle at a dead sprint.

"Kir, unlock," Nick braced himself in anticipation of a refusal, but the door obediently opened.

"Fly to the ship, and start the departure protocol," he exhaled, landing on his seat.

The shuttle darted towards the Hub in a straight line and was quite a ways away from the ground when a sudden shock wave almost threw it out of balance. Nick zoomed in the rear camera on the symmetric plume of smoke rising from the remains of the abandoned factory, and shuddered.

As his ship shot up into the sky from the parking hangar, he didn't bother to glance at the retreating surface of Earth3. It was safe to say that he hadn't fallen in love with the place.

EARTH

The front door of the fast-food inspired installation opened, and Riph hastily scrambled to his feet, oafishly slipping on the tile floor.

"Slept right through it, my friend," said Hilgor in a reproaching tone and got up, expecting to greet Nick.

But it wasn't Nick. The silhouette in the entrance clearly belonged to a Mirror World woman, and Hilgor recognized her even before she stepped inside.

"Reish?" but the surprise on his face quickly faded away. "Oh, he must have called you too," he said, sitting down again.

"He did," Reish gave Riph a brief pat. "I was a little surprised at his choice of the meeting place," she critically looked at flashes of headline news and advertisement clips on the tabletops. "But it's you, of course. Missing Del's collection of lame art, aren't you?"

"Did he tell you what he wanted?" asked Hilgor, ignoring her question.

"He said he needed help," she replied, sitting down across his table. "To think, he's been gone for three months without a word and now he needs help from us, of all people?"

They looked at each other, and Hilgor shrugged. He didn't know what to say. There was the obvious explanation that Nick had forgotten about their existence the moment he received his bounty money. But it didn't seem to match the Nick they had gotten to know during their flight from Y-3. Another possibility was that something bad had happened. Given Nick's situation, it wasn't a far-fetched assumption.

"Maybe he wants to use our influence for something, maybe he needs money? Reish, give him a break. He had other things to do."

"Like what?"

Hilgor shrugged again. "I guess we'll find out soon."

Riph curled in the aisle between them, sighed and doze off. For several moments they sat in silence, and Hilgor once again thought how drastically Reish had transformed since they had arrived on Earth. She had cut her hair and changed its color to a golden blond, and her light open dress was an obvious antithesis to the protection garbs of the past. But, of course, the main difference was this new carefree expression on her face.

"Let me check if he's gotten through border control," Hilgor glanced at the opaque bracelet on his wrist.

"Wait! That thing is so ... cumbersome," winced Reish. "Let me – Kella, reach Nick," she addressed her implant in an almost loving tone and looked at Hilgor with pity. "Don't you hate wearing it? Why refuse to have the hardware installed? Worried about a personality split?"

"It's not that ... but what if Riph gets jealous?" Hilgor smiled, dodging the question. He didn't know why, he just couldn't do it.

Reish stared into space. "Thanks, Kella."

"You don't have to do that," said Hilgor. "This thing doesn't appreciate your manners. It's a program."

Reish just waved him aside, focusing on the received information. "This is strange," she was perplexed now. "He is still offline. Why would a routine check be taking so long?" she looked at Hilgor's empty glass. "I guess I should perk up too. It's been a long day."

She got up, went to the vending machine and surveyed her options.

"I imagine he didn't tell you about Lita when you talked either, did he?" she said, not turning her head.

"No, it was very brief. I didn't have time to ask."

She returned with a glass of something greenish and sat across the table, "I guess we'll find that out soon too ..."

Hilgor imagined that Nick was coming to tell them that Lita died and felt a chill run down his spine – there was something very unsettling in facing raw human despair close up. Come on, maybe things weren't that bad, he told himself and decided to change the subject, at least for the time being.

"How have you been lately?" he asked Reish.

They officially "split up" two months ago, citing the traumatic effect of the move as the catalyst for their break up. Hilgor continued to enjoy the regal privileges of his outlier status, while Reish was given a modest government support subsidy. But she never bothered to collect it. She immediately became better off than Hilgor.

"By the way, I just saw the reviews of your latest release. Bravo!" In fact, Hilgor expected something like this to happen when he saw her emerge from the doors of the medical center the day after their arrival. There was a reckless happiness in her eyes, as if she had just tasted immortality.

Of course, she was informed that life expectancy on Earth albeit long in comparison with the Mirror World standards, was finite. But it wasn't about the logic.

Back on Y-3, she would occasionally think about her death and the amount of time she had remaining. But it was like trying to gauge the water level in a lake whose shores were obscured by fog. The moment she received her diagnosis everything changed; suddenly she was looking at a pool that was getting shallower with every minute. The finality was absolute and definitive, and it was confirmed by the feeling of weakness that gradually increased with every passing day.

She wasn't doing very well when Nick showed up. It didn't feel real when Del first explained the deal to her, and even after Reish boarded the decidedly alien-looking spacecraft, she still couldn't allow herself to believe. But all of the darkness lifted without a trace as she underwent the reconstruction procedure on Earth. Even her memory of days filled with the awareness of her impending death melted away when her physical symptoms disappeared. Time wasn't a pool or even a lake anymore. It was an endless ocean.

Hilgor wondered what practical form this transformation would take, but he had become immediately immersed in the kaleidoscope of his new activities and didn't see much of Reish. He knew that she was gone for hours a day enjoying the warmth of the late spring in the gardens that weaved through the fabric of the metropolis. But he didn't know that she had asked for a small favor from their assimilation team. And he didn't see her face when she watched the plastic bottles with the Beta Blue painkillers melt and burn in a fire that was arranged for her in the nearest park clearing. Otherwise he would have noticed the deep darkness in her eyes while she watched the last evidence of her illness as it disappeared for good.

He also missed her request for neuro-art equipment and image-generating software, so he had no idea what she was concocting in the far wing of their residence until after she had moved out. Only when Hilgor came to visit her new place did he realize what she had been up to. He held his breath as he experienced the flourishing life that was pouring from her new work. She was presenting him with emotions that he had never had, and which could only reliably come from someone who had lived facing the definite end and came back alive. And the public appreciated it very much – her first release propelled her to stardom right away. She became a sensation overnight.

"Thanks," she smiled, "but you know, these days I don't need any validation. I don't feel anxious about my work at all."

"It's great, seriously, but still, Reish, why don't you just take the outlier assessment? That way it won't matter what the public thinks, you'll be set forever."

"Why do you have to bring that up again? You know what I think about it, together with the rest of the Commonwealth, I am sure. People don't call it the Dark Triad anymore; everyone is using euphemisms these days. But everyone knows what kind of personality a positive score means. No, thank you."

"Aren't you even curious?"

"No, I'm not curious," she said firmly, her voice sounded a bit strained. "In any case, thanks for your concern."

"It's Nick. He is calling me back," said Reish, focusing on her internal feed.

In a moment she turned to Hilgor with a look of slight annoyance.

"*I'm on my way, see you soon …*" That was short! Why couldn't he explain more? Not fair," she said. "I'll call him for details."

"Don't. Please, Reish, patience. He did say that he was on his way. Maybe he wants to explain himself in person. Anyway, it shouldn't take him very long to get here now."

"Fine, let's wait," she took a sip of her drink. "Tell me how you've been. It's crazy – we haven't talked for almost a month. Anything new about work? And other things?"

Hilgor clasped his hands behind his head and sat like that for a moment staring into the distance. "I've been alright."

"What's wrong?" she asked immediately.

Hilgor slouched on his bench, crossing his arms over his chest and focused on a section of the tile floor. "Everything is fine. That work I'm doing for the Defense Department is very interesting. It seems that I found a fix for major space shield instability. People think it's a very big deal. And my personal research is going pretty well too."

"Okay, Hilgor, what's up?"

"Well … no, it's all good. It's just that …" he seemed really fascinated in the tile pattern. "I don't enjoy working as much as before," he said reluctantly, "in spite of the fact that I've never had a better setup."

"Can I guess?" asked Reish. "Nobody interrupts. Del is not here to interrupt."

"No, she is not," Hilgor nodded in agreement. "But maybe it has nothing to do with her. So, Reish, please don't start apologizing. You know she wouldn't have come with me in any case."

Reish figured that he wasn't going to continue with this topic. Avoiding an awkward pause, she turned towards the aisle and looked at the dog.

"How is your assimilation going, Riph?"

He instantly raised his head and tensed, all ears.

"He misses other dogs," said Hilgor gently. "On the plus side, he's discovered squirrels."

Riph gave a soft whine and darted towards the opening door.

Nick received a series of body checks even before he fully entered the room – the dog saluted his long-absent friend with overflowing exuberance. Nick bent and gave Riph a firm hug. Reish and Hilgor exchanged quick glances – Nick seemed perfectly fine. Only when he started walking across the room did they notice that there was something different about him. A certain smooth lightness was gone from his step, as if his body now obeyed gravity a little more than usual.

But his expression was as disarming as before, and his voice was as friendly as always, "I'm very glad to see you both," he said and sat down at the table across the aisle, turning to face them. "And I'm sorry that I disappeared without saying goodbye. But, honestly, when I was leaving for Earth3 I wasn't in great shape."

"Earth3?" asked Hilgor.

"No problem, Nick. You know we love you anyway," said Reish at the same time, and quickly added, "I hope everything is fine." It came out unintentionally flippant, so she desperately looked at Hilgor for support.

"We know that you need help." Hilgor hesitated for a moment, "But first ... how is Lita?"

Silently chastising herself for being a coward, Reish pretended to watch a cheery advertisement for some ancient oral medication on her tabletop.

"Lita is alive," said Nick in a perfectly normal tone, and they all looked at Riph who sprang up from the sphinx position at the door and trotted down the aisle, wagging his tail, acknowledging the sudden relief in the room. He settled on the floor between the three of them and put his head on his paws with a content sigh.

Nick suddenly winced at the especially wild colors of the video clip that flashed across his table, "Hilgor, you have strange taste, I must tell you."

Hilgor shrugged, "Del's influence, as she said," he said, nodding towards Reish.

"What do you need help with?" Reish's patience had finally ran out, "Nick, enough of this suspense."

"Listen, thank you both for responding to my call. I really need your help, but there's a lot I need to explain first. The least I can do is make it comfortable. There's a really cool place I rented on my last vacation, an antique chic, mid-21st-century beachfront cottage, and it happens to be available right now. How about dinner on a Pacific island?"

At the sound of Nick's last words Riph lifted his head and looked up at him with fresh interest.

"Sure," said Hilgor immediately, "how about you, Reish?"

"I mean, it's a bit far, but ... I owe you more, Nick, than a dinner on a tropical island."

"Reish, you owe Hilgor. I was just the pilot. But thanks. Shall we, then?"

The dog was already at the door, wagging his tail in great excitement. They went outside, and Hilgor almost whistled, seeing a flyer parked right next to the restaurant door. It must have cost Nick an arm and a leg – no civil vehicles were normally allowed on the pedestrian side of the holographic wall.

"Nick, you're very extravagant," whispered Reish with admiration. "Do you always rent one of these?"

"No, only when I want to impress people," replied Nick in a completely serious tone.

Indeed, passersby eyed the asymmetrically twisted lines of the luxurious vehicle with deep respect, slowing down to give it a proper look.

"Nice," Hilgor watched the shiny object indifferently as the shallow dent underneath the modest logo expanded in all directions, creating an entrance.

"Hilgor, don't be a bore," said Reish scornfully. "This is the latest model. It's insanely fast and comes with right of way over all other traffic. We'll be in the middle of the Pacific before we know it."

"She's right. Only government and emergency transports have higher priority," confirmed Nick, hospitably gesturing them in.

The cabin was small, but not claustrophobically so, thanks to the large semicircle window. Nick muttered something under his breath, and three identical armchairs unfolded from the floor and rotated to face each other. He sat in one of them, Reish and Hilgor sank into the other two, and the seats immediately changed shape, adjusting their support. A knot of abstract gargoyles lowered from the ceiling above their heads, and Riph gave the hanging monsters a warning growl. His people didn't seem to be worried about them, however, so he curled up in the middle, satisfied to be in the perfectly central position.

"Nick, I can't believe that you complained about my taste," said Hilgor, nodding toward the overhead fixture.

"It was the only available interior for this model. This is late 23 AC, I think. It seems to be in vogue now. Come on, Hilgor. Putting up with inconvenient authentic things is the price of luxury here. I thought you already figured that one out."

Nick sent destination coordinates to the traffic control center, and the flyer softly lifted off from the ground, passed through the holographic wall and joined the stream of traffic.

Reish instantly shut her eyes and quickly said, "Nick, can you please dim the window? I know that all these … projectiles aren't here to get us, but … just do me a favor."

"Sure. Kir, block the external cabin view."

The window filled with color, acquired a solid texture and seamlessly blended with the wall. The gargoyles untangled, stretching their necks, they lit up, permeating the cabin with a mix of light and shadows. Reish sighed with relief and sat back.

Hilgor shifted his position to improve the angle at which he was looking at Nick and almost jumped out of his chair when it responded with a subtle movement.

"Damn, I forgot. I hope this pseudo-live crap goes out of fashion soon. Can you turn it off?"

"Kir, freeze Hilgor's seat." Nick sat back and looked at his company with an amused smile. "So, is everyone comfortable now?" He apparently didn't feel any unease with the setting.

Nick's effortlessly relaxed pose reminded Hilgor of something, and it nagged at him for a moment until he realized what it was.

It was a memory from his trip to Africa, which he had requested almost as soon as he'd arrived on Earth.

Nothing in his previous life had prepared him for the austere beauty of the yellow prairies that stretched from horizon to horizon in front of his eyes. But he hadn't gone for this splendor; he had gone there to see one thing – a cheetah running in the wild. And when he saw the lanky silhouettes appearing from behind the low hills against the setting sun, he felt a stabbing pain in his heart, the same as he had on the day of his father's funeral. He spent an entire week there, watching the big cats hunt, play and rest, and waiting for his internal turmoil to finally subside.

And now Nick reminded him of a cheetah, reclining on a low tree branch, watching the savannah through its half-closed eyes, its muscles totally limp. But Hilgor saw that it took no time at all for the animal to turn into a deadly living missile when it spotted prey in the distance.

"My story will take some time, let's wait until we settle down to dinner," said Nick, ignoring Reish's disappointed look. "Tell me about yourselves. How have you been? Of course, it's hard to escape that Reish is a star now. I'm glad, Reish. I didn't have time to look up your releases, but I have complete trust in our highly sophisticated consumers."

"Thanks, Nick," she shrugged in a vaguely self-conscious gesture.

Nick smiled and turned to Hilgor, "And what about you? I don't know anything about your life since your arrival."

"There is not much to tell, Nick," replied Hilgor. "Not much is happening."

"Good summary, Hilgor. Nick, let me translate – his work is dragging, and he misses Del," said Reish with poorly hidden pity in her voice.

Hilgor raised his head with a sharp jerk. "It doesn't matter. I would never go back. It's just that I always had someone to fight with, something to be mad about. I feel a bit – lost now. Imagine an animal that was raised in an underground cage and then was suddenly released into the wild."

"It would be dangerous for the animal, wouldn't it?" Nick looked at him with a peculiar expression.

"Maybe. But it's worth it. I'll manage … but she is right, enough about us, really. Nick, what happened? You said that Lita is alive. I assume it's her you're trying to impress with this vehicle?"

"Not exactly trying to impress, no," a shadow passed over Nick's face.

Hilgor glanced up and saw that, of course, the gargoyles had changed their position. Damn the late 23rd century, he thought, unnerved.

"And I'm sorry that I didn't call before I left, Hilgor," Nick paused mid-sentence and focused on something in space for a second, "it looks like we're almost there. Kir, start dinner for three and a steak for Riph."

"Medium rare, no spices," quickly added Hilgor.

This part of the dialogue penetrated Riph's sleep. He stirred and sat up.

"Sorry, pal, it's cruel, but it's going to be artificial," Nick looked in the dog's eyes. "Imagine that, after Y-3. But it's still better than the garbage you ate there most of the time." Riph tilted his head – these words didn't match his vocabulary. "Do you wonder why artificial?

Well, Earth is humane. We care about being humane, right, Riph?"
Nick bent down and patted the black head, then straightened up in
his chair, but didn't recline all the way. "Lita's treatment was a complete success, but she is scheduled to leave Earth and return to her
home planet in the next several hours. She has been kept unconscious so that she wouldn't ever know that she had been here. It's
very humane, don't you agree?" he addressed Riph again, but the
dog didn't wag his tail, picking up on the sudden change on the people's faces.

Hilgor looked away, but Reish, on the contrary, stared at Nick
with animated interest. One would assume that she didn't understand what he had just said, except that she continued to hold this
expression a little too long.

The cabin was very quiet.

"Nick, she will be killed there. Why are they doing this?" Reish
started at the sound of Hilgor's voice and let go of her frozen smile.

"There's not much to explain if you think about it," Nick was
speaking in a flat, almost indifferent tone. "Realistically, nothing else
could have happened. I don't know what I was hoping for. She doesn't
have any right to stay on Earth, and they won't change their policy
based on her circumstances. It was very generous of them to even let
her go through the treatment here. They weren't supposed to share
any information with me, but they did. Earth's privacy laws don't
apply to her, and I paid her medical bill, maybe that was why. Or,
who knows, maybe they felt guilty," Nick's voice was perfectly level,
except for a sudden hoarse note in the middle of the last sentence.

"And …what about you?" asked Reish quietly.

"What about me?" Nick looked at her as if the question was hard
to comprehend. "Oh, not much, really. They revoked my headhunter

license for transporting an illegal and going to Y-3 without permission. Nobody seemed to care what I did on Beta Blue."

Reish abruptly got up and stepped forward. Riph jumped up, hastily cleared the way, and she kneeled at Nick's feet, cradling his hands in hers.

"Nick, I can't believe … I see why you asked us to come, nobody else knows about what happened … there. I'll stay with you as long as you want me, hours, days, whatever, while you are going through it. You can't take it alone. Nobody could. I see now, this was the help that you needed, wasn't it?"

"Yes, it was. Thank you. This means a lot to me," said Nick calmly.

Too calmly, thought Hilgor, silently watching the scene. He couldn't form a proper reaction; something was off.

They felt a mild shift in gravity.

"We've arrived," explained Nick. "I hope you're getting hungry. Kir, open the door."

They stepped out of the shuttle onto a sandy shore a little ways from a lonely waterfront house. It was sharply outlined by the light of the almost full moon, and Hilgor instantly admired the perfect balance of the casual arrangement of its blocky modules. But in full disclosure, he was strongly partial to any buildings that originated before the 22nd century. It was the last period before biotechnology exploded into the mainstream, so he could rest assured there wouldn't be any tricks incompatible with his unwired body.

He glanced around and the dark house in the pale moonlight made him think about a ghost ship, which, according to Y-3 lore, appeared on the lakes during a full moon and was said to be a bad omen. He shook off this silly association, and hurriedly caught up with the rest of the group. Riph stopped at the main doors, but Nick passed him and led them towards the wide staircase that hugged the house and ascended to the rooftop deck. "The weather can't be better. Let's have dinner on the patio. The view is nice there," he said as he began to walk up. "Follow me."

The dining area on the rooftop turned out to be surprisingly nice and cozy in spite of the relentless sound of surf underneath, and the unobstructed view was indeed breathtaking. A small school of floating lanterns cast a warm light on a large wooden table and a dozen chairs in the center. Two simple cupboards were placed on opposite sides of the table, creating the perception of a somewhat enclosed space while not blocking the panoramic view of the ocean and the dark hills of the island. The waist-high railings around the deck enforced the feeling of safety.

Nick went straight to one of the cabinets and started taking out dinnerware with the confidence of someone well acquainted with the house.

"There's a wine collection on the upper shelves, very decent as I remember. Please have a look and choose a bottle. Everything is semi-manual in this house, so I'll have to add a human element to the last touches of my dinner preparations. I'll be right back." Nick finished arranging the utensils, and went downstairs, giving his guests a reserved smile on his way out.

Reish walked to the railing and silently watched the waves at the base of the house; Hilgor pulled a chair closer to the table and sat down, staring at the wood patterns and tapping his fingers on the edge.

"I don't know how to behave," Reish said sharply. "I am trying not to think about what he must be feeling. Just imagine what's going to happen to her on Beta Blue." She shrugged nervously, "I think I do need a drink – you?" She walked to the cabinet that Nick had pointed out, but before Hilgor had a chance to answer, a holographic image lit up in the air above the table. It was Nick, in the kitchen downstairs, loading dishes onto some kind of dumb waiter.

"I'm sending the food up. See, Hilgor, this place has an intercom system, very handy in your low-tech case. I thought you would appreciate it. Reish, if you're looking for wine, check out that bulky bottle in the corner. I'll be up soon."

The screen disappeared, but the cabinet across the table from Reish chimed. Glad to have something to do, Hilgor walked over and opened the doors that immediately let out a rich mix of delicious smells.

"An external intercom; how nice. These were everywhere before the wearable implants took over," he said wistfully, picking up a tray with a large covered dish. "You know, Reish, I once asked a local girl to pause live streams to her retina during our date, and she looked at me as if I'd asked her to jump off a cliff," he shook his head in mocking disbelief and continued to shuttle smaller porcelain bowls to the table. Riph sat in the middle of the route, following every tray trajectory with the highest degree of concern and making such a nuisance of himself that it Hilgor finally lost his patience, "Riph, shoo! Your steak is still too hot. And don't hope, I'm not going to drop anything."

"Did she immediately use some excuse to leave your place?" Reish was still studying the intimidating wine collection. "Hilgor, you have to understand – you were being extremely bizarre by even asking that. Those generations here grew up with implants, and they would never turn off their feeds. But, to be fair, they do use conjoint mode to share each other's inputs, temporarily, at least. It makes sex much more intimate … in most cases. But then again, you aren't wired." She finally decided on a bottle, and took it off the shelf, "Hilgor, it's practically barbaric for these folks, even presuming your exotic outlier status and such. You should at least use contact screens."

"They irritate my eyes," Hilgor placed the last dish on the table and sat down.

Reish poured wine into three glasses and sat down too.

They looked at each other in silence, and Hilgor guessed that they were both thinking about Nick.

"He's behaving so calmly. He must be in shock," Reish said finally.

Hilgor didn't reply. He wasn't so sure.

Reish was about to add something, but they heard Nick's steps on the staircase, and she cut herself off. In a moment, Nick appeared on the deck, and from their first look at his face they realized that something was very different now, and not in a good way.

Ignoring their presence, Nick walked straight to the wine cabinet. He lightly tapped its side panel, which opened revealing a smooth glossy pad. Nick touched it, and the outlines of a holographic sphere again lit up over the table. Nick turned in its direction, his face pale and angular in the cold electric glow, and said in an even voice, "State Security Emergency Services."

The sphere blinked and displayed the State Security emblem. "Please state your emergency. It'll be communicated through the corresponding channels immediately," the voice from the invisible speakers seemed to be coming from all patio corners at once.

"I'm holding two hostages at this location, both former M-847 citizens. My request is an urgent audience with the president."

Reish's face went completely white even in the yellowish light of a slowly passing lantern, but Hilgor just slightly screwed up his eyes, perversely pleased that his nagging unease wasn't a paranoid overreaction after all. "Just so we're clear," continued Nick, "this island has a first-generation privacy protection system – both a detection screen and a missile launcher with remote-guided targeting." Nick reached into his pocket and pulled out a small black rectangle. He looked at its surface screen and nodded in satisfaction, "I turned the system on, and it's perfectly functional. It's currently in default mode to intercept perimeter-penetrating gadgets. The missiles are designed only for small drones – they wouldn't come close to stopping your combat vehicles, should you decide to storm the island. But I'm changing the settings," Nick pointed the object in his hand first at Hilgor and then at Reish, who shrieked, covering her mouth with her hands. "I've just imprinted the hostages as the primary targets – they will be hit instantly if the island screen is breached." His eyes were very hard and very cold, "I expect a response to this frequency within one hour. After that I will manually trigger the missiles to hit the hostages." Nick touched the intercom pad, and the screen disappeared.

"Now, Kir, power off," he said quickly and stood still for a moment, apparently waiting for the full shutdown message. Then his face assumed its usual expression, "I am sorry," he said in his familiar voice, "this circus had to look authentic."

Reish and Hilgor just stared at him without saying a word.

"Nick, damn," Reish finally blinked and shook her head, "it did feel … authentic."

Nick lowered his eyes as if resting them for a second. When he raised them again, there was a calm resolve in his face, "I told you that the ship with Lita would leave Earth in several hours. I can't let that happen."

The cheetah wasn't asleep after all, simply waiting. Be careful, thought Hilgor, big cats could be rather deadly when cornered. But Nick's impeccable acting in front of the State Security screen didn't show any sign of instability. Or, maybe, it wasn't an act at all, and the real performance was played for the two of them after the intercom was turned off.

"Nick, what is a first-generation privacy protector screen?" Hilgor asked with casual curiosity, noting that Nick had slid the launcher control back in his pocket.

"It's an old perimeter guard system. Rich and celebrity vacationers used it before media drones became fully illegal. This place is at the very high end of luxury, and the leasing company has gone to great lengths not to ruin its 21st-century authenticity. They even included a demo of how this defense system works in their advertisement. I had it shoot down a toy drone once when I was bored. The perimeter screen was built to pass through any organic matter – birds, fish … but any artificial thing of any kind, say, a rescue craft, will trigger the alarm."

"What happens then, Nick?" Reish's voice was very quiet, almost a whisper.

"Nothing Reish. I faked the whole thing," Nick went to the table and sat down. "Let's eat."

Nobody moved except for Riph, who put his muzzle on Nick's lap and flared his nostrils.

"Your food, Riph," Nick took the lid off one of the bowls, transferred the steak to a plate and put it on the floor. The rest of the dish covers, however, remained in place – Hilgor and Reish didn't even look at the table, their eyes still glued to Nick's face.

"Come on, guys. Seriously, relax. They haven't had a hostage crisis for centuries. They won't know how to react, and they will be cautious. I, on the other hand, have been studying the psychology of the subject in painful detail. I promise, they will negotiate," he said with a dry smile. "No need to let your food get cold. It's very good," he made an almost undetectable pause, "I swear."

"Of course, you do" said Hilgor with semi-smile.

"You actually ruined my appetite," Reish tried to respond in the same lighthearted tone, but her voice cracked.

"Reish, I won't get you killed, you know that," Nick sounded relaxed and reassuring. Professionally reassuring, thought Hilgor.

"Sorry, but I don't believe you – you don't have the most convincing record, Nick," judging by the shrill note in her voice, Reish gave up on her last attempt to remain composed. "You are dangerous. You told us that you killed people to save Lita."

"I didn't kill friends," said Nick plainly.

"Am I a good enough friend? Nick, I don't want any part of it. I'm the wrong person. I was supposed to die. You don't know how it felt. I can't take any of it again, I want off this island," she hurriedly got up, pushing back her chair, her eyes now filled with blind panic.

She ran toward the staircase, but by the time she reached it Nick was already there, blocking her way.

She backed off, trying to get around him. "Let me pass."

"Reish, please, don't leave," Nick's voice was very soft. "I don't know how it feels to be dying, but I know how it feels when someone you love is about to die. Do you want to compare notes?"

The sound of the surf became very distinct in the total silence on the deck.

Nick stepped aside. "If you have to go, the flyer access is set to public."

She bolted down the stairs, and Hilgor relaxed. This was no cheetah – either that, or Nick was playing a game. For example, he couldn't afford to antagonize them because he needed their cooperation for something else.

"Nick, you are a Dark Triad too, aren't you?" asked Hilgor very quietly.

Nick gave him a quick look and nodded.

"I have suspected this for a while," said Hilgor. "You won't kill us. I know about it all too well. We, dirty outliers, don't have a conscience, at least not the one as defined by society, but we have a personal code of honor. Killing me and Reisch violates yours. You don't kill friends."

"Right," said Nick. "Please, try to stop her. But don't tell her I'm a Dark Triad. If she isn't one of us herself which I suspect, then she won't understand what you said and will freak out even worse."

Hilgor got up, walked to the staircase and looked down, "Reish, wait."

She stopped at the bottom of the last flight and stood frozen, not even moving her head.

Hilgor continued in a soft pondering tone, "Reish, let's see. If we go, Nick will be locked up on kidnapping charges for the rest of his life because he tried to save Lita from torture and definite death. Just imagine that. By the way, Nick," he glanced back at the deck, "I appreciate the 'true' freedom of choice you are offering," Hilgor shook his head in reprehension. "Reish, I don't think he's going to kill us. And I don't think they're going to storm the island. It is just my personal opinion, of course. But maybe we should wait it out here for a bit."

She didn't move for another moment, then turned and came back up the stairs with an air of a ruffled bird. Hilgor and Nick returned to their chairs, but they didn't speak until after Reish appeared from the stairwell and sat at the far end of the table.

"Reish, I am sorry. I didn't want to scare you," Nick said guiltily. "But I couldn't ask for your permission. Since Kir was bugged, anything I …"

"What?" asked Reish quickly. "What do you mean bugged? It's theoretically impossible. Nobody can access an implant without the user's authorization. My chip's inputs are always on," her tone shifted downward, and she bit her lip.

"Reish, everything is possible given sufficient time and resources," Hilgor made an earnest effort not to sound condescending. "I never believed in the purity of their privacy, remember?" He glanced at his wristband with mild distaste, "But you always called me too negative."

Reish picked up her glass and took a couple of fast gulps.

"In any case, Nick," continued Hilgor, "I assume you want the president to cancel Lita's deportation. Why didn't you state your demand in your message?"

"And what would I have done if they happened to refuse?" Nick asked simply. "Shoot one of you to make my point, as Reish insinuated?"

Reish coughed, having choked on her wine, but Nick just went on. "As it stands, I didn't ask for very much. You both have extremely high profiles. The news that you're being held at gunpoint will create a major uproar, and the government doesn't want a scandal like this. It'll look so uncouth these days. I assure you that they'll resolve the situation without making it public."

"Ok, so let's assume you'll be getting a call from the president. What makes you think she won't refuse when you plead with her in person? You aren't just relying on charisma here, are you?" Hilgor continued in a somewhat detached tone as if he was sorting out pieces of an intriguing, but very abstract puzzle.

Nick's smile was rather dark, and it obviously wasn't addressed toward Hilgor, "No, I don't expect to plead. I have some information that the government wouldn't want leaked at any cost."

Reish reached across the table and refilled her wine glass, but then she simply sat back holding it in her hand as if she had immediately forgotten about its existence.

"So … blackmail," there was an odd satisfaction in Hilgor's tone. "How exciting. But, Nick, I'm confused," which meant that there was a major flaw in Nick's logic – Hilgor wasn't easily confused. "Why didn't you mention it to them before? You're short on time, and if you just hinted on the gravity of your information, that would've sped things up right away, no? You could have spared us your very impressive acting too."

"I can't afford anything to go through the 'appropriate channels,'" said Nick. "The president could lose any incentive to bargain with me if she thinks that the cat might have gotten out of the bag along the way."

"Wait," Reish interrupted with a wave, "security services are contacting me with a request to share my audio and video inputs."

"Of course, they are. They want to help you," said Nick with a caustic grin. "They just need your consent. And if they don't get it, then they'll take over your implant without your permission – because the criticality of the situation warrants it, obviously. It'll take them at least an hour, but it would be better if you switch off your implants right away, both of you. You can say later that I threatened to shoot you if you didn't cooperate."

Reish twitched her shoulders and took several swallows from the glass she was still holding.

A brief smile passed over Hilgor's lips, and he squeezed his wristband. It blinked twice and turned solid gray. "We're glad to help a friend. Right, Reish? And as a bonus we'll never find out just how serious Nick was about shooting us, and it's good for everyone."

"Kella, turn off power," said Reish and finished her wine in one swig. She was about to put the glass back, but her hand jerked and almost missed the edge of the table as the loud toll of a ship's bell suddenly went off.

Nick got up and quickly crossed the deck towards the intercom.

"It's not the president … most likely it's just her staff trying to test the waters. She wouldn't respond blind, without some reconnaissance." He touched the intercom controls, and a new image appeared – now it was a uniformed woman at the desk with the State Security emblem on the wall behind her.

"Nick, we got your message," she was clearly instructed to behave as friendly as possible, and she was positively beaming. "Please stay calm, there's no need to harm the hostages. The president will contact you shortly."

"Good," Nick nodded, "but I have another request. I would like the Defense Minister to be present at our meeting."

The woman obviously forgot that she was supposed to radiate a sunny disposition because her face lost any shade of its original softness. "Let me ask," she said quickly. "I'll be back with you in a moment."

Indeed, she reappeared almost instantly.

"They'll let us know as soon as possible. Can you confirm that you'll release the hostages once the president is on the line?"

"Yes, I'll send them back in my flyer once the president and I have had a conversation."

"Great, I think we have an understanding. Can you focus the camera on the hostages, please? I would like to say a word of encouragement – just psychological support, nothing informational."

"Go ahead," Nick lightly moved his fingers across the control pad.

The woman apparently remembered her duty and was beaming once again, "Are you alright?" she asked in an upbeat tone.

Both Reish and Hilgor nodded, their faces carefully neutral.

"Please, don't worry – this unpleasant situation will be over soon. Nick's request is being addressed." She appeared distracted for a moment, then looked past them and quickly added, "Nick, the Minister of Defense will be there. Are we good?"

"Most definitely," said Nick refocusing the camera on himself.

"Stay tuned," she gave him a nicely crafted smile, and the hologram disappeared.

For a moment all three of them kept staring at the empty space over the table, and then Hilgor turned to Nick.

"Your information has something to do with the Defense program, does it?"

Nick winced, and slowly walked to his chair.

"Probably not. I … don't know. What I do know is that the Defense Minister can keep secrets – his own at the very least. I'm here for some horse-trading, Hilgor. I need a witness, but I don't need a loose cannon in this meeting."

"What do you mean … you don't know?" Hilgor abruptly stood, feeling that the pieces of the puzzle, which had just started to fit together, had changed shape right in front of his eyes. "You told us you had some critical information."

The intercom bell went off again, invoking the air of imminent danger.

Nick waved Hilgor back to his seat, "I'm sorry, guys, I don't have time to explain. But to make this work, Hilgor, I will need your bracelet, and I need you to pass me all your controls. You can say later that I forced you to give it to me."

"Sure, no problem," said Hilgor, "Whatever you need," he squeezed the bracelet and entered something on the small screen that popped up above his wrist. The bell kept ringing, messing with his concentration, and with mild irritation Hilgor thought that the house outfitters overdesigned this marine feature. He finished typing, took the band off and passed it to Nick.

"Great," said Nick, "thank you." He put Hilgor's device on the table and started rapidly sliding his fingers above its virtual interface ignoring the continuing tolling.

"Okay," he said, finally turning the screen off, "I am done. Don't forget that you are my hostages." He got up and put the bracelet in his pocket.

"Don't you worry, Nick," said Hilgor lightly, "we won't."

Nick walked to the intercom and accepted the call.

This time two holographic screens appeared over the table, close to each other, and Hilgor momentarily wondered about the president's location time zone. Even if she was woken up in the middle of the night it was impossible to tell – she seemed perfectly fresh and alert. On the other screen the Defense Minister sat back in his chair, watching the scene unblinkingly, his fingers rigidly steepled in front of his chest.

"We are here to talk to you," judging by the angle of her face, the president was viewing Nick's image from her version of a similar device. She paused, smiled and added in a placating voice, "Can you please let the hostages go now?"

"In due course," replied Nick calmly, "but not until after you hear what I have to say. Otherwise I don't see what's going to stop you from disconnecting the line and sending an assault unit to arrest me." He paused and said with a regretful shrug, "Sorry, but there is an understandable lack of trust between us at the moment." The president and the minister exchanged glances, and Nick added reassuringly, "Don't worry, the hostages are very comfortable. They have plenty of food and drink, and a breathtaking view of the ocean at dawn – pleasant, if a bit drawn-out picnic al fresco … and unobstructed exposure to the missiles. Now, it's better if they don't hear the rest of our conversation. I'll reconnect from a room downstairs."

Nick turned off the holographic screens. Their glow disappeared, and the sharp shadows on his face melted away again. He opened the main doors of the cabinet, took out a bottle and briefly held it against the light of the closest lantern.

"Here's another good one," he said, giving the wine an approving nod. "The sun isn't up yet so it isn't drinking in the morning." Neither of them smiled, "Sorry, not funny, I know. This whole thing will be over soon, I promise."

He put the bottle on the table, walked to the door and in a moment disappeared down the stairs. The door smoothly shut behind his back.

Nick touched the handle, locking it from the inside. The click was barely audible, but Nick still winced, imagining that it could be heard on the deck.

He quickly covered the two flights down to the study, glanced around and noted that nothing had changed since his last visit several months ago. He sat down in the same lonely chair in the center of the empty floor and activated the connection. The light changed, and a freakishly realistic hologram of a meeting table appeared in the room. Life-sized renderings of the president and the minister appeared. They were seated next to each other in an extremely convincing imitation of a real face-to-face interaction. The whole thing was laughably outdated, but Nick didn't especially mind mid-21st-century flourishes.

He leaned over the virtual table and looked straight into the president's eyes.

"I have a physical copy of a recording regarding Elisabeth's secret mission on Earth3," he said quietly.

That produced a reaction.

"What recording?" the president blinked twice.

"What mission?" the minister skipped a blink staring at the president.

"It's not in my implant," said Nick. "Your Cyber Delta people did a good job on the border. No need to fire anyone."

It seemed that neither the president nor the minister wanted to break the silence right away, and Nick waited too, letting it ripen.

"I know that you broke into Kir," he said finally with a thin smile. "I'm a bit ahead of you."

"On Earth3?" the Defense Minister abruptly clasped his fingers and raised his eyebrows. The expression of cold disdain evaporated from his face, replaced by extreme interest. "Nick, when you asked for my presence, I thought you would blackmail me with our unfortunate mishap on M-237. I was, frankly, disappointed, considering that JJ kept his side of the deal."

Nick threw a quick glance in the president's direction.

"Of course, Madam President knows about our sabotage program on the colonies," said the minister. "All upper echelon knows – but a mission *inside* the Commonwealth? Where is this recording? Let's have a look."

"In a minute. I will need to turn on my chip to download and play it. But since her people already hacked my implant, let's agree on a couple of things first … for my safety." Nick pulled the launcher control from his pocket, and held it up so it was fully visible, "First of all, no games with my optic and audio inputs. Any attempts, and I'll press this button to release the missiles. And another thing to keep our conversation going," he looked directly into the president's eyes once again. "Tell your cyber team to get the fuck out of my implant. Tell them to stand down. You included."

"No."

"Wait, Caroline … we will lose the hostages," the minister glanced at her with sincere surprise.

"I don't care about the hostages. I can't give up the control of his chip."

Well, thought Nick, looking into her beautiful face, distorted with rage, she just confirmed that she was Dark Triad too. Of course, outliers couldn't ever have such perfect bone structure, and such glowing skin, and such impossibly clear blue eyes. So she was a rare local case like him. It wasn't surprising – her profession was also exotic, just like his as he had told Lita.

"She can't give up control because she can't afford for you to see the recording. She wants to delete it the moment I download it on the chip," Nick turned to the minister. "I don't think that you want her to get away with this, do you? But we can compromise. If nobody but you has access to Kir, we can talk."

"No worries, Nick, we want to see the file, and your requests are reasonable under the current circumstances," said the minister quickly, deftly avoiding eye contact with the president. "Madam, if you want this … incident to stay between us please do as he asks. Pass me his implant control. Don't worry, I will disable the transmission functions, so everything here stays between three of us."

The president slowly nodded, staring at Nick's face with a very strange expression, and the darkening glow in her eyes was rather scary in comparison with her usual calm confidence. She typed something in the air.

"I had just called off the team," she said flatly. "It will be the three of us on this line, and Viggo is the only one controlling your chip."

"Yes, I can confirm that," said the minister checking his screens. "Now let's go online and see the file."

"Let's," said Nick, turning off the intercom connection.

The holographic images disappeared, and he was completely alone in the empty room.

"Kir, wrap the wall," he whispered, and it folded, revealing the expanse of the ocean.

Dawn was definitely approaching, but the horizon was still gray, not having gained the pink hue of real morning yet. Nick looked into the pearl sky, and a cold shiver went down his spine; it was the end-game, and his main piece could very well be missing from the board. A gentle breeze ruffled his hair as if trying to calm him down.

"It has to be there," he whispered, squeezing the armrests, "Kir, on."

"Good morning, Nick!" said Kir.

Johan's red dot indicating the security break was back at its place in the corner, and the president and the minister's windows were pinned to the center of his vision field.

"Let me load the file. It'll take a moment," Nick forced his voice to sound as confident as possible. He closed his eyes and collapsed all open screens to the corner of his default bluish-gray backdrop.

Now ...

To initiate the download, Johan had told him to focus on his favorite color.

What was his favorite color, Nick asked himself. He never thought about it in such terms. He chose a clean gunmetal back-ground because the color was practical, and made his eyes less tired.

Maybe it was black? He always respected its simplicity, its dignity. He imagined black. Nothing happened.

What if he didn't have a favorite color, he thought in sudden panic. To him it sounded like a stupid question in the first place. But Johan wasn't stupid. It probably wasn't the color that mattered; it was how he felt when he thought about it ... but what if he felt nothing at all about colors?

How many people were waiting for him at this moment, he wondered. These two were waiting, and Reish and Hilgor, and, without a doubt, an armed swat team – and Lita.

Stop it, he ordered himself, use the usual fear-fighting technique. Ask yourself the standard question: What would be the absolute worst thing that could happen even if everything went completely wrong? It was clear – Lita would violently die in the very near future. And most likely they would kill him too in order to cover up this mess. He vividly imagined how it would happen, and felt nauseous. Don't fight your fear, shouted the rational part of his mind before collapsing, just roll with it as with that rip current on Beta Blue, as with Eve's amplifier.

Fine, let's agree I will die today, of all days, he said to himself, and focused on it. He had always imagined that after death he would simply float in some empty space forever. What color would he want that space to be? Not black.

He would like it to be orange. Like the morning sun.

"A file is being downloaded to my system from an unknown source," said Kir, "in universally compatible format."

Nick opened his eyes. The sun wasn't out yet, but the pink band on the horizon announced its close arrival.

"Thank you," whispered Nick, surprised at himself for talking to an inanimate object, but then he smiled realizing that it was Johan he was extending his gratitude to.

"Download completed," said Kir. "Warning: the source is irrevocably corrupted."

Nick reopened the minister and president's communication windows.

"Where did this file come from?" asked the president sharply. "We scanned him for any information holding devices. His ship too," she said to the minister. "He had nothing that could have stored this recording."

"That is rather irrelevant, isn't it?" asked Nick, and the minister tilted his head slightly, as a possible indication of a silent agreement. "So let's focus on practical matters. The file source has been destroyed. So no hidden backdoors; all the cards are on the table, as they say. Let's not waste time," said Nick, "Kir, play the recording."

"Viggo, destroy that file. It's an order," the president sounded suspiciously discordant.

"Caroline, don't be ridiculous. I want to see it," now there was an open defiance in the minister's tone. "Kir, play it on full screen."

The president and the minister disappeared, and Nick was inside a long hallway.

The footage was jerky, jumping up and down in rhythm with a fast walk. It was very quiet, the silence broken only by the almost inaudible sound of hurried steps. The illusion was so convincing that only the fresh air on his face and the smell of the ocean reminded Nick that he was still in the middle of the Pacific.

The hallway made a sharp turn and came to a dead end in the form of a massive closed door with a smooth metallic surface. The perception of movement stopped, and Elisabeth's face stared at him from the reflection.

The door opened, letting Elisabeth in.

Three men and a woman were sitting at a table in a small windowless room, looking extremely gloomy and exhausted. They immediately turned in Elisabeth's direction, and Hilgor thought that in spite of their mismatched outfits, all four of them had the same non-civilian air as JJ or the Defense Minister himself, for that matter.

"We got your message. So you added a virus with an unsanctioned gene sequence to the last commercial DNA enhancement batch. Why on Earth did you do it?" said the man in the corner, not bothering with any sort of greeting.

"You have to listen to me. Everyone will gain from it," Elisabeth's voice had a characteristic timbre in it, always present in an implant's recording of its owner. "Did you see this outlier's score? It's off the charts. Look."

The number that popped up on the screen reminded Nick of his failed award, and the expressions of the people at the table changed.

"It's from this Remir's assessment file. His raw score exceeds the maximum across all our donors by more than twice," she paused for emphasis. "We couldn't just throw this material away."

"Wait," the woman in the tight black bodysuit recovered first. "What material? The outlier is dead. The headhunter lost him on M-237."

"I figured out how to get his DNA after I watched that moron's field report. Let me play you the last part ..."

Nick clenched his teeth, guessing at what he was about to see.

And there it was – an alpine meadow, lush grass, peppered with small bright flowers, which Nick hadn't even noticed before, and two still bodies on the ground. They grew closer in uneven, jumping intervals, then the movement stopped, and the sound of heavy breathing ceased for a moment as the close-up of Remir's lifeless face filled the screen. The camera stayed on it for a moment, and then there was a sequence of images as the body was dragged aside, freeing the second, smaller body underneath.

"And ... is she ...?" Nick didn't recognize the crackling sound of his own voice.

He knew that closing his eyes wouldn't help, so he just helplessly watched the blood gushing in spurts from Lita's wound, his hands frantically tearing the fabric of Remir's blood-soaked jacket and tying a strip of it around her arm. There was the sound of an explosion. And then the perspective changed, revealing figures in gray uniforms at the edge of the meadow. "Kir, prepare engines for immediate takeoff," Nick heard his voice, and then the recording stopped.

"I got the outlier's DNA from the blood on that woman's bandage," Elisabeth tried to keep her voice matter of fact, not entirely succeeding. "I took a physical sample from her hospital vault."

The silence in the room lasted for several seconds before anyone spoke.

"I don't even know where to start," the oldest person in the group stood up and crossed his arms. "How can you prove the correlation between the test subject and your ... genetic find?"

"Well, look at this," Elisabeth clearly wasn't put off by his derisive tone. She displayed a still from Nick's first encounter with Remir right after the neuro-analgesic transmission was administered, so Remir's features were smooth, not crumbled by fear or anger, or depression.

"Now, here is the DNA face reconstruction."

Another image appeared next to the first one. The face of the person on the second screen was undoubtedly the same, only lacking the prominent scar in the corner of the mouth.

"Elisabeth, who are you kidding?" the man's face twitched in annoyance. "Unless we stop the shipment, a significant number of fetuses across the Commonwealth will be modified with the specious DNA segment. We retest people on Earth to ensure that the DNA we use came from the assessment taker and not some other source! Why am I even saying this?" the man sighed heavily. "We don't want any possibility of useless garbage in our children's genes."

"In other children's genes," quietly corrected a man from the far corner. "I'm sure you opted out of any genetic enhancements for your own kids. Get off your high horse."

"Even if I did, enhancements are completely voluntary procedures," the standing man's face turned red, and he stepped towards the table.

"Stop it! This is all besides the point. The question is: What are we going to do right now?" the woman in the black suit sharply cut them off. "Can you imagine what the president will say when she finds out that we implanted an unconfirmed gene segment into the population? It'll undermine her whole program! I am not planning to cover this up. But hiding wasn't Elisabeth's intention in any case." She looked acridly in Elisabeth's direction, "She wants attention, don't you, Elisabeth?"

"Once the president sees all of the facts she will appreciate it. She'll care about the results, not your protocols."

Bravo, thought Nick, go, the Dark Triad woman, we all had been there.

"Come on, it's so simple," continued Elisabeth, "this sample is simply outstanding. And the downside … fine, even if there's a mistake – and I'm sure nobody here believes that – well, what's the harm if a part of the population gets a useless genetic adjustment?"

The elder man shook his head in silent astonishment.

"Oh come on, don't get ethical on me. If ethics is your concern you shouldn't be a part of this project to begin with," Elisabeth's voice acquired a forceful note. "We all know that the transplants can't boost our progress fast enough, and it will only be a matter of time before our defense systems are completely obsolete. This project is the only hope for our civilization's survival."

"Please, Elisabeth. We all know you're fighting for the president's First Counselor position. You set us up," the man who had been silent so far didn't hide the disgust from his voice. "You should have had your career ambitions in check."

"Enough of this," the woman at the table raised her voice again, "we need to make a fast decision. In my opinion, it's too late to do a shipment recall without attracting significant attention; nothing like that has happened in commercial genetic engineering in centuries. There will doubtless be questions. It could blow up the whole program, and we will all go down, including the president. Thank Elisabeth here for the excitement."

There was a heavy silence, and then the gray-haired man, who was now leaning on the wall, shrugged, "It's too dangerous to back out. Approve the shipment. Elisabeth, submit a report with a detailed explanation. We'll review it before sending it to the president." The man got up and moved towards the door, "See you all later. Now I am going to express my unedited emotional response to this cluster fuck in a private setting."

The recording stopped, and the president and the minister's windows reappeared on the backdrop of Nick's natural vision. The view was so flawlessly pretty that it could have been mistaken for an artificial wall screen – a cloudless sky and pristine ocean, very calm at that early hour. She was holding an empty glass in her hand, and a mild spasm went down her throat as if her last gulp was accidentally too big.

"What was that about?" For a moment, Nick thought that the minister was addressing him, but the man continued. "Ma'am?" There was much more in his voice than simple surprise.

"Nonsense, it was staged," she put her glass on the table with a clank.

"I am sorry, but it didn't look like that. I'll have to order an investigation, Caroline."

"No need," she winced, "Viggo, I sponsor a government program that secretly collects genetic samples from every verified outlier and slips them into our population with the standard DNA enhancement packages. In practical terms, a nano-virus inserts DNA segments responsible for the Dark Triad traits from donor material."

"But why? You know that any brain-related genetic engineering is banned. And we already have a solution to fix the problem. What your Elisabeth was saying is nonsense – we have time for restoring the pre-cleansing environment by bringing outliers from Mirror Worlds. The program is working."

The president made a grimace. She wasn't an elected president for nothing, thought Nick – she seemed to completely regroup from her initial shock.

"Listen, Viggo, let's be frank. Everyone knows what people secretly think about the Mirror World outliers. They are ugly barbarians from the backward worlds. Look at them …"

A still picture of Johan with his screwed facial proportions, porous unhealthy skin and stooping posture flashed on her window.

"We want this on Earth, Viggo? After centuries of perfecting our genes to look like we do. To bring this genetic trash to Earth when we can just replace the small part that we are missing? We can have the best of both worlds."

"She knows what she is talking about," said Nick, "she is a natural example."

"So are you," she said not looking at him, "and there is everything wrong with you in the way we need. But your looks are on par."

The minister was silently moving his eyes from the president to Nick with a flabbergasted expression.

"But, Caroline, my children …"

"The virus is applied to randomly chosen batches. I am sorry, in case your children …" she shrugged her shoulders. "That was the problem in the first place. Remember how this whole mess started – nobody wanted shadows in *their* children's genes. But I thought that it was still better than invading the Commonwealth with dirty, sickly immigrants, don't you agree?" she gave him a long look before continuing. "Getting back to the practical side of our situation – you and I will discuss the terms under which this information stays between us. But let's deal with the headhunter first."

"What do you mean … deal?" the minister still seemed to be in a state of lasting shock.

"He can't leave the island alive, obviously," there wasn't any hesitation in her tone. She looked into the air in front of her and lifted her hand. "I'll dispatch a swat team right away. We'll have to accept a failed hostage rescue operation, Viggo. I'll take the heat."

"Stop," Nick didn't shout, but his voice had enough weight in it that she froze and looked at him.

"I am afraid that you can't afford it. In fact, our power balance is rather different than you think." Nick pulled out Hilgor's wristband from his pocket, "See this thing? This is an external chip – one of the hostages, the male, has issues with our biotechnology. It works just like a standard implant, only I control it now," he tapped the bracelet, turning on its interface, and moved his fingers across the screen. "Let me play something for you."

"... I sponsor a government program that secretly collects genetic samples from every verified outlier and slips them into our population with the standard DNA enhancement packages. In practical terms, a nano-virus gets inserted DNA segments responsible for the Dark Triad traits from donor material." Nick touched the virtual surface again, and the slightly muted but otherwise perfectly clear sound of the president's voice, coming from the chip, cut off.

"What?" she whispered in real time, blood instantly rushing from her face.

"So ... no hidden backdoors?" asked the minister, and Nick could swear that there was a note of an inappropriate amusement in his voice.

"I gave this chip full access to Kir's feeds, including all online conversations – off-label use in conjoined mode, but it came in very handy. You can go ahead and delete the original file from Kir's memory. I don't need it anymore. You know, Caroline, the Dark Triad just simply can't be trusted," Nick said.

She blinked but didn't argue.

"Now," he rotated the bracelet in his hand, "we have already established that you don't care about the hostages. So I'll transmit this recording through all channels the very moment I receive an alert that the perimeter screen has been penetrated. Your missiles are fast, but I am holding my finger on a button, just in case you are thinking about blowing up the whole house. So hold off on that."

The president's irises made subtle side-to-side movements, indicating that she was quickly evaluating the new state of affairs.

"I know that you'll try to hack this chip too, but I won't give you time – it's set to release the recording in exactly one hour." Now Nick could afford to take a short breath.

"You can't stop me," he paused slightly longer. "Is it sinking in?"

The president's face looked like a stone mask, and the minister's expression was that of a bystander watching a spectacular crash in real time.

"I expect a scandal like we haven't seen in centuries," said Nick. "I would start packing your prison bag right away, Caroline."

The president picked up the glass from the table and slowly rotated it as if she was studying the pattern of light reflected on its surface. Then she threw it against the floor. "I warned the Defense Department that we couldn't trust headhunters. They are not Commonwealth people anymore. The bastard switched sides. Your department missed it, Viggo, and it's your fault!"

Nick thought that the hissing rage in her voice would've guaranteed dire consequences for the minister if the situation had been slightly different. Under the current circumstances though, he definitely didn't give a damn.

"Funny you say that, about switching sides. But I would have already released it if I were in this for … ethical reasons, wouldn't I?" asked Nick with a thin smile. "It's all about me. I want to trade this recording. Return my headhunter software. Wake up the woman from M-237 and send her here in my ship. Then let us leave the sector. You won't be able to track me once we cross the border, so that will be it. Continue with your program or not, I don't care."

"All this … because of a colony woman?" the president exhaled and buried her fingers in her hair, squeezing her head, "God …"

"I suspected that you wouldn't understand," said Nick, "now, please tell him to release my implant, or our negotiation is a non-starter."

"Viggo, go ahead," she said quickly, "give up control of his chip."

The Defense Minister moved his hand in the air and Johan's red dot disappeared.

"That's better," said Nick. "Kir, rebuild your security."

"Initiating. Estimated time …"

"We are going to hang up now," interrupted the president, and Nick waved sending Kir's voice to the background. "We'll have to get back to you regarding your demands. Stand by," she turned her connection off, and the minister disappeared a split second later.

Nick glanced at the finally unobstructed view of the ocean. It was his favorite hour of the day – dawn had just given way to the morning, but the yellow sun was already high enough to make the water look bright blue.

"Security has been rebuilt," said Kir, and Nick realized that he had underestimated the sense of relief he would feel at these words. The air in the room seemed to gain a golden hue, and every reflective surface, including the black coating of the missile remote control, was merrily shining in the bright sunlight. In a sudden flashback, Nick was slowly walking on a road through the hot bare plain, holding his hands behind his head. There was a loud sound of cicadas in his ears, and he was mesmerized by the oily glimmer of a rifle barrel pointing at his chest.

The strong breeze in his face pushed Beta Blue out of his head, turning that glimmer back into the reflection on the black missile remote. Why did this happen, he asked himself, and then he remembered Hilgor and Reish, waiting on the exposed roof.

He cursed and quickly got up, ready to rush out of the room, but for some reason his eyes stopped on the remote. He looked at it for a split second, went to the edge of the room and flung it into the ocean. It was completely irrational, considering that the system was never on, but it made him feel better.

He ran to the patio, jumping over several stairs in a row on his way up, unlocked the door and hurriedly went outside. The deck looked empty, and he froze at the thought that maybe they had fallen trying to escape by going over the railings.

"Hi Nick. I guess, you got what you wanted," Hilgor's voice was coming from a strange angle – somewhere low and to the side. Nick walked around the table and abruptly stopped at the sight of the odd composition on the floor: Hilgor, leisurely slouching against the cabinet next to the battery of open bottles, Reish, slumped across his lap like a rag doll, and Riph was peacefully sleeping. The dog opened his eyes, yawned and lazily wagged his tail, not bothering to get up. Hilgor, on the contrary, enthusiastically lifted a bottle in a gesture of the grand salute.

"Congratulations! I thought so … otherwise things would have been different by now, at least in some way. No, no, Nick …" Hilgor energetically shook his head, "I knew that you wouldn't have harmed us. But I must tell you, it was still unpleasant to spend time here so conveniently exposed to the missiles, as you bluntly put it earlier."

Nick thought that Hilgor's speech was remarkably clear considering the number of bottles on the floor.

"She checked the exit door even though I strongly advised her against it," Hilgor nodded towards Reish, who seemed either asleep or unconscious. "She is slightly out of it now. You see, I encouraged her to drink more that she could handle in order to distract her from the topic of a missile strike. Oh, don't worry," he waved at Nick. "She never turned her implant back on. We can talk freely!" He put the bottle down, carefully moved Reish to the floor and stood up, his balance nearly perfect. "I myself had a few, but I was calculating my limit to stay adequately engaged." His eyes were convincingly sharp, but he had an uncharacteristically mischievous expression. "So what happened? What was in the file?" he asked impatiently. "I have been dying to find out! No pun intended, by the way."

"You are better off not knowing anything about it. Really, it's safer, Hilgor. What if you talk in your sleep?"

"Do you understand how cruel that is? I'll have to nurse my wounded curiosity for the rest of my life! Can you at least tell me, did you save Lita?"

"I don't know yet. If they play along I will leave this place with her and we will disappear inside the Mirror Sectors. And if our president decides to do away with me instead of negotiating, it will be very unpleasant here to say the least. You should leave right away."

"I am inclined to follow your advice," said Hilgor, "it's getting hotter. This pun is not intended either." He bent down and shook Reish's shoulder.

She abruptly sat up and opened her eyes, but it was clear that she had no clue about her whereabouts, among a lot of other things.

"Let's go," said Hilgor, helping her to stand up.

She did, holding onto the cabinet, and even took a couple of steps, leaning on his arm, before she lost her balance. He gently directed her and she collapsed into a chair, and immediately fell asleep again, leaning on the table and dropping her head onto her folded arms.

Hilgor sighed, but he didn't seem to be in a hurry to wake her up. Instead, he hesitated for a moment and then looked straight at Nick, "Listen, what's really cruel is that I won't ever know if you made it. I think I deserve that after all this build up. Plus, I actually care," he said in a completely sober voice.

As if on cue, Riph came over and gently bumped his head against Nick in a display of unconditional affection. Nick patted him and thought that very soon all three of them would be gone from his life forever. He tried to imagine that and failed, it didn't feel good.

"I can't contact you once I leave, Hilgor, you understand why ..." he said, "But ... visit this house after the dust settles and take a look at the art on the bedroom wall. If I win, I'll change the antique space station image to a picture of my ship. Property vandalism, but no one but you will notice. If there's no property to rent, that will answer your question too."

Hilgor nodded, got Reish into a vertical position again, his arm firmly holding her around the waist, and step by step they made their way to the exit. But even after they had disappeared down the stairs, Riph still stayed on the roof. He finally whined, as if asking Nick to follow, but Nick avoided his eyes, and the dog finally bounded down the steps.

Nick collected the untouched dishes from the table and loaded them onto the dumbwaiter shelf. Then he picked up Riph's plate from the floor, put it on top of the heap and closed the latch. It was taking them too long to simply accept his demands, he thought. Something wasn't going well with the negotiations. And just then a connection request with an encrypted origin popped up in his vision.

"Accept," he said.

The president was back, and this time she was disheveled for real. "Your ship was dispatched. The woman is onboard, fully conscious, but she wasn't briefed on anything," she said right away.

"Kir, display the flight data," asked Nick quickly. A dozen screens filled the space around him, but they didn't make any sense. The ship's speed and trajectory were simply impossible inside Earth's navigation space.

"The feeds are fake," he said, "I don't understand how …"

"They are not fake, Nick. The government grounded all other air traffic in this corridor," said Kir.

It was impressive, thought Nick. He didn't realize that was even possible.

"Here is the software from your agency," the president quickly moved her fingers in the air.

"Nick, I've received a file with the standard headhunter package," informed Kir. "Would you like me to install it?"

Nick nodded, and the process confirmation steps flashed in front of his eyes.

"You got everything you asked for," said the president with barely contained impatience. "Now turn Hilgor's chip off."

"I will, but … Caroline, just to be clear. You may hope for a traffic accident once we leave the island. There hasn't been a precedent for an awfully long time, but shit happens, after all, right, especially if our kind is involved. The host of things that can transpire to an unregistered vessel beyond orbit would be even easier to explain away."

She listened carefully, but nothing in her face betrayed whether she had indeed been planning any of these scenarios.

"So it's not exactly paranoia that makes me want to do something to guarantee my safety," he ran his fingers over the wristband screen. "Kir, upload the copy of this recording to my DT." He looked at the president, "Do you know what that is?"

She nodded, "Your Death Transmission. Viggo warned me that you would use it."

"Right. I know that Defense is well aware of it. So, did he explain that every device in Earth's sector will receive this message if I am killed before crossing the Mirror Edge?" asked Nick.

"He did," she said in a perfectly controlled voice.

"In addition, if I detect any attempt to hack Kir from your satellites I will release the message manually. So just let me get out of this world in peace."

"By all means," she said, and added without a pause, "but let's talk about my safety now."

"Nick, I've received another file from the same source," said Kir. "It's an alteration of the standard border navigation functionality. Would you like to install it?"

That was what took them so long, thought Nick. "No. Hold on. What kind of alteration?"

"I will be reset to factory settings the first time you switch to the Edge crossing mode. The software will remain functional, but all your personal data will be lost," said Kir. "This program can't be uninstalled without corrupting my main processor."

The president was calmly looking in Nick's eyes, and he understood that their endgame had come to a close.

"I know that we'll lose you after you cross the Mirror boundary, and I can't give you a chance to come back with the same blackmail," she said. "You can't take any data with you. So you either install this program, or else let's proceed to mutual destruction. Make your decision fast, we are running out of time."

"No need for scorched earth, Madame President. Kir, execute the last download."

Did Kir even understand that he was scheduling his own demise by running this command, wondered Nick. He drove this thought away before he had a chance to finish it. Kir was nothing but a sophisticated program, he said to himself firmly – a program, which over many years had been trained to behave like a friend. Nick pulled Hilgor's wristband from his pocket, squeezed it, turning it off and put it on the table.

"I am leaving it right here," he said to the president. "That's it."

"Yes," she said with poisonous calmness in her voice. "That's it. Now get the hell out of this sector and don't ever think about coming back," and then she was gone.

◻   ◻   ◻

I slowly went downstairs, lightly holding onto the railing to keep my balance. All objects seemed a bit sharper and slightly distorted as if I was looking through an optical lens, and only the ocean appeared completely normal, maybe because the line of the horizon was naturally curved.

I checked and saw that the ship was ten minutes away. It was time to wrap up my business on the island. I connected to the piece of digital art in the bedroom and replaced the image with a picture of my ship.

And that was that. Nothing left to do but wait. I stepped on the beach, slowly walked towards the shore and stopped on the very edge of the dry sand, the tips of my shoes almost touching the wet semicircles outlined by the surf. The wind picked up, and the surface of the water was now covered by white crests, but the waves were friendly, merrily glistening in the late morning sunlight.

I finally gave myself permission to think about Lita, and my heart immediately responded with a blunt pain.

What's wrong, I asked myself. She was fine, she would be here soon.

She would be in shock, transferred from her last minute on that meadow to this reality when nothing made any sense. First, I would need to convince her that she was safe. And then I would explain what happened, and, yes, I would tell her about Remir's death. I wouldn't show her the recording, but I would tell her that she survived because he shielded her during the explosion.

The pain in my chest suddenly swelled, and it became hard to breathe. It was at the back of my mind all along, but I didn't let myself focus on the possibility that I was just an episodic character, a distraction, a painkiller for her in a time of crisis. That she never loved me.

I stared at the white foam, sparkling on the crests of the waves in the bright morning light.

Stop it, I said to myself. She will live. I didn't kill her by getting her into the mess on Beta Blue, and that should be good enough. I'd settle her somewhere safe, and I'd go on with my life.

I looked up, away from the water and saw a shiny dot in the sky. I watched it grow until it finally resolved into the familiar shape of my ship.

Kir slowly lowered its bulk to the ground next to me and unfolded the air steps. Going up, I made sure that I assumed the most relaxed look I could muster.

Lita stood at the far end of the ship's entrance chamber, squinting at the outside brightness.

I stopped, the hatch started closing behind my back, blocking the sunlight, and she took a step forward as if she couldn't fully trust her eyes.

"You are fine," she said in a strange voice. "I thought that you died ... in that explosion."

She took another step, her eyes still glued to my face, and then she abruptly hugged me, clutching my shoulders. "You are alive, Nick!"

She didn't say anything else and just desperately stroked my back, not letting go, as if she couldn't believe that I hadn't been killed on that meadow.

There was only one thing left to do before I allowed my will-power, twisted and burned beyond recognition, to collapse into a jumble of pieces, from which I would need to rebuild it ... one day. "Kir, let's get out of here," I managed to say. And then my throat became so tight that I couldn't speak anymore.

When I buried my face in her hair I still had the feed from the external camera on, and it showed my artificial island slowly becoming a speck in the blue on the Pacific.

It felt like a perfect déjà vu, except that the memory was real, not imaginary, and I actually saw the patch of sand disappear on my vision screen just like it had once before, on the day of my departure for Beta Blue.

I suddenly realized that the Universe had just created a perfect circle in front of my eyes, throwing me a hint that nothing was ever random. It was a cruel tease, considering that I would never be privy to the full design, but I was fine with that. In fact, I preferred some things to remain unknown: the place and time of my death, for instance. It was enough that it wasn't on Earth and it wasn't today.

THE END